6X
LOUD, FAST AND OUT OF CONTROL

NINA MALKIN

*Hodder
Children's
Books*

a division of Hodder Headline Limited

Other  titles

6X

The Uncensored Confessions

Part One

NINA MALKIN

Hodder
Children's
Books

a division of Hachette Children's Books

A Catalogue record for this book is available from the British Library

ISBN 978 0 340 91150 1

Typeset in Bembo by Avon DataSet Ltd,
Bidford on Avon, Warwickshire

Printed and bound in Great Britain by
Bookmarquer Ltd, Croydon, Surrey

The paper and board used in this paperback are natural recyclable
products made from wood grown in sustainable forests.
The manufacturing processes conform to the environmental
regulations of the country of origin.

Hodder Children's Books
a division of Hachette Children's Books
338 Euston Road
London NW1 3BH

For Jason – rock god & goofball

(Lead item . . .)

It's midnight — do you know
where your favourite rock chick is?
The answer was a resounding
'Ummm . . . no!' last night at Otto's
Hot Stack, as a breathless crowd awaited
sensation-of-the-moment **6X**. The band
was due to hit the stage at the soiree
celebrating their debut album *Bliss de la
Mess*, and apparently all four members
of the young band — as well as a Who's
Who of Manhattan hipster elite — had
assembled earlier in the evening. But
just before showtime, lead singer
Kendall Taylor vanished in a puff of
diva vapour. Is it true major minor heart-
melter **Reid-Vincent Mitchell**
absconded with the baby-faced belter?
Page Five mustn't tell — but we can
report that fans patient enough to wait
till the wee hours did get their dose of
6X. The quartet, *in toto*, rocked Otto's
till closing time . . .

(Woo-Hoo! of the Month . . .)

Who: 6X, a three-girl, one-guy, upbeat-yet-angsty pop-rock combo.

What: *Bliss de la Mess*, a mix of self-penned tunes and quirky-cool covers from the Eighties and Nineties. The sound? Come on, doesn't the album title tell all?

When: Last summer, when Angel Blue had that super-scary skateboarding accident, 6X stepped up to replace her band on the *Steal This Pony* soundtrack. (As if you didn't know!) Now their long-awaited debut disk is out, and first single 'All Over Oliver' will have you doing the stiletto-heel stomp on that guy who had the nerve to break your heart.

Where: Band members (singer Kendall, 15; drummer Wynn, 15; bassist Stella, 16; and guitarist A/B, 17) all live in New York. But we expect they'll soon be calling a tour bus home!

Why: Because Kendall's a real role model who's not a toothpick! Because Stella's got attitude to burn! Because Wynn is a poet who makes perfect sense! Because A/B knows how to be just friends with girls . . . or does he?!

(Excerpt from the *Entertainment Now* interview . . .)

Entertainment Now: The rumour mill is grinding overtime about you guys. So what exactly *did* happen on the night of your record release party?

Stella Saunders: Look, it was all part of our make-'em-beg-for-you strategy. It's never too early to be fashionably late, all right.

EN: Yes, but two-and-a-half *hours* late? That's pretty high fashion . . .

Kendall Taylor: Oh gosh, I hope people don't think I was being intentionally rude! I'd never do that. Honestly, what happened was, what with the crazy schedule we had completing the album and all the excitement of the party, I was feeling a bit faint. I thought I might die if I didn't get a breath of fresh air. So then Reid-Vincent Mitchell — we've been friends since *Steal This Pony* — well, he's such a gentleman; he offered to take me outside. And while we were chatting, he asked if I'd ever walked across the Brooklyn Bridge before, and I said no I hadn't. But the way he was going on about how beautiful the city looks from the bridge, and Otto's being just a stone's throw from there, we decided to do it, and I just lost all track of time . . .

EN: The rest of you guys must have been going nuts.

A/B Farrelberg: Nah, we knew there was no way Kendall would skip out on a chance in the spotlight.

Wynn Morgan: The thing is, people don't know us yet — we're a young band, so maybe they expect us to act out or be immature. But *we* know us. Like for instance, we know we can always count on Kendall to be, well, Kendall . . .

PART ONE
Everybody Knows
This is Nowhere

'Everybody seems to wonder what it's like down here . . .'

— *Neil Young*

The Boss

Just when you thought you were fabulous, that you were really rolling with the big dogs, you find yourself stuck in the remix from hell. One minute you're so busy you don't have time to pee, the next you might as well be brain-dead. Talk about flipping the script!

When *Bliss de la Mess* first dropped, everybody wanted a piece of 6X – interviews, photo sessions, two *TRL* appearances. Demonically in demand, all right. Only a month, no, less than a month later, Standstill City. Yeah, the record's still a phenom, just flying off the shelves. Last I looked we were Number Five on the *Billboard* chart. But us, the actual human beings individually known as Wynn, Kendall, A/B, and the inimitable Stella Angenue Simone Saunders, what are we getting up to? Nothing. Nada. Zip. 6X business is on the back burner and the stove must be way out in the jungles of Borneo or some shit. Am I getting antsy? You might say that!

We still rehearse twice a week, but for what? With no gigs lined up, not even locally, practice is an exercise in futility. So let me tell you, I was more than happy to put this band meeting on my calendar. I am logically expecting a deep and meaningful and *specific* conversation about our tour when I head into the newly inaugurated offices of Wandweilder Worldwide. So you can maybe imagine my, ahem, dismay when I find out we've assembled to discuss endorsement deal options being heaped onto silver platters and foisted on Kendall Taylor. Can you believe I am taking time out of my day to debate the pros and cons of Kendall's chubby cheeks appearing on the wrapper of some new chocolate bar and – it gets better! – the use of the next 6X single as jingle material?

'No way!' Could I be more succinct?

And Kendall's like, 'Why not?' All petulant, throwing a glance toward her momager. (Despite all the drama that woman caused – nearly, excuse me, preventing us from finishing *Bliss de la Mess* – Mrs Taylor is still all up in our business.) A few inches of gut poke out from under Kendall's pink fleece top, and, fortunately for her, management intercedes before I can plant my boot heel in that roll of blubber.

'Kendall, Mrs Taylor, you're right, it is good money, and it would position 6X prominently.' Our man is working that I'm-Brian-Wandweilder-and-I-can-convince-you-dog-food-is-filet-mignon thing he's got. 'And of course Kendall's interests need to be represented.'

This sounds peachy to Kendall; she exchanges smug mugs with her mom.

'But you've got to think long-term,' Brian goes on.

It's the 'but' I've been waiting for. A/B's next to me on the sofa, and I pinch him to silently say, 'See?' Not like I need to school A/B on how the man operates. Brian's a master manipulator. 'Countless kids may see Kendall on candy bars, but doesn't she deserve better?' Brian gestures toward the ceiling, symbolising loftiness. It was so smart of him to bag the legal profession to launch his own management company – it's his true calling for real. 'Of course she does. Kendall deserves something that connotes credibility and class – attributes she has by the bucketful.'

This time I pinch Wynn, sitting quietly on the other side of me. For all I know A/B may have a thing for Kendall – I still don't have straight what, if anything, went down between those two – but Wynn'll be the first to bust up over anyone using the word 'class' and that trailer park escapee's name in the same sentence.

'Trouble is, something better won't be on the table if we take this. Exclusivity is, after all, Marketing 101.' Brian stands up for his summation. Gaylord, now his second-in-command at WandWorld, nods knowingly. 'So it's important to pick and choose among the many, many, many requests bound to come Kendall's way.'

Bravo, Brian. Thanks to some first-rate smooth talk, 6X won't be associated with caramel-coated, tooth-rotting, sell-out *bool*shit. Only now I'm beginning to think Brian's more than a brilliant consigliere – he's a goddamn prophet. Within a week, these perfume people start pursuing Kendall about a fragrance line and the producers of *American Dreams* – that TV show about life in the Sixties – call to dangle a possible Janis Joplin guest-star spot. This girl is getting so much smoke blown up her ass she could be a float in the Macy's Thanksgiving Day Parade. But the ultimate offer came down yesterday. Kendall's going to do it, and we all agree she should, because nothing says class and credibility like a Gap commercial.

So you'll excuse me for a minute while I scream and bang my head against the wall, all right.

The Voice

I bet a girl could work herself up into a real tizzy if she didn't have faith. My faith is my rock, my refuge. It is what allows me to hold on and be positive when it seems like evil forces are around every corner. Gosh, when it comes to trials and tribulations, I need look no further than my own kin. It's so hard to uphold solid Christian values when you find out your mother's been feeding you lies all your life, and that your long-lost father is not a dearly departed war hero, but alive and well and possibly not a very nice person to boot.

This is just one thing I have had to grapple with, so I pray for guidance. It's not like there's anyone but Jesus to help me. The people in my band? Glory, no! Fans probably think we're tight as toes, but that's an illusion. Not that we're mad at each other – I still love them all dearly. It's just that we're not really doing much as a unit at the moment; they've gone back to their hum-de-hum lives while I must endure the pressure of the limelight. Goodness, a Gap ad, can you imagine? So – lay my burdens down before Stella or Wynn? That would not be prudent. Especially when it comes to my relationship with a certain guitar player. No, I have not given up on him; our romance has simply suffered a setback. Still, it would be nice to have someone to talk to, a girlfriend who understands matters of the heart.

That's why I'm looking forward to meeting Miss Penelope Randolph. She's a friend of the Morgan family, and Wynn's mom is convinced she'd make the perfect tutor for us when we're on the road. 'After all, she *is* a Randolph, of the Rhode Island Randolphs,' Wynn's mom tells my mom, as if that's all we need to know.

Of course we wouldn't hire someone just on Wynn's mom's say-so. My mom sets up an appointment to meet this Miss Penelope Randolph herself, and she forms a real positive opinion. 'She's bright, mannerly, and grounded.' My mom gives me this review over the phone – her in New Jersey and me in my Manhattan apartment. 'And she's real spiritual, but for the life of me, Kendall, I can't recall what religion she said she is.' The vacuum cleaner drones in the background – that's *so* my mom: a successful career woman with a daughter at the top of the charts, but she still cleans her own house. 'Probably Methodist. She looks Methodist. But then, we can't all be Baptist.'

So I'm looking forward to meeting Miss Penelope myself. Even though I'm a celebrity and all – I have my fitting for that Gap commercial this very afternoon – I still believe book learning is important. One day you could be at an event and someone might ask you the capital of Argentina, and you wouldn't want to look stupid. Yet when Miss Penelope comes up here to the Teen Towers, I am taken aback.

She must've worn a whole different outfit when she

interviewed with my mom. For sure she doesn't look like someone Wynn's mom would want on her ivory linen sofa — she looks like she might *shed*. She has this purple-black hair that fans out to her waist, and she's wearing a real flouncy skirt and top and dozens of bracelets, except one of the bracelets isn't even a bracelet — it's a twisty tattoo snaking around her upper arm.

She sweeps inside my apartment, dropping a large satchel and sniffing the air like a hound. In the middle of the room, she twirls like a dancer, then stops and spreads her arms wide. 'I am Peony Randolph. Come to me, Kendahl!'

Could it be? Well, yes it could! She wants me to hug her, but even if she did shave her armpits — which she does not — my home training wouldn't permit me to be so forward with someone I don't know. Well, it's as if my thoughts are written clean across my forehead. 'If we are to trade knowledge, Kendahl, first we must embrace,' Miss Peony says. 'How can I reach your mind before we build a bridge of trust?'

Next thing I know I'm breathing through an eggplant-coloured curtain that smells like the incense the robed men sell outside Port Authority. For sure, Miss Peony's the most unusual person I've ever met. But we talk for a while and she seems awfully warm and sensitive. She asks about my interests, what I hope to learn from her, from life, and wouldn't I like to meet up with Wynn down in Tompkins Square Park for our first lesson. 'There's no better classroom than the one between earth and sky!' Miss Peony says.

Wynn gallops over when she sees us, and she and Miss Peony hug real tight for what seems like a full ten minutes.

Then we find a still-grassy spot in the park without too many bums around, and Miss Peony takes a blanket from her satchel. Once we're seated, she proceeds to draw books and pads and pens from the bottomless bag. 'You've had breakfast?' she asks.

'Yes, ma'am,' I say. 'Bacon and—'

'Bacon!' Miss Peony makes a disapproving 'tsk.' 'No wonder you're so sallow – nitrates strangle the kidneys.' She places a fingertip under my eye and pulls the lower lid down, examining it. This startles me so much I rock back on my haunches and nearly roll over. Then she delves into the bag again to retrieve a thermos. 'This will banish the toxins,' she says, handing me a cup. She pours one for Wynn as well.

'What is it?' I am more than a little iffy. The steaming liquid is grey-green and smells like country dirt.

'Just tea,' Miss Peony says.

I sniff the cup again. Under the dirty smell is the essence of mint. Wynn seems to have no problem with the stuff, and I want to make a good impression, so I drink it down. It's actually refreshing, and before I know it science is a game, Shakespeare is a song, and each one of my feet has fallen asleep twice from sitting cross-legged on the blanket. Then Miss Peony squints up at the sun through a canopy of crimson leaves. 'All right, Kendahl,' she says, 'two-thirty.' In one fluid motion she rises to standing with her ankles still crossed. 'You have half an hour to get to your fitting.' She reaches out a hand to help me up. 'I'll walk you to get a taxi.'

She tells Wynn to compose a quatrain – whatever that is – about the pigeons in the park as together we make our way towards Avenue A. There's so much I'm dying to ask her. Like how can she tell time by the sky? And how does she get her hair that colour? And why the heck does she go by Peony – isn't *Penny* short for Penelope? Her face scrunches into a pucker. 'Ask me anything, Kendahl,' she says, like she can sense the questions I'm too polite to let out. 'I'll always tell you the truth.'

'Well . . . I would like to know . . . my mom told me you're a spiritual person. But, gosh, you're not like anyone at our church. So what are you, anyway? I mean, what religion?'

Miss Peony cricks her neck left, then right, as if trying to loosen up the answer. 'Oh, Kendahl, that is a wonderful question, because I am many, many things. I have been far and wide: Palestine, Port au Prince, Cairo, Crete. I have bathed in the Ganges, breathed the rarified air of the Himalayas. Everywhere I go I gather nuggets, jewels of enlightenment.'

The way she talks is like a spell; I cannot help but listen, like it or not.

'Gurus, shamans, rabbis, priests, all have held me in thrall! Hinduism, Buddhism, Santeria, Kabbalah, all have laid ova in the nest of my soul.' Miss Peony beams like she's ready for the rapture.

'Soooo . . . you're not a Methodist?' I ask.

Miss Peony laughs like bells, and then her mouth makes that pucker shape again. 'Oh, Kendahl! This is going to be such a journey we take together. Of course, I will tell you what you wish to know. The religion I follow, Kendahl, is Wicca.'

'Oh . . .' Before I can ask anything more, a taxi pulls up to us. We smile at each other before I get into the backseat, and I

9

think Miss Peony is really going to expand my horizons. Yet the whole way down to the Gap fitting in Tribeca I can't help but wonder: *Wicca? That doesn't sound like a religion at all. That sounds like patio furniture!*

The Boy

News flash: Fame does not equal fortune. Sure, 6X got a hefty advance. Yes, *Bliss de la Mess* is selling like Spock ears at a *Star Trek* convention, but Universe still has to recoup what they spent to manufacture, distribute, and promote it. Any up-front money I got is gone. Not *gone* gone. Invested. In guitars. Like this honey of a Martin acoustic. And then, I wanted a macho axe — testosterone compensation for playing in a chick band — but since I couldn't decide between the Les Paul and the SG, I got both. You know, a stomp box here, an amp there, it adds up to lifestyles of the broke and famous.

So I've taken a job. No, nothing that involves saying 'Supersize that?' Still . . . me, A/B Farrelberg, guitar teacher at Dondi's Music Palace on Crest Crinkle Road. Yeesh. Particularly humiliating in light of recent events. Picture, if you will, my eighteenth birthday par-tay last week. A small, intimate gathering at Brian's loft. Champagne and sushi, courtesy of the world's best manager. Weed and babes courtesy of my buddy Moth. You know Alan Slushinger who produced our record? Moth's his French wife's kid brother. That makes him French, too, and here's a little secret you might already know: Chicks dig French accents. So he's invited these very friendly ladies along and after a while – after a certain lead singer split (she had to appear at family court at the crack of dawn) – one of these ladies, whose name, if I remember correctly, is Debby, decides to get even friendlier. I mean, she licks me! First on the ear, then on the neck. Did I neglect to mention that she is hot? Well, she is. And she's leading me astray, straight to the king-sized bed in the master suite. Actually says, between licks, 'I wanna do the birthday boy!' Am I going to decline? A gorgeous girl with her own condoms and no strings?

Yes, sadly, I am. I do. I won't bore you with the harrowing blow-by-blows of my lack of debauchery, but suffice to say Debby doesn't handle rejection very well. There it was, the perfect score . . . and I just said no. Now I've thought about this a lot – what the blazes is *wrong* with me – and guess what I've discovered?

I *want* strings.

Great big sweet swells and crashing crescendos of strings – violins, violas, cellos. When I lose my virginity I want the New York Philharmonic passionately, intensely, deliriously in the background. And until I get that, the real deal, I'm not going to settle for some synthesized facsimile.

Anyway, it's a beautiful day as I head towards Dondi's in my dad's Buick – fall foliage on suburban lawns singes my eyeballs. Seventies Detroit bands on the stereo make me hopeful today's four students will want to learn 'Kick Out the Jams' or 'I Wanna Be Your Dog.'

Um, no.

My first student, Morris (first, name? last? who knows?),

has a real Santa Claus vibe. Round-bellied, white-haired, merry twinkle in the eye. Except the wardrobe throws me – he's wearing flip-flops, baggy shorts, and a Hawaiian shirt. When I spy the sheet music he's brought, it all makes sense: surf sounds from the Sixties – Beach Boys, the Ventures, awesome stuff.

'So you're into surf music.' I nod appreciatively 'Cool.'

'WHAT?!' Morris is smiling, twinkling . . . and screaming.

'Surf music?' I say.

'WHAT?!' he screams.

'SURF MUSIC!' I scream back. 'YOU LIKE SURF MUSIC!'

Despite the twinkle, Morris looks perplexed, so I mime my way onto an imaginary board, arms out, body weaving while I ride that sucker to shore.

'WHAT ARE YOU DOING?'

OK, Morris doesn't dig my Kelly Slater imitation. I don't think he remembered his hearing aid. *Cowabunga!* This is going to be one loooong day. At two, another geezer hoping to recapture his misspent youth, and after a short break my three-thirty – a sadistic fifth-grader who can't strike a G7th without kicking me in the shins. So when the door to Dondi's back room opens at four-thirty I am naturally pessimistic.

'This is A/B,' rasps Dondi. 'This is Edie.'

'Hi, A/B – it's amazing to meet you.'

'Yah, yah . . .' I toss my issue of *Gearhead* magazine. 'Hi, you . . . toooo . . .'

It *is* amazing to meet her. Amazing, incredible, astounding. Not just because she's cute. No, not cute. Beautiful. In a cute way. Her hair is short but not too short; it flips out all over her head however it wants, and it's this rich, shiny espresso-bean brown. Her eyes are green, with these flecks. And her lips? Juicy. Like sections of tangerine. Best of all is her smile. It sparkles, and her braces have nothing to do with that. See, that's why the visual Edie is only part of why it's so amazing to meet her. Emanating from that smile is Edie the person – a little bit bouncy, a little bit badass.

'I'm really a fan,' Edie confesses. Though petite, she's what my Grandma Sophie would call zaftig, meaning round, curvy – a plum, not a twig. An extra-large Nirvana tee, worn out to perfection, fits her snugly since she's cleverly cut it up and tied it along the sides. Below it she wears a skirt DIYed from old Levis and duct tape, striped knee socks, and Converse One-Stars. *My* shoes. 'I hope that's OK.'

'Oh, uh, sure,' I say in a stream of unparalleled eloquence. 'That's cool.'

'I guess you told them here they couldn't advertise it was actually *you* giving lessons.' She dips a shoulder to drop her guitar case. 'It would have been such a scene. When I called to schedule and that Dondi guy said someone named A/B could teach me I'm thinking it couldn't be you. But . . . here you are.'

I'm – what's the word? – smitten. And trying not to be obvious about it.

'So, you want to see what I can do?'

Oh yeah. If she's doing the doing, I want in. Trouble is, I can't seem to tell her so.

'On guitar?' Edie watches me expectantly. 'I'm not a total beginner, you know, but there's just so much you can learn on your own . . .'

The word *learn* brings me back to what's ostensibly occurring between us. 'Yeah – yes, please.' I offer a professorial nod, gesture toward the stools. She takes out a battered, sticker-strewn Yamaha, and as she sits, her skirt rides up, baring the skin above those socks. There's a scab on her left knee.

Edie focuses on her fret board and strikes a chord – D minor, I'll never forget – then blushes. 'Wait,' she says, glancing up at me. 'Guess I'm nervous.'

'Don't be,' I squawk. 'Pretend I'm not here.'

Espresso-bean curls do a jig as she shakes her head. 'They say when you're nervous in front of someone to imagine them in their underwear.'

Embarrassment begins somewhere around my testicles, surges up and out. 'Oh, no, please . . . don't do that.' I rake my hand through my mop. 'Don't be nervous. Just, you know, whenever you're ready.'

Edie takes a deep breath and charges through 'Chain-Link Fish,' the Ayn Rand single currently chewing up the charts. She gets a few chord changes wrong, but I recognise what she's playing and it's a cool tune. Grinning like Mongo the Monkey Boy, I realise I was dreading she'd picked some lame song. Now the effect is complete. I can say without hesitation that I am amazingly, incredibly, astoundingly in love.

The Body

If you are a nice, calm, relaxed sort of person, you probably shouldn't take up the drums. Try, I don't know, maybe the viola. Or the oboe. But if you are neurotic, just prone to anxiety and jumpiness, definitely investigate percussion. Because with me, when I'm not at my kit, I am banging on things. Anything, everything, the table, my knee, bang-bangetty-tap-tap. Actually, it's a newly developed tic; it first came on when being in 6X started to feel like a farce. I mean, if you're in a rock band you're supposed to rock, because if you don't you're not a musician, you're a . . . a celebrity.

Ick.

I'm sorry, I don't want to insult anyone who *aspires* to that kind of popularity, but the whole fame part of what we do is just weird to me. The way people look at you in the deli or the drugstore, like why would you need a bottle of water or a box of tampons? And then you've got designers sending you clothes you'd never wear anyplace normal. And television actors you don't even know asking you out. Of course, to be accurate, the actor doesn't ask you out — his publicist contacts your publicist and the rendezvous is arranged. Isn't it romantic?

So tonight Kieran Dennis and I will do the town. Yes, that Kieran Dennis, star of *Thrift Stories*, the crown prince of The WB. I've never even seen the show and I try to get out of it, but Stella is adamant.

'You're going!' she informs me in no uncertain terms. By her reasoning, it doesn't matter if I *want* to date Kieran Dennis, I have to do it for the good of the band.

'Look, stop being so selfish,' she says. 'You get spotted with Kieran, it'll make the gossips – and there's no such thing as bad publicity.'

Oh, joy! I think. But my groan is inside me, silent.

'Besides, *Thrift Stories* has a killer soundtrack, and Kieran clearly has taste in music if 6X is on his radar. So you get in good with him, we get a song on the show.'

The effort required to ditch would be enormous. After all, as I said, publicists are involved. Plus my mom is practically hyperventilating over the prospect of me on a 'proper date.' It will be easier to just go. Six-second wardrobe scan for appropriate outfit (long skirt, cashmere tee, heap of beads, flats). Muss my hair a bit – sorry, Kieran, if you go for the sleek, well-groomed type. Stare at my make-up table. I guess I should, I don't know . . . *apply* something. Mascara. Glitter. I'm not a glitter person, but glitter seems to be the mandate. When going out with the 'It' boy of teen TV it seems imperative to first dust your cheekbones and cleavage with something sparkly and shimmery and above all fake.

Door chimes summon, and there's this comedy of manners between my date, my parents, and myself that's straight out of Oscar Wilde. My attitude's as Zen as I can manage. I don't ask where we're going or how we're getting there. I'm simply along for the ride. But a ripple of ick runs through me when we get outside and I see the limo. God forbid a Hollywood boy wonder should take the subway or hail a cab. Off to Mondo Titos, which I presume is very 'in.'

'I burn out on Mexican in LA,' Kieran says, 'but I hear this place has the best tapas outside of España.'

Not only does he say Espana instead of Spain, he uses the Castilian pronunciation, lisp and all: 'Ethpanya.' But he's very . . . inquisitive – actually asks me questions about where I like to shop, if I've checked out the new Dolce & Gabbana boutique yet. I make polite inquiries back, and try to keep my fingers from using the table as a tom-tom.

Kieran is kind of loud, and he keeps glancing around to see if we've been spotted yet. As he rambles on about 'retail therapy' and how he's been 'living at Bendel's,' I wonder if Kieran Dennis might be gay. I mean, who else but Roger and Phillip, our neighbours in the Hamptons, know that much about the Henri Bendel shoe department? I almost burst out laughing when I think of all those girls who tune into *Thrift Stories* for their Tuesday night droolfest; in fact, I can hear Stella moaning now: Shut up! The boy eats Queerios for breakfast? Wynn, don't tell me!'

Of course, what transpires next changes my mind in a big fat hurry.

We've been dining for what feels like half a century, and after Kieran finally pays the bill he suggests we cruise Central Park. Cool by me; I've committed to this, and I'm not having a miserable time.

18

'Check it out – you're going to love this!' Kieran promises, popping in a CD he says is his own special mix. Cheesy Eighties New Wave blasts through the speakers, and at first I'm in shock – how did he know I'm addicted to that stuff? – but I guess his publicist could have asked mine. Anyway, it's Depeche Mode and Duran Duran and all that, and I can't help singing along. Kieran cracks champagne. Bubbles spurt all over his shirt; it makes me shriek but he doesn't care. We're swilling from the bottle, whooping it up in this time warp, and when the Human League classic comes on we're like, 'Don't you want me, bay-bee . . .'

That's when Kieran grabs my wrist.

'Don't you, Wynn? Don't you want me?'

Completely out of nowhere – he hasn't made a move all night. I'm trying to gauge if he's gone psycho or if this is some game. Then he goes, 'Now, now, don't say no till you check out the merchandise!' And he . . . I guess he uses his free hand to undo his pants. He lifts his butt up to yank them down a little . . . and he – he shows me his . . . *area*.

And it is *enormous*! It's not even sticking up the way it's supposed to – not that I've ever seen a . . . an erect one – but it's just . . . *reclining* there. Like this hairless pink ferret. Inside I am all *ick!* but I'm staring, speechless, flabbergasted. The only thing that saves me is the next song. Kajagoogoo's 'Too Shy.' I just start screaming at the top of my lungs: 'I'm too shy-yiiii, too shy . . .'

Kieran gets the point, I guess. He lets go of my arm and he puts . . . that thing away. Zips up and starts talking about the Monet water lilies at the Met, like nothing happened.

I blink. I smile. I yawn. I say: 'Kieran, I think I'd like to go home now.'

Now if this sounds like your idea of a dream date, be a celebrity – be my guest. Me, I'd rather just go on tour.

The Boss

Enough is enough. I am on my way to Wandweilder Worldwide. My agenda? Easy: I'm gonna waltz in and give Brian thirty seconds to deliver some 6X tour dates. Or else.

Or else what? Rant and rave? Trash the place? I see it unfold in my mind. Sweeping my arm across Brian's desk, spilling shit to the carpet. Grabbing his ever-present bottle of mineral water and hurling it at the platinum records on the wall. Not gonna happen. Stella Angenue Simone Saunders does not lose control. Diva histrionics lie in the province of Kendalland. I will conduct myself with the chill demeanour of the consummate professional I am.

Up on the ninth floor, I try to swing through the double doors but the damn handle is stuck. As usual. The Wand World digs are so ghetto. Once I get in, I'm greeted – sort of – by Susan, Brian's secretary and the Wand World receptionist. She gives me this gesture – part wave, part halt signal – as she takes a phone message.

'Yes, got it, hold on . . .' Then to me: 'Hi, Stella, he's . . .' Then to the phone, 'I said I've got it, please . . .' To me: 'Stella, wait . . .' Phone: 'Yes! Thank you!' Herself: 'Ugh!

Some people!' Me: 'Stella! He's in a meeting. You can't just barge in there.'

I stop in my tracks. Double back. 'Excuse me, Susan?' I am ever so polite. 'Are you telling me I can't go into Brian's office?'

Susan removes her glasses. 'Spare me the attitude, Stella,' she says. 'I raised two teenagers – I'm immune to it. You don't have an appointment so plant your fanny.'

Gotta love Susan – the woman takes no mess. I shoot her an obligatory grimace anyway, rustle through the magazines, and sit down to stew with a copy of *Blender*. Moments later, the entrance to Brian's inner sanctum opens. I'm on my feet. Here comes Gaylord, Brian, and . . . check it out, I'm a city girl, all right. My experience with the country is limited to a couple of trips upstate in the winter to go skiing. But this person emerging from the office with her hand in the crook of Brian's arm smells like a field of daisies. Fresh, sunny, and primed to send you into an allergic sneezing fit. She looks like she belongs in that field, butterflies perching on her lustrous chestnut ponytail. Oh, and Brian looks ready to join her, maybe carry a picnic basket or a goddamn fishing pole.

At first I think this trio's gonna glide right past me. They don't acknowledge my presence till they're close enough to step on my feet.

'Oh, hey, Stella! What a surprise,' says Brian.

'Yeah, hey, Sass.' Gaylord has taken to calling me Sass ever since he figured out it's my personal acronym. 'What's up?'

I waste no time. 'That's what I'd like to know, but—'

Yeah, well, rhetorical question. Neither Gaylord nor Brian has any interest in what's up with me. Not with Miss Farm

Stand Special around. She, however, is looking at me, and her peaches-and-cream complexion splits to reveal a crooked smile.

'Oh, where are my manners! Let me introduce you ladies.' Brian snaps to. 'Stella, meet Cara Lee Ballantine. Cara Lee, Stella's the bass player in 6X, one of Wand World's rock bands.'

One of their rock bands?! The phrase inflames my brain while Cara Lee puts on a mock-mad face. 'Come now, Brian, I do dig out of the tumbleweeds occasionally.' At first her accent is so sugary she makes Kendall sound like she comes from the South Bronx. Then she switches to her real voice – a twang, yeah, but a flat, gutsy one: 'I know all about 6X.' With her slant-tooth smile still in place, she stretches out her hand. 'Nice to meet you,' she says. She's got a good grip. 'I like your record a whole lot.'

'Thanks,' I say. Part of me wants to spit something snarky, or just snort, roll my eyes, and dismiss her. But I don't. This Cara Lee Ballantine commands respect.

'Come on, Cara Lee, you don't want to miss this sale at Guitar Centre, trust me,' Brian says, beginning to steer her towards the exit.

Cara Lee grins. 'Well, this has been a great meeting – I like how you guys think,' she says. 'Gaylord, a pleasure, truly.' She goes for the goodbye shake, then opts to give him an impromptu kiss, her left foot actually leaving the floor as she leans in. Gaylord turns pink, like a girl's lips have never brushed his cheek before. It cracks me up, all right – and distracts me from the fact that Brian intends to usher this girl down to Guitar Centre himself, completely disregarding me. They sail out on a whiff of wildflowers. At which point I narrow my glare onto Gaylord. Do I blow a fuse? I do not. I keep it light when I ask, 'So who's this Cara Lee Ballantine?'

'Cara Lee Ballantine?' Gaylord replies. 'Cara Lee Ballantine is the female Ryan Adams. The hip Faith Hill. A Miss Loretta Lynn for a new generation.'

Oh, he's beaming so bright you could land planes at Kennedy with his head.

'Or at least,' he adds, 'that's what we hope to turn her into . . .'

The Boy

I consider myself a fairly intelligent fella with a decent grasp of the English language. Yet the simplest of sentences — 'You want to go out sometime?' — is a hairball I can't seem to cough up. Edie's collecting her picks and her tuner, packing up her guitar. She's pulling on her jacket, pushing her sunglasses from the crown of her head to the bridge of her nose. Now, man, now!

'So, you like coffee?'

Edie cocks her head. 'Coffee? Never heard of them.'

What? Oh! Music's been our sole topic of discussion. 'It's not a band, or who knows, maybe there is some band called Coffee,' I say. 'But I'm talking about regular coffee. Or cappuccino if you prefer. Even decaf. You know, coffee. The beverage?'

Rambling on, I spy a half smile tugging Edie's tangerine lips. 'Sure, coffee's cool.' With that, she takes my hand and writes her digits on my wrist. Then she's out the door.

Now, I don't play games. I *scorn* games. Games are for self-destructive, insecure jerks who make up for their insecurity by toying with a chick's head. I am not that jerk. I wait for one minute, then I scramble for my cell, jab the numbers inked to my skin.

'Hello?'

'Edie?'

'A/B?'

'Yeah. It's me. So where are you?'

'Where am I? I'm still here in Dondi's. I'm waiting for my mom to pick me up.'

'So, about that coffee. You know, I could really go for a cup right now.'

A beat, followed by a barrage: 'Look, A/B, I don't work that way. If you want to see me, you have to ask me out in advance. Because I'm not some starry-eyed little groupie willing to drop everything to spend ten minutes with you, and I apologise if somehow you got that impression.'

OK, what's the cutest image you could conjure up? A kitten with its back up and its tail puffed out, right? That's Edie. Keep your wimpy, wussy girls. What I'm discovering, right there in that moment, is the best thing about an assertive female, the thing a lot of guys don't get, is that they don't whip you, they motivate you – they help make you the best you can be.

'How about Brew-Ha-Ha this Friday? Coffee. Comedy. Killer biscotti. Around six, six thirty . . . ?'

She says yes. Yes!

I can't stand stand-up, and you could crack a tooth on Brew-Ha-Ha's brittle biscotti. Even the coffee sucks. But the java joint sits on the Long Beach boardwalk, and what better way to burn off a caffeine-and-sugar buzz than a seaside stroll? Waves crashing. Sun setting. Seagulls screaming.

So we go. And it's perfect. There are six tiny plastic turtle barrettes in Edie's hair. I mention this because I'm usually blind to stuff like that. Except now, with Edie, I'm a paragon of perception. I soak up every subtle shift, every nuance, every inflection. In other words, I pay attention to her. We order lattes that taste like they were brewed in ancient Rome. A plate of brick-like biscotti, too, and get this: We both dunk! Only it's more than cookie etiquette we have in common. Between comedians we talk, and it flows – we agree a lot (great), and when we don't things get more intense (better!).

After a while, sneakers off, jeans rolled up, we hit the beach, up to our ankles in surf. We stick close together so we can hear each other over the waves. Or maybe just because we want to. Eventually we wend our way back to the slatted wooden path and park it on a bench. The sun says 'See ya,' and dusk settles in all warm and fuzzy. An ideal opportunity for a kiss. Except what we do surpasses kissing.

Maybe we're both musing on kissing as we turn towards each other, then suddenly drop our eyes. Mine fall into Edie's lap, where her hands lie like a pair of pale, folded wings. Whoa, they're so small – how did I miss that during our lessons? I reach out – careful, careful, as if the wings might fly away – till the fingers of my right hand contact the fingers of her left. The wrinkles of the knuckles, the shiny, shell-like surface of her nails. The warm cradle where etched lines spell out Edie's future – our future. Here my fingers come to rest and are greeted by a sweet, significant pressure, a squeeze of excitement that matches my own. Then our fingers interlace, fit smoothly into each other's niches, naturally inseparable.

My fingers will never ever do anything – scratch an itch or lift a spoon or strum a chord – the same way again.

The Voice

Gosh, you think you know the devil you know, then the nasty old imp goes and flip-flops on you! As of today's rehearsal, 6X seems to be a whole different box of animal crackers. The Nervous Nelly otherwise called Wynn Morgan is all lah-di-dah relaxed, while Stella's the one walking around with her face screwed up in a worried frown. And A/B? If anyone understands that boy it's me, but who is this person with the cotton-candy halo, noodling sappy Top 40 songs? Lord, what I wouldn't do for a little consistency around here!

Our practice is all off-kilter from the get-go, since *I'm* the first to arrive and everyone else is late. Then it takes them for ever to even pick up their instruments. Wynn's new carelessness has her missing the beat, and Stella, who can usually be relied on to keep Wynn on her toes, is so preoccupied she doesn't even notice. It seems this whole band is going you-know-where in a handbasket – until something incredible happens. We're hog-slopping through 'Bliss de la Mess' when A/B floats over to my microphone, leans in close with this dreamy expression, and starts going, 'Ooh, la-la-laaah; ooh-ooh, la-laah . . .' Yes, out of the clear blue sky the boy decides to sing harmony! And you know what? It sounds wonderful! What's more, I'm not the only one who thinks so.

'That's terrific, A/B! Truly inspired!' I hadn't even noticed Mr Wandweilder come in. But there he is, applauding as we finish the song. 'But it's just a start,' he says. 'I mean it, you guys — you're going to have to start putting a lot more effort in.'

The way Stella reacts you'd think Mr Wandweilder told her she'll have to live on a diet of gravel from this day forward.

'More *effort?*!' she explodes. 'You're the one that's been sleeping. We've been working our behinds off, Brian, but it's like being on a freakin' hamster wheel. Why haven't we played a single show since our album dropped, huh? Why aren't we on the road?'

Truth be told, Stella and I don't see eye-to-eye much, but it occurs to me she is one hundred per cent right! 6X is stuck in the mud! This makes me mad, and I give Mr Wandweilder a piece of my mind. 'Yes, I'd like to know that too. I . . . we . . . 6X has fans, we have to serve our public, we need to perform.' I stand by Stella to pose a united front. 'We're just wasting our time rehearsing while you've been dawdling.'

Stella snorts. 'Dawdling! You wanna know what he's really been up to? Let me tell you. He's letting our record sales pay his rent while he sucks up to new acts.'

I have no idea what Stella means by this, but Mr Wandweilder rears back like he's been slapped. Stella finds a certain satisfaction in that, so she keeps on, darting poison like a copperhead: 'You guys should have seen him, bowing and scraping to some nobody, some hayseed calls herself Cara Lee Ballantine.'

So much steam's coming out of Mr Wandweilder's ears right now you could cook a pot of corn. Meanwhile, A/B's watching like he's got ringside seats at an especially brutal boxing match. Even Wynn appears to be tuning in for the first time today. But when she jumps in she throws us all for a loop.

'Stop it, you guys, come on. Do you really think Brian's screwing us?' She steps away from her drum kit. 'You know how much he cares about us.'

As Wynn defends him, Mr Wandweilder just studies the floor. With his glasses askew and hair all in his face, he looks like a little boy getting bullied at recess.

'Did you ever think maybe there's another reason we're not on tour?' Wynn asks. 'I mean, maybe it's cosmic, beyond our comprehension – like no matter how bad we want it, fate has other plans. There are things you can't explain . . . that you basically have to accept.' She squeezes her drumsticks. 'That's why – please don't be mad, but I think I'm going to take off for a while. I've been e-mailing with my dad a lot, and he's been really making sense about me coming to Europe. I'm at a point where I should explore, be free.'

Thank goodness no flies are buzzing around or we could catch them in our open mouths. Then Mr Wandweilder lets out a low whistle. 'Oh, that's just perfect,' he says. 'Look, you guys, I hear your frustration – but I've got some of my own. Wynn's interesting metaphysical theory aside, the reason you're not on the road is rooted in hard reality. Fact: Despite your sales and the many media and promotional opportunities, 6X is not exactly a slam-dunk to book. Promoters are wary. Why? Because 6X has played, what, five shows total?'

Listening to Mr Wandweilder, we're all a different shade of shocked; the fury drains from Stella's face, and my indignation changes to shame. 'So go ahead, Wynn, pack your bags.'

Oh, no! What is he saying? Has Mr Wandweilder given up on us? Then a little grin sneaks up on him. 'Only Europe? I don't think so. You're going to Florida. That's what I popped in to tell you guys today. The 6X club tour – the 6X get-your-shit-together tour – kicks off in Orlando, right after Kendall wraps her shoot for the Gap.'

The Boy

'OK, rock star . . .'

The way Dondi says 'rock star,' he might as well be saying 'Nazi.' But hey, I warned him I had one foot on the road. So I'm not too concerned about his feelings as he doles out my final week's earnings in cash. Edie's feelings, however . . .

Her I didn't warn. Never said, between kisses (yep, we've been Siamese twins since our first date): 'Oh, by the way, savour this smooch because I'll be dropping out of your life any minute.'

Not fair! Soon as I secure a real girlfriend I have to abandon her. And I have no idea how she's going to react to the news. It'd be one thing if I'd been drafted, but state-hopping with my guitar and three hot women can't really be construed as serving my country. Making matters trickier is I'm so excited I can barely contain myself. But I won't beat around the bush. I'll tell her. Right after dinner. And dessert. And clearing the table.

Edie and I are baby-sitting her sisters, Roz, seven, and, Lily, twelve, who generally won't be caught dead hanging together but tonight join forces to tease us mercilessly. They sprawl on the living-room floor with Barbie and Ken, only they don't call them Barbie and Ken as they make the dolls hump with demented lust.

'Ooooh, suck my face, A/B! I looooove it!' squeals Lily.

'Ooooh, suck *my* face, Edie!' shrieks Roz.

'Thank Heaven for Little Girls?' I think not. 'Is there anything you can *do* about them?' I plead.

Edie positions my arm across her shoulders and snuggles against me on the couch. 'You can't let them know they annoy you,' she whispers, then sneaks a quick kiss on my neck.

'Yeah, but Edie . . .' Guilt grumbles like a burp I can't suppress. 'I have to talk to you.' Gulp. 'It's important.'

Man, does she switch gears fast. 'You!' she says, hopping up. 'Both of you. In your room. Now.'

Roz and Lily instantly know, through some uncanny sisterly cognition, that Edie isn't kidding. Without a whimper they collect their dolls and trudge upstairs.

Edie stands in front of me, hands on hips. 'I'm not going to like it, am I?' Her tone is soft — which makes it harder. Her lower lip quivers — which makes it impossible.

'No . . .' I say morosely. I pat the crocheted afghan on the sofa, inviting Edie to sit back down. A gesture she chooses to ignore. So I lean forward, take her hand off her hip and gently yank her to my side. 'The band . . . our tour . . . I've got to leave, Edie. I'm going on tour.' It feels exhilarating to say it. I hope it doesn't show.

She pulls her bottom lip tight to the top one to stem the tremulous action. Through those tight lips she mews: 'When?'

'We leave Wednesday.'

'This coming Wednesday . . . ?'

'Yeah.' In a way I wish she'd get mad, give me a dose of that trademark Edie spit and vinegar. But her eyes are big green globes and her lips are doing their damnedest to be brave.

'How long?'

'Not long,' I say. I'm holding her hands, but they seem to be getting smaller; I hold tighter so they won't disappear. 'Not even two months.'

'*Two months!* You mean you'll be gone for the holidays?' Edie is horrified. Just because we're Jewish doesn't mean we don't get caught up in the whole happy-merry vibe. I'm still a sucker for Hanukkah, even though it's a kids' holiday.

'If there was anything I could do about it, Edie, I would. But I can't. And, well, I'll be back for New Year's.'

She brightens slightly. 'New Year's? Oh . . . I've never actually had a date for New Year's Eve.'

'You do now,' I vow. 'I mean, if you want – I mean, Edie, will you go out with me on New Year's Eve?'

She sniffs again, then sits up straight. 'Yes,' she says. 'On one condition.'

'Anything,' I tell her.

'I get to meet the girls before you leave.' She's adorable when she's demanding. 'If I'm going to let you take off with them, I get to look them each in the eye.' With a whip of her pinwheel curls, Edie looks *me* in the eye. 'So set it up.'

The Boss

It's not friendship or obligation that gets us down to Sticky Thai – it's morbid fascination, the kind that makes you gawk at a car wreck. Because, be real, maybe A/B can sit around with his thumb up his butt but the rest of us are pretty busy, tour-prep-wise. Are we really motivated to hook up for lunch? Not so much. We'll be spending the next month in close quarters, stinking up the van with Taco Bell or Mickey Ds or whatever slim excuse for nutrition we can grab off the interstate.

'Come on, Stella, this is important to me.' Guilt-tripping is A/B's forte, and he's working it big-time on the phone. 'Wynn and Kendall already said OK, so you have to.'

'What do you mean *have* to?' I retort, booking it to my hair appointment. 'I *have* to get a 'fro mow, I *have* to buy Wynn a birthday present, I do not *have* to sit down to pad thai with you people.'

'It's not just us,' he baits me. 'It's . . . you have to meet someone.'

I am not playing; I don't bite, just swing into the salon with a 'yo!' So A/B's like: 'Stella? You there?' and I'm like, 'I gotta go, A/B, so stop fooling and get to the point.'

'OK, OK – I want you to come meet Edie,' he says, and before I can hit him with a 'who?' he rushes out, 'my girlfriend.'

Girlfriend? Girlfriend! 'Fine. Sticky Thai. One-thirty. I'll be there.'

My next move is to have my stylist add a hot oil treatment to my trim. I just want my hair in good shape for the road. What do I care if this Edie sees me looking busted? Kendall, now, she's gotta be losing her shit. That concerns me. The last thing I want is her going off the rails before we leave. Plus, truth, she hasn't been bugging me so much lately. Look, she was the only one who stood up with me when I called Brian out about our tour plans. And we're both on the same page as to the specifics – i.e., how bad they suck. Club tour, ha! More like Poverty Tour. Brian's having us hit every shithole between Orlando and Las Vegas so we can 'hone our chops' and 'become a mean, lean performing machine' and blah-blah-blah. No private rooms – we've got to share. No swank tour bus – just a crappy van.

Whatever. I go to the Thai place convinced I'm gonna be picking up little pieces of Kendall Taylor before the green-tea ice cream is served.

The Voice

It's nice that my mom took the morning off to bring me to the Gap shoot. Nice for her, that is. At her core, my mom is still a simple country person, so she gets awfully excited about the glitzy side of my career. Gosh, is she tickled pink to meet Delta Burke, the big-haired actress from that old TV show *Designing Women*. See, the holiday line of Gap stuff has a Nineties retro feel, and the theme for the ad campaign is old-meets-new: hot, young, cool stars like me and people who were popular back then.

Well, my mom's about as gooey as a one-minute egg, reciting plot lines from her favourite, *Designing Women*, and begging autographs not just for herself but half our hometown of Frog Level, South Carolina. Miss Burke is a lady about it, signing every piece of paper my mom thrusts at her.

Finally my mom checks her watch, gasps, and rushes off to work – thank goodness. I get into my outfit and meet up with the other stars on the seamless – that's a long, long, long sheet of blank paper that starts at the ceiling and reaches the floor like a giant roll of Bounty. An assistant turns on an enormous fan that blows our hair around – to think we've been two hours in the hair chair just to have it made mussy.

'OK, people – just . . . *relate*!' shouts the director, and we all start acting like we're at a crazy party, dancing around and singing along to the music. It's pretty fun, more free and easy than any video shoot I've been on. Time flies, and before I know it we're done – it's a wrap. The Gap people send me off with a gift bag packed with goodies, just for being in the commercial, which puts me in a super-duper mood as I head off for what is probably the silliest, most ridiculous lunch that never made the Guinness Book of World Records.

I'm just a teensy bit late as I stroll in, but I'm sure they understand – it is rather inconvenient for me to be rushing over there after the shoot. But I couldn't skip the lunch; that would be bad manners. And I couldn't be rude to Edie – that would be beneath my dignity. You know, when A/B first told me about her I was aghast; but then I figured out what this whole how-do-you-do is about. That gave me a sigh of relief and I knew exactly how to conduct myself.

'Well heyyyy, Edie!' I say before they can even greet me. 'I'm Kendall. It's so nice to meet you! A/B has told me so much about you.' Well, that last one is a little white lie, since A/B sprang this girl like a jack-in-the-box clown. I sit down and open my menu with a smile.

Edie smiles back, then turns to A/B. 'Do you want to share an appetizer, sweetie?'

Sweetie. I hear that and I think, *Poor thing!* Poor, sweet, simple, ordinary thing. She believes A/B is really her boyfriend and, well . . . it's not my place to dissuade her. We order a whole bunch of food – noodles and satay and coconut soup – and then I ask how they all met.

Edie narrows her green eyes for a second. 'I thought he told you all about me . . .' she says.

'Oh, you know A/B,' says Wynn. 'He told us how cool you were, how pretty—'

'And how nice,' I chime in.

Wynn nods in agreement. 'But how you met? What guy would go into that kind of detail?'

Edie balls a fist, gives A/B a playful chuck on the bicep. 'Obviously not my guy,' she says with a sigh. 'He was my guitar teacher. Only now I get my lessons free.'

Now Stella, who's been mighty quiet, leaps on this like a blue jay after a peanut. 'You play?'

'She's great,' says A/B, putting his arm around Edie proudly. 'She's got a killer ear and can figure out just about anything—'

'Yeah, anything that doesn't involve a B flat seventh,' she says. 'My stubby little fingers can't—'

'Hey, you're talking about the fingers I love!' A/B grabs Edie's hand and, Lord in heaven, pecks each fingertip in turn. He sure is putting on a show. 'I've taught her a couple of leads, and she's got a real knack for bass lines too.'

An all-too-familiar zigzag of heat lightning flashes in Stella's eyes, but she blinks it out. It's as though she wants to be pleasant – or at least not overtly hostile – but can't quite manage it. The way she stirs her Thai iced coffee you'd think she wants to bore a hole in the bottom of the glass. Why would Stella be in the least bit perturbed by this no-account girl? Because Edie fiddles around on guitar? Or is Stella being unnecessarily protective of me? Well, I am fully bewildered.

Lunch is served and food sort of neutralises the conversation. Throughout the meal, I steal peeks at A/B and Edie. They eat off each other's plates, and comment after every few morsels with a 'Yum!' Edie seems so . . . utterly average, and again I'm stricken by how sad it is. Not that A/B would consciously be cruel, but he couldn't possibly be serious about romance now, right before our tour, so this dalliance with – well, just about any girl who came down the pike would do – it's obviously an attempt to make me jealous.

I must get all lost in thought, musing on how heartbroken Edie is bound to be, and whether green-tea ice cream might actually be any good, when Stella elbows me in the ribs with a 'Yo!' Startled, I look up to see Wynn absent from the booth and A/B and Edie making mushy faces. 'Wynn went to pee, so I wanted to ask – you wanna go shop for her birthday present after this? We could chip in on something.'

That iced coffee must've given Stella brain freeze – the way she's suddenly making like my best friend. Truth is I haven't given a kernel of thought to Wynn's gift, so shopping with Stella would certainly get it out of the way, but I've been running around doing for other people all day long and I have had my fill. 'Ooh, Stella, I would, only you know what time I had to be on set this morning? Five thirty! I tell you what, why don't you pick out something real nice – you know Wynn's taste better than I do – and I'll pay you back.'

I beg off like I could lie down and sleep till Sunday, gathering up my stuff and saying my goodbyes. But once I get outside, I don't really feel tired, exactly, but I start to feel . . . funny, off. At first I lose my bearings, like I'm not sure which direction to walk in. Then something strange and clammy seems to seize me by the throat, like a plastic garbage bag closing over my head. I can see . . . but barely. I can breathe . . . but barely. Forcing myself to put one foot in front of the other, I make my way up the street as if against a vicious wall of wind. Every face looks to be wearing an iron mask – mean and cold. I turn my eyes up to one of the tall buildings, and I get all dizzy.

Then I see it. A sign. Bright and blinking and beckoning. I hurry inside, sit down at a table to collect myself. An aroma fills my nostrils – it is sent to me from heaven! I'm still a little shaky, and I realise that even though I just came from lunch, it feels as though I haven't touched a morsel all day. I can't explain, I just know I'm starving. Thank you, Jesus, for leading me into the salvation of Carolina Fried Chicken. I'm hungry, that's all. So very, very hungry.

PART TWO
Clubland

'Don't pass out now, there's no refund . . .'

— *Elvis Costello*

The Body

I-95 is a far cry from the Champs-Elysées — but I'll take it. We're jangly as a charm bracelet as we rocket toward Orlando on my sixteenth birthday, a heartbeat-quickening, anything-can-happen near-hysteria infecting all of us (including our chaperones, Gaylord and Peony). We stop for lunch at a roadside Applebee's, and they go into a hammy 'Happy Birthday' and present me with a journal — leather bound, moiré-patterned endpapers, my initials on the front — plus this elegant fountain pen. They all chipped in, not just money but thought, and I appreciate the gift because it's the thought that counts.

After all, I'll probably never use it. I'm not the type of writer who'd *want* fancy paper and a gold pen. I'm strictly a composition notebook and Uni-Ball kind of girl. Looking at the journal, the embossed monogram almost mocks me. I open it, run my finger down a page, and the fine-milled powdery texture seems to tense away from my touch the way my mom might inhale on a crowded elevator. I'll keep the journal in my suitcase the whole tour, then shove it in a drawer at home. I'll look at it occasionally and it will remind me of the band;

hopefully perspective will make it a completely happy memory. Because right now? I'm a little disappointed. I mean, I wouldn't expect Kendall to choose something I'd like; she is so self-involved it's scary. And A/B just shelled out his share, I'm sure – he was probably as surprised as I was when I opened the gift. Only I guess I was hoping that Stella would know better . . . know *me*. Instead, she and Kendall actually appear to be bonding. Talk about an unholy alliance! Ooh, that was mean. It's just that those two aren't oil and water, they're lava and lightning – a combustible combo that would ordinarily make you break out the asbestos jumpsuit. But there they are sharing chilli fries, and no one nearby has burst into flame.

The Boss

A lert MTV News – this is huge news, all right. Wynn is being idolised. Only it's not some toenail-clipping collector stalker. The sick thing about it is Wynn Morgan's superfan is as famous in her world – no, forget that, more famous – than 6X is in ours.

So here's the scene. If you thought Orlando was all cutsey-wootsey theme park plastic, you're ninety-nine per cent right. But there's a wrong side of the tracks – and the jewel in its tarnished crown is Goudy's, this grimy, broken-down bar. We roll in around five PM, thinking this *can't* be the place – there's not even a stage in the backroom, just a platform about six inches off the ground. A/B groans, saying he used to play dives like this when he was twelve, the novelty prodigy in his uncle's cover band. Forget about a sound check; forget about a sound *guy* – except for a few geezers at the bar, the place is deserted. We figure we'll unload our gear, then find our hotel, chill, get a snack.

Just then the door busts open. 'SEEKS-X is in the house, yes?' A cross between a trumpet and a bullhorn, a booming screech. 'WEEN MORGAN is in the house, yes?' We're all thinking, *What tha . . . ?* since none of us knows a soul in Orlando. The owner of the voice strides forward, followed by a small posse, and we stare at this . . . this giantess. Six-feet-something, short spiked hair, bronzed limbs bulging.

'WEEEEN! WEEN MORGAN!'

To everyone's holy-shit astonishment the Amazon with an accent grabs Wynn in a wrestling hold and lifts her off the ground. To our even greater astonishment Wynn exuberantly returns the hug.

'Oh my God!' cries Wynn. 'I can't believe – Malinka!'

They stand stock-still, smiling into each other's faces. Then, suddenly, they start jumping up and down while holding on to each other's arms, a thunderous partner pogo that makes the whole bar shake. A few seconds later they stop, and Malinka smoothes a wisp out of Wynn's eyes.

'Malinka, what are you *doing* here?' Wynn asks.

I still have no idea who this chick is, but Wynn clearly does.

'Here is where I live, where I train.' The big girl squeezes Wynn's shoulders. 'You are not mad, Ween? When I saw Seeks-X would play here, I was so excited I could not even wait for the night.'

'No, yes, I'm sorry – of course!' says Wynn, all flustered. 'It's amazing to see you. I mean, I thought you'd have forgotten about us by now.'

'Oh no!' Malinka laughs, and touches Wynn's hair again. 'I love Seeks-X.'

The two of them are having a moment, and everyone else – me, the rest of the band, Gaylord, Peony, Malinka's crew, the hard-core Goudy's clientele – we pretty much cease to exist.

Then some vestigial traces of ESPN must wander across A/B's brain. 'Holy crap!' he says softly. 'That's Malinka Kolakova – the Brutal Butterfly.'

And then we're all kicking ourselves. Because not even the most sports-ignorant clod on the planet hasn't heard of the teenage tennis ace who's been bringing the pain at tournaments left and right. We'd even met her before – she was one of the random celebs who hit our record release party in New York. The nickname? Sure, I remember from back pages of the *Post* and last minutes of the ten o'clock news: Apparently, the Russian eighteen-year-old emerged out of nowhere – as if from a chrysalis – and every time she administers a beat-down on the court, she busts this signature arm-flap move. Looking at those arms, now happily enveloping Wynn again, gives me a funny little shiver, like I'm glad she likes our band. I sure as hell wouldn't want to be on the hating end of those arms, all right.

The Body

As far as birthday surprises go, this is one for the record books: Malinka showing up like we're long-lost friends finally reunited, instead of two people who met casually at a party. Of course, we hit it off immediately, even with the language barrier. Talking to Malinka is so much fun. Not funny, like you're laughing at her — it's more like a game trying to understand her skewed hybrid of textbook English and American slang. It's not like she's stupid or anything; I swear, she's pretty smart . . . for a jock. Basically, though, the best thing about having her here is she helps my nerves — I'm having serious first-night-of-the-tour jitters, but as far as Malinka's concerned, I can do no wrong.

When she finds us at Goudy's and offers me a lift to the hotel, I'm like, *Yes!* A respite from that stifling van. I don't even care if my bandmates are envious as I slide into the passenger side of this brand-new bright red sports car, a Porsche I think, with an open roof. Malinka drives like a maniac, but it feels sublime speeding along, sun on our skin, hair a riot in the wind. In the hotel parking lot we keep gabbing away. It's like she won't let me go to the room without her. Only when

I point out she's still wearing her tennis whites does she agree to go home and change. I check in and race upstairs to the shower before the van pulls in and Stella, my roommate, commandeers it.

'I hate you so much right now,' Stella informs me. She's sitting on the bed near the window, selecting clothes from her suitcase, as I exit the steamy bathroom. 'Utter, extreme loathing and contempt are coming off me in waves.'

Her expression, thankfully, denies this. In fact, she seems amused, intrigued. 'Ooh, I feel it,' I say, falling on the other bed, flailing in mock agony. 'Please, make it stop! Make it stop!'

'You want to at least begin explaining what all this is about?' Stella asks.

Sitting up, I unwrap my towel turban. 'Malinka? I have no clue,' I tell her. 'I mean, we met at the Otto's thingee – I knew she was into the band, but . . .' I trail off. 'I don't know, I guess Orlando's boring. She heard we were playing, and—'

'Don't give me that,' Stella says. 'Your girl Malinka acts like you two were separated at birth.' She pulls off her jeans and tosses them aside in a ball. 'There's this major megabucks athlete following 6X – you can't buy that kind of publicity. So do us all a favour, Wynn, and don't screw it up.' Shaking her head, she hits the bathroom.

'Malinka lives here,' I yell at the door. 'I'd hardly call that *following* the band!'

'What-Ehhh-Ver!' Stella retorts over the whoosh of the shower.

★ ★ ★

Later, back at Goudy's, I realise how glad I am Malinka's coming. Orlando's entire population of disenfranchised youth has converged on the bar, but these kids are not here for 6X. The black-clad contingent has come for a megadose of homegrown goth, courtesy of Dead for Centuries, who go on at nine. The rest will soon be clamouring for Clovis Knot, which someone describes to me as *creamo* – cracker rock meets emo.

DFC are grinding through their encore when Malinka makes an entrance that distracts from the sanguine spectacle on the make-shift stage. She is . . . gleaming – and while it could just be good moisturiser, I think it's something more, this magnetic quality. Of course, she's not alone. The squat, muscular man (her trainer?) and thin, leathery woman (some other sort of handler?) who hovered around earlier, as well as four girls Malinka introduces as her cousins – Cousin Letya, Cousin Lina, Cousin Cosima, and Cousin Yelena. I don't know if the cousins are serious about tennis, too, but they're certainly serious about partying. Boisterous and beautiful, with imposing jawlines and slanted eyes, they're like a pack of Slavic supermodels, screaming toasts and tossing back Stoli Vanil. While the cousins opt for designer garb – lingerie tops, swishy skirts, too much jewellery – Malinka's more low-key in her cropped jeans and wifebeater. Still, she's the one you can't peel your eyes off. The Brutal Butterfly. A superstar.

The Voice

Far be it from me to judge, but the way people fawn over athletes nowadays gets my goat. Gosh, what does it take to smack some silly ball across a net? You could teach a chimpanzee to do the same thing. So when Gaylord comes in to breakfast waving the *Orlando Orange Press* and hooting about how we made the gossip page, it's just plain peevesome to find the item all about Malinka Kolakova with scarcely a nod to 6X.

Irksome as it is, I don't say a word, just finish my wheat toast and fruit salad. That's one of the few meals that passes Miss Peony's scrutiny. She sure is critical when it comes to food, her being vegan and all. We've only been on the road two days, and she's already found cause to make that disapproving puckery face. But how are you supposed to be healthy, not to mention politically correct, at a turnpike McDonald's? Last night, before the gig, she gave me grief about my room-service burger, too, at which point I had to remind Miss Peony that her job is to tutor me, not lecture on nutrition or animal rights. That pretty much put her in her place. Although the thing with Miss Peony is, when you win you feel like you lose, and when you lose you feel like you win. I'm probably not explaining that too well, but that's Miss Peony all over – hard to explain.

Anyway, I could sit here and list all the irritations of this tour so far. The cramped van. The crummy venues (if that nasty Goudy's is any indication!). Sharing a room with Miss Peony (who hogs the bathroom, despite her lackadaisical notions about body hair). But I ought to stop or I'll short-circuit the camera. And I don't want to be a grump. So I take a seat, put on my headphones so Miss Peony won't start filling my ear (two hours of lessons a day ought to be enough!), and gaze out the window as we head west towards Alabama. To keep my thoughts positive, I think about how A/B sang background vocals on two songs last night, leaning over and la-la-laing in my mike.

The situation with A/B – I've pledged to rectify it during this road trip. But being forward with boys – well, I was not raised that way. Plus, A/B is shy in his way. Double-plus, although I don't believe for one little second he's serious about that Edie girl, he went to such trouble putting up a front about her. I could never make a play for a boy who's attached – or says he is. That would be breaking a commandment: coveting thy neighbour's wife. I peek over to where he's sitting, next to Stella, the two of them arguing over his Game Boy. She sticks her tongue out at him, and he gives her a little shove, but it's just joshing. They get along so easily.

Suddenly, the sight of her with A/B – she's got him in a headlock now, and she's giving him a noogie – sends a hard lump to my throat. *What if? But no!* Swallowing the lump, I can see beyond the physical contact – they're like brother and sister.

Watching Stella act goofy instead of all attitude-y gives me a happy feeling. Right then I decide that the next time we have a minute alone, I'll find a way to get some advice about A/B. Because Stella is experienced, assertive – she knows how to go for what she wants. I'll ask her for some tips on how to make things right with A/B. You know, get him back – because back with me is where that boy is meant to be.

The Boy

Please do not engage me on a secret mission. I suck at them, royally. I can handle a secret. I can deal with a mission. But the combo of mission and secret, that's too much. So when we check into the motel in Mobile and I dig my cell out of my pack, I get a little *ping!* of alarm at Brian's message. 'Call me when you're alone. There's something I need to discuss with you *mano a mano*.' Well, OK, I could have blown him off, but I defy you to show me the guy who can resist anything presented as '*mano a mano*.'

Once Gaylord – in eye mask and earplugs – conks out for his power nap, I give Brian a jingle. 'It's A/B, what's up?' I'm all business.

Brian, however, comes on like he just poured a piña colada. 'A/B! What's happening? How was last night?' He sticks to the blasé bit for a whole minute, then pushes past the pleasantries. 'Ahhh, A/B, I need you to do me a favour. I need you to look after our little girl.'

What is he talking about? And please let it not have anything to do with Kendall!

'Look, this club tour is meant to prime you guys for

something bigger, and everyone needs to focus. Everyone. I know I can trust you to make sure Kendall doesn't . . . do anything. Like get loaded, run off with some guy. Or any other diva antics.'

'Um, I'm not sure what you mean, Brian. I don't think Kendall's touched a drop since that incident with Reid-Vincent Mitchell.'

'A/B. This is *me*. And we're talking about Kendall. Kendall Taylor. Can you honestly tell me you don't think that sweet, lovely, innocent girl could succumb to the dark side at the slightest provocation?' Brian's stirring himself into one of his televangelist-type verbal riffs. 'And who's better suited to be her valiant knight than you?'

My head is spinning from all these mixed references – James Bond, Star Wars, King Arthur – sheesh!

'Gaylord's road managing. He's got enough on his plate. Peony Randolph? She's still an outsider. It has to be you. You've got to look out for Kendall, make sure she doesn't get into trouble. Because it won't take much for that mother of hers to pull The Voice out by the scruff of her neck. Out of the tour, out of the band. And no one wants that.'

Does the guy even need *oxygen?* I wonder.

'Besides, Kendall is crazy about you. There are no jealousy issues like she might have with the girls. She sees you as an equal, talent-wise, so there's that respect. Most important, she trusts you. You're like a big brother to her.'

There, Brian Wandweilder, there you are wrong. Because I know something you don't: I know about a certain lip-lock that Kendall and I shared on the red-eye from LA earlier this year.

So I can assert with absolute certainty that Kendall Taylor does *not* see me as a brother.

The Boss

Thumbing through the Yellow Pages in my Mobile, Alabama motel room, I locate a couple of thrift stores – and I'm itching to check them out. It's not like I don't love dropping a wad of paper at a cute boutique. And you know I bought myself a trophy bag the day that advance cheque from Universe arrived. But combing through a Salvation Army or Goodwill is like a shopping safari. Plus I do pick up old-school T-shirts and funky jewellery. And vinyl records? They practically give them away! Not that I have a turntable, but A/B does, so I figure I'll go motivate his lazy ass, get him to come thrifting with me while Kendall and Wynn are at their lesson. I'm just about to go knock on his door when someone taps on mine.

'Ken Doll!' I can't resist clowning on Peonut's whackass accent. 'Aren't you late for your daily academic interlude? Wynn's already out of here.'

'Yes, that's what I was hoping,' she says. 'Can I come in?'

I step aside. Kendall sits on the bed, stands up, sits down again. I plunk down in the desk chair and segue into shrink mode: 'So what's your problem?'

'Who says I have a problem, Stella? I don't have a problem!' Kendall's defensive, evasive – and I think: *This is gonna be pointless.* 'I just want to talk to you is all. I want you to help me with . . . uhhh . . .'

'With your problem? Come on, Kendall, just spit it.' Then, ever so kindly, 'Really. I want to help. Really.'

'Well, OK, here it is.' She tilts towards me, inching off the bed, and I lean forward too, like the fate of the universe is at stake. 'That girl, that Edie – you don't think A/B could possibly be serious about her, do you? I mean, gosh, what kind of fool gets involved with someone right before going away for two months!'

Truth? I've already pondered and dismissed that myself. I nod encouragingly at Kendall.

'So I've determined that he's using her to get to me. To remind me how attractive he is, how desirable. Because, you know, A/B and I, we had . . . well, we almost . . .'

So that's it! 'Yeah, Kendall, I know.' I do not add: '. . . that you were deluding yourself that A/B was sweating you.'

She smiles, seeing I'm so understanding. 'Well, then, you know A/B and I are destined to be together. But he's too shy, and I, well, it's just not my upbringing to pursue a boy, so, umm, if you could . . .'

'If I could what?' Suddenly this conversation is starting to bug me, and I'm not sure why. 'Get you the hookup? Find out what he's feeling? Praise you to the skies?'

'Oh, Stella, yes!' Kendall claps her hands in sheer delight. 'Exactly!' She stands up and heads for the door. 'Oh, I knew deep down you were a good, decent person. I knew you were

60

my friend, Stella!' To my utter shock, Kendall throws herself on me for a quick, tight hug. 'Thanks, Stella, thanks so much! I can't wait to hear everything.'

The Body

Just because someone you respect and admire disagrees with you, you shouldn't take it as a slam. It's not an act of cruelty or malicious rejection. They just don't happen to share that particular idea or opinion. Except now that I'm getting tutored by P – that's what I've always called Penelope Randolph – she's always planting interesting or challenging stuff in my brain. But if I mention it to Stella, she just sneers. And that sneer feels like a steel-toed kick, Crazy, right? I mean, she's trashing P, not me. Or am I a retard by extension for buying into the oh-so-alternative, deliberately, defiantly weirdo routine P waves like she's doing a left-of-centre Dance of the Seven Veils?

I don't know. I guess I just want – need – Stella to . . . approve of me. When she does, I'm good. When she doesn't, it hurts. Physically. In my heart, my head, all over, flitting twinges of burn and ache. This bothers me. The power she has over me. I doubt she's even aware that my self-esteem is completely contingent upon her perception of me at any given moment. What a mushy, pliable substance, my self-esteem. Play-Doh . . . no. A marshmallow . . . no. A gerbil – yes, that's it. When Stella high-fives or compliments me after a gig, or simply gives me a sharp nod, my self-esteem's a happy, healthy little rodent. When Stella sneers or snorts or sucks her teeth, *splat!* – gerbil pancake.

Stella's self-esteem? It's a string of freshwater pearls. Natural. Enviable. Hard.

You'd think after Florida, with Malinka . . . I mean, if anyone's approval ought to make me feel validated . . . But when I try to figure out what I've done to deserve her iron-clad, vice-grip of instant devotion, all I can come up with is that Malinka thinks I'm cool. I play in a platinum-selling band and I'm . . . you know . . . how I look, and she's from another country so to her I represent the American Dream. The rich WASP rock goddess. Ick. Malinka probably has a new best friend every week. I'm a fleeting fancy. Today Wynn Morgan, tomorrow Crimson Snow or whoever. Not that I blame Malinka. I mean, she doesn't know me.

Nobody does. That's the thing. The raw ugly meat of the thing that sits undigested in my stomach and gets bigger and fatter by the minute. People see me – what I look like, what I do, the surface – and they stop. It's enough for them. It's not enough for me.

The Boss

Ready for a real mind-thwack? I've got a thing for A/B! A minor thing, possibly just a virus: here today, what–the–hell–was–I–smoking tomorrow. Could be an early symptom of road burn — away from all that's familiar, I'm casting my line at the most convenient fish. Whatever the cause, there it is, small but gooey, a caramel stuck in a corner of my consciousness. Incompre–freakin'–hensible, but if it doesn't exist, what else is keeping me from making good on my promise to Kendall?

It's not like I haven't had a chance to big her up. Prime example: this wild–goose chase me and A/B get up to. After bailing in Mobile, he swore he'd thrift with me here in Jackson — so off we go, searching for an elusive Goodwill. Wandering around, we mostly talk business. The shit factor of the tour — and the necessity of it.

'I know the venues suck,' he says, 'but comparatively speaking so do we.'

'Yo, speak for yourself, dude!' Of course he can't speak for himself — we both know he's got the talent thing covered.

'Hey, having a hit record doesn't make us a powerhouse performing entity,' he says. 'Brian's right. We need to hone our chops. And where would you rather mess up – in Bumdunk, Mississippi . . . or on *Saturday Night Live?*'

I cringe accordingly – screwing up on *SNL* is such a benchmark no-no in the post-Ashlee era. And suddenly I start to feel bad. Real bad. 'You know what, forget this,' I say. 'I don't wanna search for this stupid Goodwill any more.'

'Um, OK – your call, Stella. How 'bout we just grab some coffee?'

'Only if we can get it to go.' I put a hand on A/B's arm. 'Look, I'm so mad at myself right now. I don't wanna be the reason concert promoters won't book 6X. No, don't make excuses for me – I know I need to work on my game. And it's not just my playing . . . I need to have a breakthrough with background vocals. I know Brian wants me to.' Self-flagellation is really not my style, but here I am, whipping myself into a frenzy. 'It's so freakin' frustrating! I hear harmonies in my head, but singing while slamming out a beat? I don't know how Wynn does it. And you! Mister I'll-Just-Stand-Here-and-Flick-Licks, now you're singing too – I'm the only one who can't make the leap.'

Am I yelling? I must be, since conservatively attired Jacksonians are cutting this raging rock chick a wide berth on the sidewalk. A/B puts his hands on my shoulders. 'Shhh, come on, it's OK, calm down. Jesus, Stella – you're always so intense.'

For half a second I want to shake him off, except his hands, his voice, those warm brown eyes brimming with concern plus a twist of humour, they're stabilising me. Yet at the same time I'm getting stirred up – an oh–damn different kind of stirred up.

A/B is touching me.

And not in a gimme-back-my-Game-Boy way. His long, strong, fret-ministering fingers melt my T-shirted shoulders. And did I never notice how delectable his lips are? The subtle ginger tang of his breath? That supercute sloppy sprout of curls and that new grooming addition – the sexy sideburns?

If this is happening – and I'm not one hundred per cent sure it's not some trick of the light – it has to stop. Right. Now. So I say: 'Stop!'

'Stop?' A/B doesn't have a clue. Or does he? 'Stop what, Stella?'

'Oh – I'm talking to myself.' The answer comes too quick, pulled at random off a shelf in the lie library. 'I do that, when I'm freaking. I tell myself "stop" out loud.' I should manoeuvre away from his touch, but I can't, or won't – whatever, I don't. '*Pffff!* Check me out.' I look in his eyes. 'I was on the verge there, wasn't I?'

Now A/B steps back; his hands fall to his sides. 'Yeah, well, I'm glad you got it together. Because if you lost it, I probably would have too. And a Jew boy and a black girl getting hysterical in public – they can arrest you for that in Mississippi.'

I laugh. Nervously. Damn it!

Then A/B says he's cool to go back to his room and run through the set, jam a little, coax my vocal chords. And we do. That's *all* we do. But Kendall? Edie? Yeah, well, somehow they don't come up. After our one-on-one practise, I'm feeling pretty high on life, until guess who chases me down in the hallway to jack my good mood.

'Stella!' Kendall cries my name.

Really, all the world's a stage to that one. All I say is, 'Hey . . .'

'Hay is for horses, Stella!' Kendall tails me back to my room. 'What the heck is going on around here?'

'What are you talking about?' I ask, Ms Indifferent, slinging off my bass. Where's Wynn when I need her? Her presence would get Kendall off my back, but she's probably meditating or tied up in some other kind of bullshit bugaboo with Peony.

'Didn't I see you coming out of A/B's room just now?' Kendall wants to know.

'Yeah, so? We were practising, do you mind?' She buys it – I watch the wind of accusation deflate from her sails.

'Oh, well of course, I figured *that* out!' She covers her ass, then gets all cajoling. 'I meant what's going on? What did you find out? About the Edie girl, about A/B and me?'

I plop on the bed, unlace my Docs. 'Oh . . . that,' I say. 'Didn't really discuss it.'

'What!' She's instantly enraged again. 'Stella, you said—'

I show her the hand to cut her off. 'Look, Kendall, I don't know who told you the solar system revolves around you, but you've been misinformed.' *Clunk!* I throw one big boot against the wall. 'A/B and I were *busy*, we were *working;* we are trying to ensure that when this Poverty Tour is over, 6X is ready to play with the big dogs.' *Ba-boom!* The other boot. I stand-up, all regal – but I'm fronting, feeling more like Brutus than Caesar. 'So maybe your love life is not my highest priority. Now if you don't mind I'm gonna shower. We've got sound check in less than an hour.'

The Boy

Am I on the road with three ladies – or three linebackers? If you ever watched my bandmates put away a meal, you'd be confused too. Definitely not a bunch of 'I'll just have a salad' girls. This is not a complaint – I'm glad they hype the non-emaciated look. My own love-bug Edie's got some junk in the trunk, as they say, and I'm all for it. Trouble is, we're all getting a little sick of the same-old road food, so when we get lost looking for a Cracker Barrel and wind up in front of this place with a weather-beaten sign proclaiming authentic home cooking, we're psyched.

Then we walk inside. Buford's Tavern is authentic uh-huh – authentically chainsaw massacre. Smoke hangs like cobwebs above the bar. The floor is sticky, and I could be wrong but I'm thinking it's not from Silly String. Three old guys roost up on stools, beer in one hand, cigarette in the other; they've probably been there since the Clinton administration. All the men are fixated on one of two static-stricken televisions on either end of the bar – each tuned to a different channel. Behind the bar another Methuselah clutches a grey dishrag. He smiles. There is not a tooth in his head.

'Kin I get y'alls something?' he asks.

We all just gape in response, except for Peony. Apparently she's seen her share of beggars, lepers, and hobos – she's not the least bit fazed.

'Yes, sir,' she says. 'A table for six, please.'

This takes a few seconds to register on Old Man Buford. He hawks deep in his throat, spits into the cloth, scratches his head. 'Y'alls not from around here, are you?'

A groan escapes me. Stella giggles in answer and pokes me in the ribs.

'No sir, we're not,' Peony says. 'But we are hungry. That is, if you're serving. If not, perhaps you can recommend a –'

'Oh, no, that'd be dandy – glad to have you! My daughter May Verna's the best cook in the county.' He drops his rag and navigates around the bar. 'We just don't get many folks for dinner, since they built that derned Cracker Barrel. Feeding y'alls is just about going to make May Verna's year – mostly she just puts on the spread for me and them children. Come on back, y'all have a seat.'

This is the part where we wonder if perhaps the best move is a hasty exit, followed by a tip-off to the health department. But Peony admonishes us with a vibe of 'Nonsense!' There are three more TV sets going full blast in the back room, and we each pick one to stare at as Buford toddles off, hollering 'May Verrr-na!' Out comes a sturdy, apple-cheeked woman, wearing an apron and a smile containing a reassuring number of teeth. May Verna tells us they haven't had menus since the fire of '98, but she could fix us up just about anything, then rattles off a tempting list. Peony tells her to 'go off and create,' and once

69

May Verna realises that means we'll eat anything, she bustles toward her kitchen.

Fifteen minutes later, the most amazing smells drift our way. And when May Verna, accompanied by several sturdy, apple-cheeked, ample-teethed children, proudly hauls out plates of food, we fill our faces like there's no tomorrow. Smothered pork chops, chicken and dumplings, black-eyed peas, mac and cheese. Pitchers of sweet iced tea wash it all down to make room for more. I feel a little sorry for Peony. For all her posturing she won't pig out with the rest of us. Nibbles a biscuit. Sniffs the sweet potatoes suspiciously. Hey, even the vegetables taste a bit like bacon here at Buford's Tavern, so what's a vegan to do? Hope Gaylord will pull into a Tofu Hut after the gig, I guess!

But the rest of us are scarfing like there's no tomorrow – until suddenly Wynn gasps with her mouth full and points to one of the TV sets. 'Everyone look!'

The Body

I'm not much of a TV person; I guess that's why all the flickering sets at Buford's Tavern are driving me nuts. They're so distracting I think I might have a seizure, but I'm glad I can't ignore them because I'm the one who notices Kendall's commercial. 'Everyone look!' I shriek. And there she is, dancing around with Alinda Monserat – remember her? She had this ginormous album in the Nineties and then, *floop!*, disappeared. The camera cuts away to another set of celebs, then a third, then back to Kendall and Alinda. We all start clapping and whoo-ing over Kendall's advertising debut.

Everyone but Kendall. And I doubt she is attempting false modesty. Kendall's accustomed to handling praise with a clumsy kind of aplomb. When she does her thank yous onstage, she maintains that unspoiled sweetness. Only now she looks mortified – her pout, her pallor, the way her posture clenches. The way she pushes her plate away.

Maybe I should ask what's wrong, but I chicken out. My imagination's been known to run away with me – I'll sense something on an emotional level that's just me projecting my own insecurities. Plus, sometimes, with Kendall, you don't ask because you don't want to get her started. We still have a show to do, and I'd rather not incite a pre-gig meltdown.

And it turns out to be our best date yet. A/B's on a roll with his background vocals, and tonight, instead of singing into Kendall's mike, he ambles over to Stella, and they la-la-la cheek-to-cheek. I'm not saying I actually *hear* Stella sing, but she's trying. Best of all is Kendall. Just when I think she can't get any more mountain-high-valley-low, she goes off the charts, her voice coming from some primal place within her core.

So I don't know. I tell myself I was hallucinating when I thought she was upset at dinner. And I believe myself. Until around three the next morning.

Stella's conked out in the next bed, but I've been tossing and turning. The motel pillows are flat as pantyliners, and the coverlet is scratchy. I think about grabbing my journal but don't want to risk waking Stella, so after a while I creep towards the window and crack the curtains to check out the moon. It's nearly full – a huge, bright, benevolent ball, golden rather than silver, the proverbial harvest moon. Incredibly bright, it illuminates the parking lot, the road, and the swimming pool outside my window. As I sweep my gaze down, I'm confused; then distressed by what I see.

A lone, robe-swathed figure on a lounge chair. Surrounded by scraps of coloured paper. Butterfinger, Kit Kat, Snickers, Crunch. Could it be? Yes, who else? Kendall must have hit the vending machines in the hallway, raided, ransacked, looted, and pillaged them. Deliberately, methodically, she unwraps a candy bar, stuffs it in her mouth, swigs from a can of Dr Pepper, and goes for another. The air outside is still; the litter of wrappers barely flutters as, piece by piece, Kendall devours her cache.

The Boy

Who knew Oklahoma City was such a hotbed of rock-and-roll activity? I thought Flaming Lips – and that's it. Yeah, well, the place is apparently crawling with bands, psyching me up for our Halloween performance. The town's hipster strip – lined with clubs and coffee houses, comic book stores, skate shops, and 'usedtique' emporiums – got special open-all-night permission for the annual Sick 'Ween Scene event. The music won't stop till six AM. The best part? No adult supervision!

See, Peony, Halloween is a sacred night for her, so she'll hook up with some local witches she tracked down online. And Gaylord? Poor dude has some kind of twenty-four-hour thing that's been wrecking his system for the last thirty. No picnic for me, either – I drove the van while he moaned in back; plus, rooming with him has been not-so-fragrant. But that means 6X in O-K can get as loud, fast, and out of control as we want. Whoo!

In keeping with the spirit of things, we decide to costume up, cosmetically. All three of the girls empty their make-up bags, and Wynn -unleashes her visually artsy side, painting our faces in the glamour-ghoul look. We catch a few acts before our own gig – we're on a bill with Land of Rotten, who've got the psychobilly thing down to a psychoscience. They're a tough act to follow, but that just amps our intensity – that plus the mask of make-up and the vibe of the night cranks our kick-ass factor even higher. Afterwards we wander around from club to club. A little before two, I escort Kendall back to the turn-of-the-century hotel we're staying at, and I don't know if she's as pooped as she says she is, but she keeps her head on my shoulder the whole time. Wynn hits the wall around three thirty, and me and Stella – night-crawling overachievers that we are – see she gets safely to their room.

'So, where to next?' I ask.

Me and Stella wedge into an alley doorway – attempting to gain shelter from the crowd, which is pretty punch-drunk delirious by now. She consults her Sick 'Ween Scene programme, then shrugs. 'You know what? I don't care what we see next, but if I don't get some caffeine in me soon, you're gonna be peeling me off the sidewalk.'

She doesn't have to twist my arm! We clamber into the first Java joint we spy, find a table, and order triple-espresso-infused tall ones. The spindly stage is barren, but the place is roaring loud, and we're so wired-tired, we don't even talk; instead we stare vacantly, like zombies. Then I become aware that someone has taken the stage. This guy, about my age, just seems to appear – hocuspocus, abracadabra, *voilà*. Looks like Jimi Hendrix – wild hair, high cheekbones, fledgling moustache, sienna skin. Dressed like Malcolm X – sombre suit with narrow lapels, white button-down, skinny tie. He stands at the mike and gazes, calm yet intent, at the meleé, until slowly but surely, one by one, partying patrons notice he's there. From the first flicker of attention, this smile starts to form on his face – a smile of almost child-like satisfaction. Once he's got about half of us he puts on his guitar, a Gibson acoustic. This puts more eyes on him, but still he waits, practising some kind of hypnotism. Eventually he gets what he wants. Eeerily, everyone goes from roaring mindlessly to murmuring with anticipation.

'Welcome to the Didion Jones Show,' he says in a sleepy bottom-drawer baritone. 'I am Didion Jones.'

At that moment, Stella's heart, soul, and mind airlift out of her body and abandon me.

The Boss

Well, now I know. I freakin' know, all right. I *know*.

I know what Romeo and Juliet knew, what Tristan and Isolde knew, what Sid and Nancy knew.

I know that anything I thought I knew – about Brian, about A/B, about any other guy on the planet – was not true, that those thoughts of not-knowing or near-knowing were just a set-up, so that when I really knew, I'd know. I'd know for sure. Like I know now.

I don't know if he knows, but I know that I know. How could he know? He can't, of course. He never even saw me. But I saw him. From the instant I saw him, I knew. Something was different – wonderful. His eyes, his hair, his hands. He stood there, letting me look at him, letting me know. Then he opened his mouth and I heard him, and I knew more. Then he played, and it was all confirmed.

Wanna know *where* I know it? I know it in the convolutions of my brain. And on my skin; I know it in every pore. Here, in my heart. Here, in my gut. Where else? In my coochie – oh yeah, there, all right. I definitely know it there. I know it there like crazy.

Now I just need to know what to do about it.

The Voice

Love, love, love! That's what it's all about – and that's what I get the whole time I am onstage. Almost every night, I get to step out and greet a new slew of adoring, devoted fans. I sing to them and they reach out to me. Sometimes I'll slap palms with the entire front row or take the hand of one lucky person, but I wish I could touch them all. Of course, I *do* touch them – with my voice. They touch me, too, with their applause. The great thing about playing a small club is the fans are right there, there's no distance, yet when I perform I also feel as close to God as I feel to them. It's like Jesus is in heaven – but in the crowd too. Jesus is one of my fans.

Gosh, I am so blessed! Although it seems like there are tons of entertainers out there, compared with all the other people on God's green earth, there are really only a very special few who get to experience this kind of stardom. It's not as though my bandmates do. Oh, the audience definitely likes how they play. But when you're the leader, the focus, the vessel of all that love . . . well, it's different, that's all.

That's why those guys seek love from other sources. It's only natural that they'd want something akin to what I receive in their lives, even a cheap imitation. So A/B has his Edie – they're constantly phoning and texting and IMing, and he can't go into a truck stop without picking up silly souvenirs for her (it rankles me a little, the way he insists on keeping up the charade). Then Wynn, with that Russian girl calling all the time. Apparently Malinka will meet up with 6X in Texas. Since it's not tennis season, and she has tons of money, she can hop on a plane as she pleases.

Now Stella's got somebody to not shut up about too.

'You guys, listen to me, he's freakin' fantastic!' Stella is shouting, even though you'd think she'd be subdued our second night in O-K City – I don't think she's had a wink of sleep – she's carrying on like that battery bunny. 'Tell them, A/B.'

A/B is trying to restring his guitar in a hurry – we're on in a few minutes – so I wish she'd stop harping on him. On all of us. The object of her obsession is playing again tonight, after our set, and Stella's using strong-arm tactics so we'll go see him. A/B fusses over his tuning pegs, but he's so nice – he doesn't brush her off. 'He's the shit, that's for sure,' he says. 'I've never seen or heard anyone like Didion Jones.'

Didion Jones, Didion Jones, Didion Jones! Gracious, I am sick of the name already. Only saying no to Stella is like a daisy defying a bulldozer, so we agree to catch his show, though frankly I'm still pooped from last night. At least the social excursion, though not officially a date, will be a baby step for A/B and me.

Once we get to the coffee house, though, I don't even think about A/B at all, not for one second. I never expected to be even mildly entertained by someone who dresses like Mr

O'Fallon, my eighth-grade maths teacher. But Stella was so right, A/B too – Didion Jones is the most original and pure-hearted singer-songwriter I've ever seen. Each one of his songs has a one-word title – an emotion: 'Anger,' 'Pity,' 'Frustration,' 'Joy.' And when he performs them, he *becomes* them. On fierce songs he is an avenger – his eyes bug, his body shakes, his veins bulge, and his wingtips stomp up dust. But on gentle songs he is a shepherd, an angel; he is Moses in the bullrushes, Jesus in the manger. You wouldn't think someone who bellows with such terrifying force could also sing so beautifully. A deep, sweet molasses lullaby of a voice, that's what he's got.

Everyone in the coffeehouse claps like crazy and calls for an encore, but Didion Jones slips away after 'Hurt.' The sound engineer passes around an empty pitcher for folks to fill with bills, and that realisation – he plays for tips! – makes me dizzy. I wish I had a hundred-dollar bill in my purse, I'd stuff it in that pitcher. In fact I'm embarrassed that all I have on me is a few fives and ones, but my mom cautioned about going around with a lot of cash. Well, I stuff the contents of my wallet into the pitcher and remind myself that Didion Jones *is* rich. In that same way that I am rich when I perform. Rich in love.

Suddenly, though, I need to be out of there. Stella, Wynn, and A/B are yammering away; they want to stay and talk to Didion Jones, who will have to reappear at some point to collect his wages of crumpled singles and small change. But I can't, I just can't. I ask Miss Peony to take me back. I don't want to drag the others away. I don't even want to say good night to them. More than anything, I don't want to look into the eyes of Didion Jones. Because I feel so bad for him.

Or do I feel bad for me? Oh, that's just foolish. I am no less an artist because Didion Jones is one too. His gift does not diminish mine. It makes my head hurt to think about this, but even once I go to bed and say my prayers, the thoughts swirl around my head like no-see-ums. Ultimately, I do puzzle it out. I feel bad for Didion Jones *and* myself, because we are both in the same boat. We both get that love when we are onstage, and it fills us up so much we could cry. But then everyone goes home. The applause fades away. And even though you *know* that a couple of nights later you'll get back onstage, and the love will rise again, it doesn't *feel* that way. It feels like the love will never come back, it feels like you have lost it forever.

The Body

Texas is endless. My butt is killing me, and since Gaylord is phobic about rest stops, the second we pull up at the Austin Holiday Inn, I have to bolt for the lobby ladies' room – the most satisfying pee of my life. When I rejoin the band at reception, there's a lot of groaning going on. Looks like someone neglected to request early check-in, and our rooms won't be ready till three. We want showers, we want naps, we want room service. We are crabby. Very crabby. Sorry, but it's hard to be Zen when you've been driving all night.

Saved by the ring tone: Ayn Rand's 'Chain-Link Fish.' 'Ween? Ween! How are you doing now, Ween?'

'Ohhh, Malinka, hey! I'm good, I guess.'

'Me too. I am good! Where are you?'

'Well, we just got into town but it kind of sucks because our rooms won't be ready for hours.'

Malinka laughs. The honking clatter of a symphony's brass section dropping their instruments on linoleum. 'You are at the stinky Holiday Inn and they won't even let you in? Ween, that sucks very much. But is not a problem. You come here to the Four Seasons. Is very nice.'

I am so tempted. I'm not spoiled, I swear, but when I travel with my mom and stepdad, we stay at the best places, and while I've tried to be a sport on this cut-rate road trip, the thought of stretching out poolside at the poshest place in town . . . mmmm! But I can't just dump the band.

'Ween? Ween, are you there? Come on, I have cabana and everything.' See, I knew she was at the pool! 'You can bring the band, is OK.' Wow, maybe Malinka's psychic. 'The more the hairier!'

'Merrier,' I automatically correct. 'The more the merrier. Are you sure?'

More clanking trombones and trumpets. Then: 'Ween, wait for second. Hello, cabana boy! Yes, please, you! I am needing more towel, you can bring? Sorry, Ween. Yes, of course is OK. I love 6X! I came all this way to see you . . . you guys. So get it on over here to my hotel now!'

It's not like I have to beg – 6X eagerly adopts rock star mode. Spotting Malinka is easy. Although her entourage is down to one (Cousin Cosima), the two of them lay atop their chaises in boy-cut bikinis – golden, glazed, and warm as fresh-off-the-conveyer-belt Krispy Kremes. Malinka sees me and leaps off the lounge with a whoop. Fortunately this is not a very stuffy Four Seasons; the Bloody Mary set seems to enjoy watching Malinka's rippling, glistening muscles barrel toward me at warp speed. Since last I saw her, she's dyed her spiky hair candy-apple red.

Malinka leads us straight to her cabana to change. 'What are you kidding me? No boys!' She bars the door against A/B and Gaylord. 'You will have to be waiting here. No peeking! No imaginations either!'

Hair up, shades on, it's oh-so-nice to settle back and enjoy Malinka's generosity. Mango smoothies, iced coffees, shrimp tacos – and my fave, pomegranate spritzers – all billed to Kolakova, room 502. Even P, who aims for that back-packing, hill-hiking earth-mother thing, lets her to-the-manor-born side slip. After tossing back a Cristal mimosa, she takes off in search of the spa – a mud massage and a chakra tune-up are absolute musts. Gaylord and A/B take a quick dip, then sling wet towels over their eyes and sack out, leaving us girls to an assortment of SPFs, a stack of tabloids, and, well, girl talk. Which Stella dominates. After all, she's got four new ears to fill with the *dernier cri* that is Didion Jones.

I'd give Kendall a 'here we go' eye-lock, but I'm too zonked to peer over my shades. Besides, it's . . . amusing hearing Stella carry on about a crush. Stella doesn't get crushes (not that she'll cop to, anyway – I don't know what you'd call that thing she's had for Brian since day one). Stella considers boyfriends to be an obsolete concept – she's all about friends with benefits. But you should have seen her after Didion's set – she was virtually a shrinking violet, hovering around him, starstruck, but almost too shy to speak. The way she talks about him now, though, it is clear that she intends to make him hers. And I don't doubt her – even if she knows nothing about him (like his phone number, e-mail address – you know, essential pertinences like that).

So, yes, it's cute to see Stella all starry-eyed, but then she segues from romantic musings to more explicit specifics on what she'd like to do to every square inch of him. Kendall blushes. The Russians squeal for more. Me, I'm in between. On one hand Stella's rapturous rap is arousing – I mean, I can't help it, sex is sexy! But on the other, I don't know, it's like something's off. It makes me think about those times I tried to masturbate and it didn't work, and it got, well, frankly, annoying. Anyway, things really degenerate when Cosima asks Stella if she expects Didion to have – and I quote, I swear! – 'an impressive package of meat in his boy panties.' As Stella glances slyly at me, I know where this is going – she wants me to spill the story of Kieran Dennis, Hollywood flash dancer. 'It's hot!' I blurt abruptly and, dropping shades to chaise, dive into the deep end.

The Voice

Reading, writing, and arithmetic are all well and good, but it may be time to ask Miss Peony for an elective. Yes, I am talking about sex education! Of course I know where babies come from – I'm fifteen years old for goodness sakes. Of course I am saving myself for marriage – true love waits. Yet listening to Stella and those Russian girls – I couldn't help but listen, I just couldn't! – I realised things are not that simple.

Like, I know you can tell that a girl is not a virgin, because she has a broken hymen, but how can you tell with a boy? Is there a way to tell just by looking? I'm positive A/B was a virgin when we kissed – but since he's been with Edie, has he 'been' with her . . . biblically? In his heart A/B is bound to me, but I've heard boys can be ruled by their nether regions – could his have led him astray? If so, could I ever forgive him? Also, I'd like to know what sex feels like – really, what all the hoop-dee-hoo is about. And when does something go from being sweet and romantic to a 'sexual activity'? Most important: How do you keep from crossing the line?

That's the one I wonder about most – that's dangerous territory, a slippery slope. Because when I think about kissing

A/B that time on the plane, I remember how natural it was. An instinct. The way my lips opened and my arms went around his neck. That sigh that came out of me at the end. And how I wanted another kiss, and another – I wanted to make out! – but the captain came on the speaker to say prepare for landing and we quit it. The point is, I wanted more kisses, so if I had gotten them would I have wanted A/B to touch me above the waist, and then below, and then . . . See what I mean about a slippery slope? Maybe it's better to never kiss at all until your wedding night, but it's too late for me.

Days go by and I don't think about kissing A/B. I think about *him* – how we belong together, and how nobody's buying that crazy talk about his 'girlfriend.' Then I'll get these . . . surges. Sometimes out of nowhere. I'll be watching TV and – uh-oh. Other times there's an obvious cause, like the conversation out by the pool. Can you believe them, talking like that in broad daylight, and in public? Just the nastiest girls ever!

Anyway, when I get these surges – ideas, images, feelings on my . . . in my . . . organs – on occasion I will touch my own body. Now I know what that is (I don't have to say the word). Nor am I such a fool as to think it will strike me blind. It's like watching scenes from a PG-rated movie; I'm not even in them myself, and neither is A/B – I wouldn't taint what we have. If I keep it up, it gets to where my heart's about to explode, then – *fooosh! ahh!* – this plummet into paradise. And before I can think about how you're supposed to go up, not down, to paradise, I'm asleep.

Anyway, I can scarcely believe I'm talking about it this bluntly to my camera, but it's actually easy. I haven't been able to broach the subject with Miss Peony, though. Saying these things to a person, even her, would be awfully hard. Maybe when it comes to . . . intimate matters, words go out the window. I know that when I look at A/B, my heart speaks for me. And once we clear up that pesky Edie problem, nothing will come between us.

The Body

We've got two shows in Austin, with days off in between and on either side, before heading to the Dallas gig. It's a bit of a breather, not to mention, with the Russians around, a break from each other – at least Malinka and Cosima are two other people to talk to. I'm a human being, not a drum machine – I'd be content to veg by the pool . . . but Malinka has other plans.

'I have been such a lazy person – is not good for my colon,' she announces. 'I think we will go water-skiing. I have made already the reservations and everything. Lake Austin is very beautiful, Ween, you will like.'

So we go. And it is beautiful. Fun too. I've been water-skiing before in the Caribbean; I'm not great but I can get up and hang on. Malinka, naturally, drops a ski and leaps the wake – her body has got to be the eighth or ninth wonder of the world. I'm sure her colon feels much better after an hour of slicing through lake water. After we ski, we take the Four Seasons's haute cuisine picnic and find a good spot to lay out.

'Ween, you think I am big slut I bet,' Malinka says, out of the blue.

'Malinka! I do not!' I insist. 'Why would you say that?'

She turns to lie on her side and gives me a one-shoulder shrug. 'Because of yesterday, talking all those dirty things with Stella. She is big slut, no?'

'Don't be ridiculous.' I jump to Stella's defence. 'Stella may make it sound like she's been with half of Brooklyn, but I know for a fact she's only had sex with one guy.'

Malinka's quiet for a minute, dips her fork into a crab-stuffed avocado. 'Can I tell you something, Ween? I too talk big – but I have not had sex once even.'

'Really? You're a virgin?' I sound surprised, but for some reason I'm not really.

'Yes. It is true, Ween. No man has ever put it in me. And you?'

'Yes – I mean, no. I mean, I'm a virgin too.' I sit up, cross-legged, and sample the ceviche. 'I'm interested in sex, definitely, but actually doing it with a guy? I just, I don't know, I can't even go there in my mind.'

'I hear what you say.' Malinka nods. 'But I bet you have a million boys all the time trying to invade your panties. You are hot rock star and celebrity and everything.'

This last remark kind of rankles me. 'You know, Malinka, I really don't think of myself that way,' I inform her huffily. 'And it's actually rather irksome that people do, and like me because of that. And not just guys either, friends too.'

'Whoa, Ween, wait! Fold your forces!'

I'm upset, so I don't bother correcting her. But she seems authentically disturbed, too, when she sits on her knees and rakes her raspberry coif.

'You don't . . . my English . . . you take me wrong, Ween. You think I like you because you are famous? Because you are rock star? You are wrong, Ween.' She sits back on her heels and stares at me. 'You are very much wrong.'

But I'm not convinced. I mean, why else would she like me – why would anyone? 'It's all right, Malinka,' I say. 'I'm used to it. Even before I was famous, people liked me because I was rich, or because I'm . . . because of what I look like. I mean, I don't like it, but it's cool.' Unbelievably, I quote Whitney Houston: 'It's not right, but it's OK . . .'

'No, Ween, is not OK,' Malinka insists. 'I will tell you why I like you: I don't like you because you are in 6X, I like you because you write the words of 6X. The song about the true father who lives far away and makes pretend of caring. The 'Lingerie Model' song, about people who measure you by your bra size. These songs, I, Malinka, I hear these words, and I feel . . . I just *feel*.' She shakes her head. 'You know? Or am I not saying it right?'

And I think: *Oh. My. God.* Because she is saying it exactly right. Malinka is speaking to the poet in me. And no one has ever done that. Most pointedly, no one in my band. Oh, they're glad my random scribbles ovulate our material, and maybe once someone uttered 'cool' over a turn of phrase or whatever, but not one of them ever mentioned *feeling* anything. So right now I am overwhelmed. I duck my head; I can't face her. I'm so touched. First-cut touched.

'Ween,' Malinka says, and I have to look up. 'Here is why I like you . . .' She puts her fingertips against her mouth and kisses them, leans forward and grazes my cheek, then very

lightly lays her hand on my chest, on my heart. '*Dusha . . .*'
Malinka says. Then she translates for me: 'Soul . . .'

The Boy

Texas girls are a species unto themselves. A spectacular species. Take it from me – I'm surrounded by awesome women in my band, I have an amazing girlfriend, but man, these girls are like no chicks I've ever come in contact with before. In Austin I thought maybe it was a fluke – but then we hit Dallas. It's like there's a biogenetic lab hidden under Dealey Plaza churning out Dallas Cowboy Cheerleader types: killer curves. Button noses. Toothpaste-commercial smiles. Mountains of hair. But the clincher? They all know how to talk to guys.

After our Austin gigs, dozens of them just sashayed over to say hi. They're like: 'Hi, I'm Lindsay!' or 'Hey, I'm Bobbi!' even 'Howdy!' – *howdy!* – 'I'm Felicity!' And they're not cat-fighty about it either – get this, if they see one of their fellow Texanettes chatting me up, they wait their turn. Unless, of course, they're friends. Then it's like: 'Hi, I'm Michelle and this is Taryn!' You see what I'm saying – they're willing to *share* you. How alternative universe is that?

Plus, it's not like they say hi and leave the ball in your court. Nope, a Texas girl follows up a salutation with a compliment, then sinks the shot with a question, like: 'How in the world did you learn to play so good?' or, 'Have they named a street after you in your hometown yet?' Then there's the way they seem to be having a great time all the time. (What, the Lone Star State has patented an immunity to PMS? Poe and Kafka are banned from the public libraries?)

Anyway, Austin was merely the prelims. We get to the venue in Dallas, and guess who's waiting to greet me? My fan club. No shit. Not the 6X Fan Club, the A/B Farrelberg Fan Club. Never in my wildest dreams – but there they are, five of them, with a banner the size of a Seventies Coupe de Ville. And when I exit the van, they do a little rah-rah thing – 'Gimme an A! Gimme a B!' – and a midair kick-split, the whole nine.

'Hi, I'm Keeley Spencer and I'm the founder and president of the A/B Farrelberg Fan Club!' She's barely even winded by her gymnastic display.

'You've got to be kidding me . . .' If I believed I was famous enough for *Punk'd*, I'd be scoping Ashton Kutcher.

'Nope! Not kidding!' Keeley says, and insinuates her arm through mine. 'Come on, A/B, we are all so excited to see you we could bust a lung.' She turns on her heel, spinning me with her, then flips over her shoulder to shout to Kendall, Wynn, and Stella, who stand there like they just got shock treatment. 'Hey, girls! We love you too! Only not as much!' Her compatriots in the A/BFFC collapse into good-natured giggles and wave at my bandmates, then descend on me. We enter the club together, and I sign their CDs and T-shirts, and the upper portion of flesh that swells from the scalloped edge of Keeley's bra cup. Yes, this is for my memoirs: the chapter entitled 'The Day I Signed a Breast.'

I disentangle myself long enough to ask my bandmates if it's OK if the fan club stays for sound check.

Wynn and Kendall couldn't care less – or make like they don't. But ever the boss, Stella wants to know: 'What's in it for us? Like, are they popular? Influential? They got a website or something? Then fine, I'm down – they'll get kids to come out tonight. But if they're losers, please. We're not about to be giving a free show for your five fans.'

'Look at them, Stella,' I say. 'Do they look like losers to you?'

Stella glances at the bevy of Texas's finest, tightens her lips the way she does when she's pissed but not pissed enough to hurt you. 'Yeah, they all look like big-boob girls on campus. Better tell them to bring their friends later.' Stella grabs me before I can hustle back to my minions. 'And A/B? Read my lips: No guest list. They pay or no way.'

I'm OK with that – not only because Stella says so. Somehow I doubt Edie would be too high on the idea of me giving five rabid female fans free passes to our show. Not that she'd go for my John Hancock sliding into another girl's cleavage, either.

The Boss

The rest of this tour, the rest of my freakin' life, will drag on interminably until the next time I land in some speck on the map and see a hand-lettered flyer, stapled to a telephone pole, hyping the Didion Jones Show. When will that be? Ha! Might as well have Witchy-Poo Peony consult her tarot cards. Does he have a website? No. A mailing list? No. A clue this is the 21st century?

In Oklahoma City, we only talked to Didion long enough to tell him how off the hook he is and learn that his upcoming appearances lie in the hands of fate. Basically, he hitches from town to town, lining up gigs where he lands. As he put it: 'Have guitar, will travel . . .'

Me, I don't leave shit up to chance. Yet on some level I admire his MO – if it's even true. Didion works this sort of self-mocking thing, or maybe it's *you* he's mocking; all I'm saying is I know from the start not to take him at face value. All slo-mo voice and half-closed eyes and superfine physique, Didion Jones is part panther, part spider, and pure trouble. The kind of trouble I can deal with. Butterscotch trouble. You know I was dying to ask him to ride with us to Texas, but

1) no room unless we strapped him to the hood and 2) I was trying to be chill.

But pop it forward to Albuquerque, where I spy, could it be, a Didion Jones flyer? Clearly Didion committed to memory the 6X itinerary I happened to drop, then willed his hitching thumb to bring him here. Of course I was hoping he'd be at our show, but disappointment doesn't deter me from going to his. Anybody see a pattern developing? 6X plays, then dashes off to another club for the soul-stompin', heart-chompin', sweat-flingin' phenomenon that is Didion Jones.

Afterwards, us and Didion, we're like old friends. When it comes up that he has no place to crash, I throw Wynn an 'I will so owe you' look. She's insightful, I never have to break shit down for her – but her face is ambivalent. Almost like she wants me to be happy but isn't sure inviting Didion into our room is the direct route to nirvana. Yeah, well, I take her no answer as a yes and say casually that our floor is available. Floor, right.

Didion smiles and accepts. Back at the Ramada, he breaks out a bottle of Maker's Mark, asks permission to remove his shoes. Damn, he's got big feet! Me and Wynn snicker, and it's off with our kicks too. Then we pick a bed. All three of us. I lean against the headboard, and so does Didion, but he angles himself so he can see me and Wynn, who sits yoga style toward the foot of the bed. There's a silence, but not an awkward one – it's the waiting-for-a-second-wind lull, a quiet touring musicians in that space between gig and dawn know well. I get my second wind first: 'So who the hell are you, Didion Jones?'

As Didion lets loose his tale, his tie comes off, then his coal-grey jacket, then one by one his shirt buttons get undone. Around his neck, a silver chain with what looks like a medal the size of a dime.

'Well, I'm *from* New Orleans . . .'

The simple statement – all bruised blues in his tone – sums it up. Didion doesn't need to go into detail; I assume he lost his home to that annihilating banshee-bitch Hurricane Katrina.

'But I loved growing up there,' he goes on. 'Even though my mother . . . let's just say our relationship was . . . amorphous.' He swigs at the bourbon – I watch his neck as it courses down his throat – then passes the bottle to me. 'She came in and out of my life a lot. Granddad kept threatening to install a cat flap so she wouldn't have to worry about losing her key. Then she did lose it. Lost it for ever. Granddad, he's the one who really raised me.'

Raised you right too, I think as I tilt the bottle toward my mouth, while my eyes are slaves to Didion's face – the glow in his amber eyes, his high-planed Choctaw cheekbones and the straggly moustache crowning his sculpted upper lip. So of course I choke on the hot, hard liquor; actually spew my shot all over the paisley bedspread, then can't stop sputtering, like a trickle of bourbon went down the wrong pipe.

'Stella, oh God – are you all right?' Wynn rushes to the bathroom to run me some water. By the time she gets back, Didion has cured me. With the knuckle of his index finger, he chucks me under the chin, coaxing my head back, like you'd do to a cat to make it purr. Bam! I'm better, breathing easy. And jealous of the damn cat, wishing I *could* purr.

'So . . .' I say, unable to remember ever being so glad to cede the floor to someone else's story. 'Your grandpa . . . granddad?'

Didion tells us how it's his theory that his mom went wild to rebel against her dad. Morrison Jones was Somebody. Capital S. First tenured Creole-Choctaw professor at Tulane University. Not some token subject either: mathematics. Married a Swedish-Nigerian violin virtuoso. Sired three sons, who grew up to pursue engineering, medicine, and law. Then, once the youngest was already in his teens, oops, accident – out pops Didion's mother. Didn't help that *her* mother died when she was two, as if the professor weren't sour on the deal as it was. But if Gramps was less than cool to his late-in-life daughter, he atoned with her son.

'He let me be,' Didion explains. 'Gave me all the advantages but let me pick and choose for myself. Never tried to force me in a cage, like he did with her. My uncles – his sons – they don't care much for me, but Granddad loved me. Respected me too.'

'Past tense?' I venture softly, wondering if Didion's vagabond ways are a symptom of being alone in the world. I flick my eyes at Wynn's and see that they're wet.

'Passed, burned, scattered. Three years next month.'

Wynn and I don't know what to say. Us, with our comparatively normal lives and traditionally dysfunctional families.

'But it's all good,' Didion says for us, and toys with the silver circle lying against his chest. 'What I got from Granddad? My wits, my will – and my suits. I wear his suits in memory.'

'Wait, really?' Wynn lapses into a fashion moment. 'You never wear jeans?'

Didion smiles. 'Only on Sunday. And sometimes I wear the checks.'

'The checks?'

'You never been backstage in a restaurant? Black-and-white checkered pants, what kitchen help wears. Wherever I roam, I pick up work in kitchens.' He looks at me and Wynn, then back at me and smiles. 'I hate to brag, but I can *cook*. Maybe one day I'll be able to repay tonight's hospitality, prepare some fine Creole cuisine for you girls.'

Damn, is there anything Didion Jones can't do? 'So from your grandmother you got talent, clearly,' I say to put us back on track.

'That, and passion. Talent's a trap without passion.'

Me and Wynn let that sink in a second. Then she asks what I won't. 'And your mom? What did you get from her?'

Didion doesn't miss a beat. 'I don't want to know,' he says.

'Stella, I have to kiss you.'

It's hours later, Wynn's in her own bed, and me and Didion are inching closer, talking softer, till we can't get much closer and we're nearly all out of words. And I am ready, all right, primed. He warned me. Said he was gonna lay one on me. But when he does I am *not* ready, I am *not* primed, I have never . . . I have kissed guys – all right, I have done a lot more than kiss – but *this* kiss, this honey-dripping, fire-stoking, soul-nudging, spellcasting, voodoo-dude kiss . . . Oh. No. Nothing. Ever. Like. This.

A millennium passes, and when Didion draws slightly away I need another kiss like crack. But I cannot grab his shoulder, roll on top of him; I cannot take his kiss like I'd take anything else I want. All I can do is wait. Hope. For more.

Of course he'll give me more. That's what boys live for: more. They have to have more, go further; every guy I've ever met was on the verge of blue balls.

Yeah. Well. Not Didion Jones. He does not put his weight on me. He does not slip his hand under my shirt – although he has to know, he *has* to, that he can make my shirt evaporate. That kiss was not a step towards a goal; it was . . . itself. The curl of contentment in his smile tells me this. And when he shifts off his elbow to lie on his back, a sliver of electrified air between us, I realise I am contented too. I'm not gonna be greedy. A single perfect kiss is plenty. It is.

All around us, the world goes on about its business. Trucks eat up the highway. Wynn snores and mumbles. Objects in the room become distinct as shadow gives way to light. I'm just assuming this – I'm not technically conscious of it. My entire awareness is Didion Jones. A sigh comes out of me, so unfamiliar, so simultaneously light and loaded, it hurts.

That's when he tells me: 'Don't, Stella.' His eyes are cast on the ceiling. The book of my heart must be open there. 'Don't fall in love with me. Please, Stella, don't . . .'

Yeah, uh-huh. I understand. I understand completely. I understand about Didion Jones. How he cautions me not to fall for him because he's terrified of taking that same spill in my direction. How could he not be scared of love, a boy like that, an orphan, an orphan of the storm, too – he's lost so much, love is like wildfire to him. Too hot to touch. Impossible to predict.

Likely to burn out in a fierce flash, scarring you in the process. Love is the antithesis of survival to Didion.

So it's my mission to prove otherwise. Because if there's one thing Didion Jones needs, it's for us to fall in love. Fall hard. Fall fast. Fall forever.

The Boy

Three more dates – Phoenix, Salt Lake, Vegas – and then we fly home. I miss my girl, I want to see her so bad, but home? Home to what? The road is a tick, a tapeworm; it gets inside you. I can understand going back for a visit, a personal-life pit stop, but sticking around, settling in, doesn't seem . . . normal any more.

One thing's for sure – it's weird skipping Thankstuffing with the fam. Mom sneaking sips of Dubonnet to maintain her cool while my little cousins ravage the living room. Dad keeping vigil, watching for the little red 'done' button to pop on the bird. The Battle of the Bubbies – Grandma Ann versus Grandma Doris in verbal combat: 'You call this green bean casserole?' 'You call that gravy?' Blah-blah-comfy-homey-blah.

Instead, we're sitting down to Tex-Mex Turkey Day in Arizona, where the menu boasts cranberry salsa, sweet potato enchiladas, and other sacrilege. But hey, we make the best of it, even get relatively spruced up – remarkable since we've been to a Laundromat exactly once this whole trip and are really scraping the bottom of the suitcase. Peony, however, totally transforms herself — in deference to our special guest Mrs Taylor, who flew out for the weekend. She's got her hair pulled up and a blouse buttoned over her tats. It's Peony, in fact, who asks Mrs Taylor to honour us by saying grace. Post-prayer, she and her patron peck at Kendall like two hens with an ear of corn between them.

Kendall seems to take solace in her food, chowing with glum gusto, then suddenly brightens. 'I know!' she cries. 'Let's go around the table and say what all we're thankful for.' No one groans aloud, but we're not chomping at the bit either. Kendall ignores this. 'I'll start,' she volunteers. 'Wow. Gosh. There's so much. Well, first of all I'm thankful to God for granting me so many, many gifts. And I want to officially thank my mom for coming all this way. We've been through some hardships, but I appreciate everything you've done for me, Mom.'

She and Taylor the Elder exchange a dewy, gooey glance before Kendall lets her eyes rest briefly yet theatrically on everyone else in turn. 'I am also thankful that the Lord sent me Miss Peony, the best tutor ever. And I'm thankful for Mr. Gaylord, who puts up with our shenanigans and keeps us safe. And, well, maybe it isn't fair to say most of all but my greatest gratefulness is for my band. Wynn . . . Stella . . . A/B . . .' She delivers the rest with her Bambi browns on me. 'I know you love me as much as I love you.'

Man, she's a tough act to follow! We hollowly echo Kendall's sentiments, but if we were being absolutely honest I bet we'd sound more like this:

Gaylord: 'I'm thankful there are only three dates left on this tour. I don't know what I expected when I got into management but being a glorified bus driver was not it!'

Peony: 'I'm thankful Kendall's rooming with her mom in Phoenix, freeing me to chant incantations or draw pentagrams or whatever it is I normally do.'

Wynn: 'I'm so thankful that none of us has slit anyone's throat so far, because I swear, I really can't handle that kind of emotional distress.'

Stella: 'First, I'm thankful that I didn't just leap across the table with my butter knife and cut Kendall up for calling us "her" band, like we're some backup hacks she hired. But the main thing I am thankful for is Didion Jones. I'm thankful that he exists, that I got to experience him, and that I have the brains to find a way to be with him.'

Me: 'I am thankful for my Edie. I only hope I can avoid doing anything stupid that would cause her to dump me.'

Gremlins conspire against me, though – that night I rack up serious dumpworthy demerits. The digital clock displays the irrefutable fact that it is 2:26 AM when I am raised to consciousness by insistent tapping. 'Gaylord . . .' I grumble. 'Someone's at the door.' A knock at 2:26 AM equals a problem, and solving problems basically *is* a road manager's job description. But the tapping continues and Gaylord does nothing. Moments later I realise that's because Gaylord is not present – not in the next bed, not in the can, not in the room.

Aha, so it must be him – he went for a soda and left his key card. Half-asleep, I grant him entrance wearing nothing but my skivvies. Only it's not him – it's Kendall. She throws her arms around me, the momentum hurtling us both inside. Her cotton nightgown is warm against my bare chest; her body, underneath it, even warmer.

'Oh, A/B!' she whispers violently in my ear.

I want to shed some light on things, literally – I try to find the wall switch.

'No, A/B! Please! Don't turn on the light.' Kendall clutches me tighter. 'I don't want to wake Mr Gaylord; I just, I had to make sure you're all right—'

'Kendall, relax!' I'm telling *her* to relax? I'm ninety-five-per cent naked in the clutches of Kendall Taylor! She does release me, yet manages to manoeuvre me against the door, my face in her hands, (seemingly) blissfully oblivious to my near nudity. 'What do you mean? Why wouldn't I be? Really, check it out, it's Gaylord I'm worried about. He's not even here!'

Kendall takes on a new tone – alarmed, excited. 'He's not?'

Stumbling away, I bang my shin against an inconveniently placed piece of hotel furniture. 'Ow! Shit! Ow!'

'Oh! A/B! A/B!'

Kendall's touch lands somewhere along my left flank as I fumble toward the cursed desk and the lamp on top of it. I flick it. Kendall and I blink at each other.

'Oh, A/B! Did you hurt yourself? Oh, I'm so sorry.'

'It's fine!' I lie. It hurts like a bastard. 'Ow, no, really, it's fine.'

'Are you bleeding?' She crouches, white nightie billowing around her. 'Let me see – ooh, you broke the skin.' Gingerly, she touches the spot, which sends me into a spastic flinch. Kendall, thrown off balance, lands flat on her butt. So I get down beside her to make sure *she's* all right. A silly position, a silly situation, nothing more – just a boy and a girl in minimal clothing in the middle of the night because . . . because why?

'Kendall, what's going on? What are you doing here?'

She turns away, then looks back. 'I – I'm sorry, I . . . I had a dream, a nightmare, and you were – oh, gosh, A/B, I can't remember any more. But I know you were in danger, terrible danger, and even though it was a dream, it was so real, well, when I woke up I snuck out of my room. I just had to make sure nothing had happened to you.'

What a sweetie, her eyes peering intently into mine. I can see concern on her face . . . and a trace of make-up. Also, her hair is not bed-heady. Hmm. So she struggles awake, throat closing with fear for my mortal soul, yet takes a few seconds to daub on lip gloss and run a comb through her locks? I need to get off the floor . . . now, stat, pronto. I do that, and Kendall follows. We can't just stand there. So we sit. On the bed.

'Oh, A/B, I'm sorry – I'm just . . . gosh, aren't you cold?' Damn skippy, I'm cold! Shivering in my boxers and socks, to be precise.

'Why don't you get under the covers?' she suggests, hopping up, very Florence Nightingale, to pull at the sheets. I get under, drawing my knees to my chest, the blankets with them. Kendall mumbles, 'I'm chilly too,' and next thing I know she's climbing in on the other side, a shred of cotton between her flesh and mine. This is not good. But what am I supposed to do, toss her out? Kendall is . . . fragile. And I took a solemn oath to make sure she doesn't flip out.

'Look, Kendall, first things first.' I strive for comforting yet business-like. 'What's wrong, really?'

'I told you!' she wails. 'I had a bad dream! I was worried about you!'

'OK, shhh! I hear you, I know – but I'm perfectly fine. Right? A little damaged in the shin, maybe . . .' I test out a chuckle.

'Oh, A/B. How can you laugh? It's not funny.'

'What's not funny? What's going on? You can tell me . . .'

'Nothing. Everything. I don't know.' Kendall sighs. 'I'm just so tired. The tour, being the frontperson – you have no idea how draining it is. Lessons every day on top of it. And just feeling, I don't know, alone somehow. Like the girls, I hoped we'd really bond on tour, get close the way girlfriends are supposed to. Goodness, sometimes I feel like they scarcely tolerate me!'

'Now come on, Kendall. That's not true.' *OK, how am I going to finesse this one?* 'You know what I think?' I take a stab. 'I think because you're such a kind, generous person, you naturally think everyone is the same as you. But they're not. Like Stella, it's not that she doesn't care about you, it's just that ballsy Brooklyn mode is all she knows. And Wynn, well, she's full of feelings, but with her upbringing, that icy WASP thing, being demonstrative is considered tacky. So she puts into her writing and her drumming what she can't outwardly express.'

As Kendall's head drops to my shoulder, considering this, I think I did pretty good – Wandweilder would be proud of my spiel. 'You're right, A/B,' she says, then adds cheerily: 'You know what? You really are a prince!' She kisses me – small, chaste, on the cheek – then sort of smushes her body around in the sheets. Getting cosy. Too cosy. Inside I remind myself she must not – *cannot!* – stay the night. I roil over my next move as her breath warms my neck. Then, finally: Eureka!

'So hey . . .' I say. 'Where do you think Gaylord has got to?'

The Voice

People who don't believe in Jesus Christ are so blind! There are so many signs of His divine self wherever you look. Take Thanksgiving night. When I knock on A/B's door, all I hope to do is show him some concern. I certainly don't expect us to wind up in bed! Now if that is not a gift from God I don't know what is. Then, to make things better, we now have a secret between us. Because of course I'd never think to stay all night, and he knows it isn't proper either, so he brings up the missing Mr Gaylord again.

'We should go find him.' A/B throws back the blankets and pulls on a pair of track pants. 'He can't be in the bar; it must have closed by two. And he can't be in the lobby, on the phone with New York — it's not even dawn there yet.'

'Gosh, A/B, you'd make a brilliant detective,' I tell him. I am simply thrilled — romance and a mystery! 'What should we do?'

'I don't know. Maybe he went to the vending machines and got a brain embolism. Something like that can kill you in seconds.' He snaps his fingers.

That is scary! It would be awful if something horrible

happened when everything else was proceeding so well. I put my fears behind me. 'Let's go check.'

'Yeah,' he says, grabbing his key card and stuffing his feet into his Converse. 'Which way is vending?' We take off down the hall to the left. No luck. As we head back in the other direction, we hear a sound and quickly duck behind the stairwell door. Peeking out, we see Mr Gaylord, oh, we sure enough do! And he looks as right as rain – with Miss Peony holding on to him like a monkey on a vine. She's wearing this flimsy and flowy and, good Lord, see-through robe! And not a stitch underneath! Well, A/B and I are about to bust. We clamp our hands over our mouths as we huddle in the stairwell. Then Miss Peony and Mr Gaylord start kissing passionately right there in the hall.

A/B pulls me back into the stairwell. 'I've got to get back to the room!' he hisses. 'I don't want him to know we know!'

I nod in furious agreement.

'Do you have your key card?' he asks.

I pull it from the pocket of my nightgown.

'Good,' he says. 'Are you OK to wait here till they . . . uh, finish?'

Again I nod.

'OK, well, shush about this, right? No one needs to know but us.'

My eyes shine my answer, and A/B makes the 'shh' gesture – fingertip to lips – before he tippy-toes down the hall and slips into his room. Finally, Miss Peony and Mr Gaylord part, and she lounges in the door frame watching him go towards his room. I bet A/B jumped into bed with his sweatpants and sneakers still on. Miss Peony steps inside, and I creep back to my door, slip in the key, and open it with care lest it creak. The last thing I want to do is wake my mother!

The Boss

On a musical tip, everything Brian hoped for is happening. We are bow-down-and-worship-us *performers* now. When I step up to the mike, harmonies actually come out of my mouth. Must be connected to Didion – I want his respect as an artist when he comes to see us. Notice I didn't say if? There is no if. Me and Didion are gonna be together; I just have to figure out how. Believe me, the wheels are turning. Just as I am deliberating this, sitting in the van on the way to Salt Lake, an unknown caller hits my cell.

'Stella?'

It takes me a second. 'Brian?' I haven't heard from him once since we left. 'Yo, what's up?'

'A million things, Stella,' he says. 'But as Willie Nelson says, "You are always on my mind."'

Whoa, I am snapped like a rubber band. He's been thinking about me the whole time, probably dying to call, but letting me go to do my thing, spread my wings or whatever. A flash of something like guilt smacks me. Now that I've met Didion, kissed Didion . . . everything's different.

'Stella, you there?'

'Yeah, Brian, sure,' I say.

'You know, my spies tell me great things about you.'

'Shut up.'

'I'm not kidding. All Gaylord can talk about is how hot you are onstage. He says you started doing this move, this strut? And singing your head off.'

Black girls do blush, all right. Only me? Not so much. Till right this second. 'With these holes you booked us into?' I say. 'They're so small, I strut about three paces before I bang into a wall. But the singing, yeah, I've been working it.'

'I can't wait to see you, Stella. I really can't.'

'Well, you better line us up some shit in New York.' I snark him – I know he loves it.

'I have,' he says. 'Another single, a new video, definitely. *Saturday Night Live* – we're so close. But I'll tell you more in detail on Friday.'

'Friday?' *What is he talking about?*

'Didn't Gaylord tell you?' There's mirth in his voice. 'I'm coming to Vegas. I'm in LA right now for meetings, so I figured what the hell? Stay an extra day, then meet up with my favourite band. We can party in Vegas, then all fly home together.'

This is so outta left field – yet pure Brian. Let you loose, then reel you in.

'Stella? Am I losing you?'

I don't know, Brian. I thought you already had. 'No, I'm here,' I say. 'That'll be cool. I – it will be great to see you.'

'I know,' he says. 'Just a couple of days. Can't wait!'

The Body

By now road burn has really set in. A/B's incessant Edie chatter was cute at first, but now he's a broken record. I swear, I'd rather hear him talk about chord progressions or fuzz boxes. Kendall's stubborn denial of this is starting to crack too. Onstage she's a pro, but the other twenty-three hours of the day she's either morose and withdrawn or acting like a pep-squad captain. What's more – and I know this is going to sound terrible and mean – she's gaining weight. It's hard to eat healthy when careening from one drive-thru to the next, and we all want to ménage à trois with Ben and Jerry occasionally, but ever since I caught her scarfing candy alone in the moonlight . . . well, that's just disturbed.

I'm just lucky I have my journal; I can vent in ink. Because that's when a writer writes, when conflicting feelings square off – bittersweet versus melancholy, irritation versus isolation. I'd probably be writing more if I had any privacy, but rooming with Stella has its own set of challenges. It's like, I'm sick of washing out my *own* undies in the sink every night, but now she's taken to leaving hers strewn on the bathroom floor, knowing I'll pick them up and do them with mine. I swear, talk about TMI – too much intimacy. When did I become her maid? Plus, I've had to deal with two Stellas, pre-Didion and post-Didion; we're in the post-Didion phase now and she will not shut up – she makes A/B look like a monk who's taken dual vows of silence and celibacy.

It's not like I don't get what Stella sees in the guy. Talented. Gorgeous. Rangy tall, sultry tongued. There's this purity about him too . . . or is that just what he wants everyone to think? The whole bad boy troubadour routine, his crusty suits, the way he rejects the traditional route to success – I mean, if it's real, cool, but wouldn't it make great copy for his record company bio? That sounds awful – I'm usually so not cynical. Except when it comes to men, I guess.

Of course, Stella's not Kendall. Stella has her head screwed on, she's streetwise, she can smell a phony a mile off. Yet Didion still unnerves me. It's not like he's called her once since they spent the night together. Maybe I believe she deserves someone she knows is more than flash, someone with substance and loyalty, with soul . . . *dusha*. Anyway, as we get into Salt Lake City, her life develops yet further complexities.

'You wanna guess who that was?' She closes her cell, shakes her head, grins like a pumpkin. 'Brian.' I guess 'guess' is a figure of speech. 'He's coming to Vegas. What's up with that? Do you think he knows?'

'Knows?' I say. 'Knows what?' Oh, I'm pretty sure what she's driving at, but I play dumb, especially since Stella's feelings for Brian – obvious as they are, or were – is a topic we never actually bandied about.

She looks at me like I'm a complete moron – apparently I

play dumb quite well. 'Knows about Didion. Gaylord has such a big mouth – it's gotta be him that told. Why else would Brian be calling, all, "Oh, Stella, I hear you're on fire" and "Oh, Stella, I can't wait to see you."'

I don't know how to respond. On one hand it does seem odd that Brian's interest in Stella has suddenly been resuscitated – I certainly didn't get a personal call announcing his visit. On the other, she's probably misreading him. She makes it sound like his sole purpose for coming to Vegas is to whisk her off to the Elvis Chapel! Whatever. If Stella wants to revel in this 'torn between two lovers' drama, I'm not going to stop her. So I feed her a non-committal, 'Wow, yeah, that is weird . . .' and shift my focus out the window.

The Boss

Vegas, baby! Lights unlimited, the sizzle scent of desert air, the manic vibe of all that money lost and won and lost again. And those massive theme hotels, one wackier than the next. Screw the Holiday Inn, we're staying at the newest, ritziest place in town. Le Rousseau, inspired by the post-Impressionist painter, is a magical jungle enclosed in a palace — rooms, restaurants, and the sprawling casino — all homage to the old French dude's lush, weird work. Hey, it's rewarding to wind up the tour at a cool spot, especially since we're not playing the Hard Rock or the House of Blues. In fact, this has gotta be the Poverty Tour's sleaziest venue yet. Not that it bothers me, but it is freakin' hilarious watching Kendall wrap her mind around just what kind of club Peekers is.

I'll give you some hints: It's in a *strip* mall miles from the famous *Strip*. And the silhouette on the sign outside is a shape you see on truckers' mud flaps. A/B and I get it immediately, cracking up as we walk in. Wynn catches on when she sees the poles onstage. But Kendall? Clueless.

'So what do you think, Kendall?' I can't resist.

'Well, gosh,' she says. 'No worse than the other dives we've been at.'

'Are you sure?' I swing around a pole, then grab hold, jump up, and slide down. 'Hey, this is fun!'

'You're a natural, Stella. If this rock thing doesn't pan out, you have something to fall back on.'

Do I detect bitchiness in Wynn's remark? 'Speak for yourself, Bimbo Barbie,' I tell her. 'Those look like your ta-tas up there on the sign, not mine!'

Guitar in one hand, amp in the other, A/B follows Gaylord backstage. 'I'm staying out of this!' he calls over his shoulder.

'Will someone please tell me what's going on?' Kendall asks.

'She's teasing you, Kendall.' Wynn gestures lamely. 'Peekers is . . . it's the kind of place where men . . . where women . . . exotic dancers—'

Slowly recognition crumbles Kendall's face. 'Ding, ding, ding!' I crow. 'That's right, you win, Peekers is a strip club!'

'Hey!' A familiar voice calls from the front. 'A *former* strip club.' I can't see him – the bar area is murky – but I know who it is strolling leisurely toward the stage.

Brian! 'Yo, yo, Brian – check me out!' I twirl around the pole then bump off, gyrating in my best hoochie-mama impersonation.

Brian whistles and claps, which naturally encourages me to get on all fours and crawl to the foot of the stage. When I look up, there he is, still clapping, still whistling. Brian always did get me – my crazy ways, my sick sense of humour. Trouble is, he's not alone.

'You remember Cara Lee Ballantine, don't you, Stella?'

120

Sure I do. Only last time I saw her she was in jeans – today she's rocking a white linen peasant top and ruffled prairie skirt. Practically Little Bo Peep. Very not strip club. 'Yeah,' I say, hopping off the stage, searching for my dignity and wondering what the hell that heifer is doing here.

The Voice

This is an awfully important show for us. The fate of 6X hangs in the balance. If we wow all the important folks Mr Wandweilder has brought to Vegas – promoters, radio station programme directors, the editor of *Pollstar*, the magazine that covers the concert industry – we're practically guaranteed a real tour come the New Year. Gosh, wouldn't that be wonderful? A real tour bus with an entertainment centre and everything. We wouldn't be headlining yet, but we'd open for someone huge, and play big theatres or maybe even arenas with genuine dressing rooms. Oh, and we'd get a rider! That's a contract detailing all your on-the-road demands – like Butterfingers and Dr Pepper backstage and plenty of underwear and socks so you don't have to worry about clean laundry.

Fortunately I don't get stage fright, and I always say a special prayer right before showtime so I know the Lord is with me. (At the start of the tour I tried to include the whole band, but, well, it's their prerogative if they don't want to be saved.) Tonight I decide to pray extra, since the show means so much, and frankly, Peekers being a place where people used to take their clothes off, I don't think the Lord has had cause to come around here before. Just as I'm thinking about the best way to word this for Jesus, Stella and Wynn burst in. Oh, my. Things could go downhill at breakneck speed from here.

'Get the F-word away from me, Wynn! I do what I want,' Stella says, her tone quiet yet riddled with malice.

'No, F-word you, Stella!' Wynn is much less in control. 'You're F-wording drunk and if you F-word up onstage you're not just F-wording yourself, you're F-wording all of us.'

'Uch, I can't F-wording stand you! You're not my F-wording mother, all right!'

Wynn does not like to fight; unlike Stella, she's not good at it. She's trying not to cry, stifling sniffles, wiping snot on the back of her hand. 'Stella, please, you've been throwing them back since six o'clock – you need to put that drink down right now!'

A/B and Gaylord enter the stuffy backstage area and instantly look like they want to turn around, but Wynn and Stella ignore the lot of us. Wynn wrings her hands. Stella gulps from a can of spiked Red Bull and goes, 'Ahhh!' but if she has been drinking for three hours she doesn't seem worse for wear. Gosh, the time I accidentally got drunk, I don't recollect many details but I do believe throw-up was involved. Stella isn't yelling or slurring. Her movements are a little exaggerated, her limbs sort of whipping around, but she's not discombobulated. She takes a seat near me, legs splayed, Red Bull dangling between two fingers. 'You are such a wuss, such a F-wording baby!' she says to Wynn.

'*I'm* a baby?!' Wynn shouts. 'Look at you, getting wasted to get attention. But go ahead – make a spectacle of yourself in front of our Vegas fans and the industry people Brian got to come out. You don't have to worry as long as your *crush* isn't around.' Oh, this gets a rise out of Stella! 'Yes, that's right,' Wynn goes on, 'I sincerely doubt you'd be acting like such an A-word-hole if Didion Jones was here.'

Stella leaps up. 'How dare you!' Now she's shouting too. 'How dare you mention Didion! You're not even fit to say his name!'

Oh my goodness, she is hopping mad. But she puts down her Red Bull right quick.

The Body

War is one thing I will never comprehend. How governments convince a bunch of people to go out and massacre another bunch of people they've never even met. I mean, how could a perfect stranger make you that angry? And how would you attack? OK, the point is moot if you have chemical weapons or an atom bomb, but if you're going hand to hand – or snipe for snipe – you need an idea where to land your blows. The only thing that makes sense is to know your enemy. It probably helps if you love her too.

The smackdown with Stella? I start it, no question. Yes, namby-pamby me picking on the queen of confrontation. Of course, it's not that I plan it; hidden and therefore more twisted forces are afoot. I guess it's been building for a while and I'm waiting for my shot. Stella's drinking provides a convenient excuse. She's hardly girl-gone-wild rowdy or anything. It's more *why* she's drinking that infuriates me. Frustrated over darling Didion not being at her disposal, she hears from Brian and gets all worked up over him – but when he arrives with Cara Lee, she decides he's playing her. So she hits the bottle, jeopardizing our biggest show so far. How soap opera is that?

A real friend, a good person, would be sympathetic – apparently I'm neither. Stella's drowning in romantic miasma. Do I dive in to rescue her? Throw her a life preserver? No. All I say, sweetly and sincerely, is, 'Do you really think you need another Red Flag?'

The fight impulse kicks in with a wallop. What a sick, nasty energy – a foreign, bitter taste at the back of your throat, a twitchy tightness in your muscles. Yet it's irresistible, the pull is so strong. And just because something interrupts it – your manager, say, scoffs at your blood-thirstiness and scoots you toward the stage like a kindergarten teacher at a holiday pageant – it doesn't automatically go away. The only good thing I can say about the bilious, spasmodic sensation is it spurs our show. I swear, Stella and I are going at it like wolverines, only to deliver the performance of our lives minutes later.

Alcohol must modulate the fight impulse in Stella. Rage is a stimulant and booze sets it loose, making the rhythm flow. Consciously, maybe, there's a bit of 'I'll show Wynn; I'll show them all!' to her tonight. When she leans into the mike for background vocals, she spits cobra-style. She is *on* it.

Me, I feel poisoned, and the only antidote is to pummel my drums like a chariot racer. I need to beat this out of me, sweat it out. I'm lucky our set list tonight doesn't have me singing till the fourth number. It's not that I'm in control by then – far from it – I'm just more in touch with being out of control. There's also this undercurrent of competition, which is utterly bizarre; I am so not a competitive person. But if Stella's coming from an 'I'll show Wynn!' place, I need to counter with an acre of 'I'll show her!' of my own.

126

As for A/B and Kendall, they can't know that the fight impulse will actually function in our favour, so they strive even harder. A/B's slinging his guitar around like they're partners in a jitterbug contest on Mercury, leaping, mugging, wind-milling like a man possessed. Naturally, Kendall can't be outshined by mere members of 'her' band, so she kicks it into high. Some singers, their voices get weaker as a tour goes on, but the more Kendall exercises her instrument, the clearer and sweeter it gets. Tonight, though, there's a new dimension to it. Maybe it's rooted in the fight scene she witnessed earlier; maybe it's due to other demons she's wrestling with. I don't know, but there's an alien wailing edge to her delivery that takes us to the precipice and throws us – the band, the fans, even the industry people – straight over and out, into the void.

But the voice is only part of it. Kendall's putting her body into it too. The way she sings is physical to begin with – she belts from the gut, and it contorts her involuntarily. And since she insists on performing in the skinniest stilettos she can find, when she makes deliberate moves – straddling the mike stand, stomping to the beat – she's sort of stilted and gawky, which is part of her charm. Only tonight she's going over the top swinging, swaying, and spinning like the spawn of Stevie Nicks and a capuchin monkey.

Everything's cool – until 'Put This in Your Purse (Ashley).' The chorus is frenetic, really fast and jumpy, with an abrupt little pause before the bridge. Kendall decides that's the place for a swoop-and-lunge – think the proud warrior pose in yoga. Left leg bent, right leg straight, arms high, head flung back. She throws herself into it, teetering slightly on her heels, but when

127

she springs off the forward foot to come out of it: – *skr-r-r-ip!* Her pants split all the way up the back. White cotton panties bloom out the chasm. From my vantage point, behind her at the kit, I see it all. She has *got* to be freaking! I remember when my boob popped out at our NYC showcase, and wonder if clothing catastrophes are some kind of 6X curse.

Kendall clamps her knees together and keeps on singing. As A/B sears into his solo, she darts panicked looks left and right but stands stock still, then finishes the song atop a scree of feedback and bows deeply from the hips. Only once the applause starts crashing does she dash for the wings. A/B and Stella don't know that her seams rebelled – all they know is we have three songs left to play – and they give each other looks, like 'What . . . ?' I don't hesitate: I bolt from my stool, grabbing the hoodie I shrugged off after our first tune, and head after Kendall.

'Ohhh, Wynn!' Kendall looks about to hyperventilate. 'You saw?!'

'Yes, but don't worry – no one else did.' I glance at the stage. Stella and A/B shuffle uncomfortably, wondering whether to walk off or what. Then the audience starts yowling 'More!' and 'Encore!' A/B noodles a few notes; Stella plucks some strings, desperate to find a bass line for his ad-lib. 'Look, it's OK,' I say, but Kendall's shell-shocked – I might as well be speaking Portuguese. 'Damn it, Kendall!' I shake her shoulder with one hand and thrust my sweatshirt at her with the other 'Tie this around your waist and get your butt back out there!'

I start for my kit, and the crowd takes notice, their whoops renewed. Then Kendall waltzes out in my wake, causing a new wave of approving screams. 'Thank you! Thank you so, so much!' she says demurely, then pumps up the volume. 'Whooo! Now I know what Elvis meant when he said "Viva Las Vegas!"' She rambles off a little speech about how this show is the culmination of our first tour, and how great it is for us to have such an amazing audience to wind things up with. Then she literally says, 'Aw, shucks!' and introduces 'Hello Kitty Creeps Me Out.'

So we finish our set, and afterwards, well, you would not believe how well Stella and I manage to avoid each other's eyes till past midnight, when Brian announces he's moving the soiree to Le Rousseau. Stella and Kendall ride with him, Cara Lee, and several hand-selected industry types in the limo; I go with A/B, Peony, and Gaylord in the van. Once we're back, though, I can't bring myself to join the party. I step over the litter of Stella's clothes and shoes in our room, wash my face, pull on sweats. I think about taking out my journal or talking to this camera, but no – the fight with Stella, how I feel about the tour ending and going home, I'm just not ready to preserve it for posterity yet.

At first I think my only other option is to crawl into bed and feign sleep, so when Stella stumbles in later I won't have to say anything. Problem is, I'm too wired to pull that off convincingly. My breathing is volcanic; I can hear my hair grow. Then I realise: This is Vegas. I stick my key card in my pocket and start wandering the verdant, tiger-eye-haunted halls of Le Rousseau.

That's when I spy Kendall. She's not at the party either; she's also in sweats, baggy ones, and she's making a run for Jungle

Indulgence, an all-you-can-eat dessert buffet. *Oh, yes!* I think. *Brilliant!* Hurrying, I catch up with her, pinch her sleeve. She starts when she sees me, eyes wide, mouth a grim line, cheeks aflame. Of course she's embarrassed. This is the last place she wants to be seen after splitting her pants, and as the only one who knows about it, I'm the last person she wants to be seen by.

But there's no judgment in my smile. Kendall has got to know that. I slip my arm through hers. 'Great minds think alike,' I tell her, softly, reassuring, and lead her inside.

PART THREE
Road Trippin'

'Have love, will travel . . .'

– The Sonics

The Boss

Here's how I do: I get mad. I blow up. I get over it. And I keep it moving. Wynn, of course, wants to deconstruct the minutiae of our fight the next morning, but I am too hungover to go there. What's to analyse? Shit happens. We've been rooming together for months. That's rough. Adding insult to injury, I was the one dripping male attention, not her. So she attacked me. Really tapped into her inner mean girl, all right – but it's better she get it out in the open than use it to fuel her neurosis. My response is the epitome of Stella style: I forgive her. Consider yourself exonerated, bitch – don't let it happen again.

Now, back in New York, it's all good. We're busy. Meetings at Universe re: our next video – the label wants Wynn in the foreground, so it's between 'Hello Kitty' and 'Lingerie Model.' Plus, I'm prepping for the SAT *and* the ACT *and* my GED. During downtime, Christmas shopping. A cell phone for Didion – that's part of my master plan. A picture phone, of course. Preloaded with shots of guess who.

Me and Wynn hit Soho, hoping to avoid the Midtown mob scene, but it's gridlock there too. The mayor should charge an entrance fee or something. Weaving in and out of package-toting tourists is exhausting, so when Wynn suggests Mexican hot chocolate, I say lead the way.

'We should pick a day to exchange gifts as a band,' she says over a steaming mug.

Out come our PDAs. 'Better do it soon – when's Kendall leaving for Hog Level?'

'Frog Level.'

Pffff! 'Excuse me, but *Hog* Level's more like it. You look at your girl lately?'

'Stella, you are so mean.' Wynn inhales her chocolate narcotic, 'All that fattening road food, I probably gained five pounds too.'

Please. Barbie needs Mattel stamped on her ass to remind her how great her body is. 'So what're you doing for New Year's?'

Wynn nibbles a cookie. 'My real dad's coming in. Naturally my mom greeted this info by booking a flight to St Bart's – Manhattan is not big enough for both of them. Anyway, he'll be with his girlfriend, so we'll probably just have dinner and I'll stay at their hotel – I don't want to go back to an empty house – and it'll be nice to see him . . . them.' She shrugs. 'You?'

'You heard Brian at the label meeting. He's getting a table for that Ramones tribute – the cancer fund-raiser,' I remind her. 'Skip out after dinner with your dad, we'll hook up.' Wynn's no doubt dying to ask if I'm cool with the Cara Lee thing. Truth? I still don't know if Brian's mixing business with pleasure, but I do know that hokey Okie is home for the holidays so not an issue. Wynn's got a chocolate moustache. I must have one too. I lick my lips and a second later she does the same. That's when her cell rings.

'Hey you!' Wynn says cheerily. 'What's up?'

That bray – Malinka. Wynn holds the phone an inch from her ear.

'Really? Cool!' Wynn says. 'No, my parents fly out that day. No, don't be silly. Yes, of course. Yay! Fun!'

Wynn snaps her cell with a goofy smile. 'Looks like I don't have to worry about being alone in the house . . .'

The Voice

Now that I'm famous my cousin Carlene is on me like glaze on a roast ham. Last time I saw her, she acted all superior, her with her promise ring and her fiancé; now she's my best friend. Does she think my sparkle rubs off? I act real gracious as she shepherds me around, flaunting me. Thank goodness I brought plenty of press kit photos. A little gesture on my part – for the people of Frog Level, a treasure for ever.

It's nice seeing everyone, having the whole town at my feet, but I'm distracted, disconnected. Lately, the whole idea of home is an itch I can't reach. Is home here in South Carolina, where I was born? Or up in New Jersey, at my mom's house? Or in my fabulous Teen Towers apartment, which I haven't been to once since we came off tour. I ought to be completely at ease down South, yet instead I feel more 'on' than ever. In the East Village, with so many people – students and artists, professionals, bums, just everybody – you can be anonymous. Even if you're recognised, people show respect; they won't fawn all over you unless it's a die-hard fan about to wet his britches. Here, whether in the Piggly Wiggly or the Dairy Queen, people come over and talk to you like they have every right.

Well, I take that in my stride, but I'm glad we're leaving soon. Not that I have any hoop-de-hoo New Year's plans. I know *who* I want to spend it with – I just can't figure out how to wrangle it, until Jane Marie Fulton starts gushing over my earrings.

'They're real unusual,' she says, reaching out to touch them. We're all at the Dairy Queen, me and Carlene and her girlfriends. I pray Jesus will prevent Jane Marie from leaving greasy fingerprints on my most cherished Christmas present. 'They sure don't have anything like them over at the Claire's.'

Claire's! As if A/B would have bought my gift at some old chain store. 'Thank you, Jane Marie.' Semiprecious stones glitter and swing as I toss my head. Jane Marie's fingers retreat. 'They were a gift from A/B.'

'Really?' Jane Marie and Carlene and Devon are more interested now – they start asking all about A/B. It's like feeding fish in a pond; throw a couple of crumbs and they gobble them up. But I say, 'Oh, I can't talk about that,' so it gets through their cinder-block brains that it's rude to intrude. Still, I look kindly at Jane Marie – thanks to her a great idea occurs to me. 'Tell you what, I can call A/B and find out where he got them,' I say. 'I'm sure it's some exclusive boutique, but maybe they take phone orders.'

'Would you, Kendall?' Jane Marie lights up. 'Wow, that would be so nice!'

I pat her hand. 'I sure will,' I say. Well, then they all gawk at me like I'm going to call A/B right then and there! 'Later . . .'

Only when will I get a moment's peace to do so? My grandparents' house is small, and me and my mom share what was her room growing up. What with the close quarters and all the company coming and going, it's not till eleven at night when my mom takes her shower. I slip out my cell.

'Heyyyy, Kendall.'

Gosh, it's good to hear his voice! 'Hey, A/B! Did you have a good Christmas? I sure hope so!'

'Cool, you know, your basic Jewish Christmas: a movie and Chinese food.'

It always slips my mind that A/B is Jewish – another river to cross. 'Well, mine was wonderful. One day, A/B, you'll have to experience a country Christmas. But look here, the reason I'm calling . . .' I get that out of the way, then progress, doodling hearts on my notepad. 'We're coming back the day after tomorrow. I've pretty much had my fill of Frog Level, but, well, things have been so hectic since the tour and rushing on down here and all, I haven't made a single plan for New Year's. Isn't that hilarious? Kendall Taylor with nothing to do on the biggest party night of the year.'

I let it sink in a second. The thing with A/B is, if I set him up with the right signals and let him know it's OK for him to be forward, he does the right thing. Of course he does! That's why I love him so!

The Body

My mom and stepdad are so thrilled that my world-famous friend is coming for a visit, they risk missing their flight to welcome her into our home. I don't warn them how potentially bone-crushing that is.

'Mrs Ween's mother!' Malinka booms, dropping luggage in our foyer and securing my mom for a left-cheek, right-cheek, left-cheek kiss. And I mean cheek, not air in vicinity of cheek. This gives my stepdad the smirks, until he's caught by the Brutal Butterfly. Faintly bruised and rattled, they're off for the airport. Malinka and I are alone.

'Is beautiful house, Ween.' Malinka's gaze traverses high ceilings, heavy drapes, parquet floors. 'You have many servants?'

'Just day, not live-in. And we don't call them servants, silly,' I tell her. 'You want a tour?'

We don't get farther than the library before the doorbell rings. Federal Express.

'I bet is my Christmas present!' Malinka says eagerly as I sign.

'You shouldn't have bought me a Christmas present!'

'Why should I not? You did not buy one for me?'

'Of course I did,' I say somewhat guiltily – she wasn't even on my list till she invited herself up here. I carry the large box to the living room. Our crystal-encrusted tree holds centre stage, and Malinka 'oohs' approval. She arranges herself on the Persian as I push her present toward her. 'Teefany!' She pounces on the signature blue box, tears at it excitedly. 'Oh, Ween! Is beautiful!'

'Do you really like it?' I really hope she does. 'Pins are so in now, but a butterfly – not too cheesy?'

'Ween!' She nearly knocks me over with her hug, then holds the silver creature up to the light. 'Is gorgeous, I love it, I will wear it New Year's and tell your father it is gift from you. It will be conversation piece. I will pin it here, against my bosom, and look très chic.' She places the pin back on its bed of cotton, picks up the ribbon and fiddles with it. 'Now you mine . . .' She sounds almost timid. 'Is not anything compared to your gift. But I was certain it would upright your valley.'

'What?' I unravel the contorted colloquialism. 'Oh, right up my alley. I'm sure it will be.' I undo the wrappings. 'Oh, wow! Malinka, you're awesome!' An oblong crate, baring the stickers 'Imported from Morocco' and 'Fresh, Ripe. Pomegranates.' Nestled amid protective strings of jute lie rows of bloodred, leather-skinned fruit. They might as well be imported from Jupiter. 'Malinka, this is incredible,' I tell her, then confess, 'I love pomegranate juice – you're so thoughtful to remember – but I've never had an actual pomegranate before.' I take one from its crinkly nest, stroke the mottled peel, then poke at the nipplelike crusty knob at the top. It's so . . . foreign, so alien.

'Try it,' Malinka says.

'Well . . . um . . .' I turn the fruit over in my hand, scratch the skin with a fingernail. 'How the hell . . . how do you eat it?'

Malinka laughs, that symphonic smashup. 'You need knife, and bowl — big bowl. Maybe we should go into your kitchen, Ween.'

'No, wait, I'll get a knife and come right back,' I say. 'You relax.'

'You are sure you want to eat pomegranate in your mother's so elegantly decorated living room?' She puts a singsong in her voice. 'Ver-ry mess-y.'

This makes me more psyched. 'What do I care? No one's home.' And I trot off for implements of pomegranate destruction, returning in a blink with a porcelain bowl and a sharp paring knife. Malinka and I sit on the floor, facing each other, and when she pierces the peel, I suck in a terrified breath — she's cut herself! But it's not Malinka; it's the pomegranate that's bleeding. When she has it open, I gasp again. It's like she split a geode. Ruby-red globules, glistening polished jewels, cradled in a parchment of cream-coloured pith.

Malinka now quarters the fruit and hands me a piece. Yet still, I'm clueless. I smile into Malinka's smile. 'OK, I'm a moron . . . what do you do?'

Malinka's eyes brim with almost menacing know-how. 'Is easy,' she says. 'Bite, suck, tear, suck, spit.'

'Huh . . . ?'

She points to the succulent quadrant. 'See, they are seeds. You should not swallow . . . or you grow pomegranate bush in your stomach.'

We both giggle.

'So: Bite, suck, tear, suck, spit. Here, for you I demonstrate.' Malinka opens her mouth to receive the fruit, sucking extra slurpily for effect, then rips seeds from rind. The skin around her mouth goes red. She sucks some more and finally spits the mess of pith and pit into the bowl between us. Then she grins. 'You go!'

I bite, suck, tear, suck, spit. Then howl. 'Oh my god, that is so delicious!'

'Is funny though,' Malinka laughs. 'I feel like I am giving you drug abuse.'

I go for the rest of my slice. Bite, suck, tear, suck, spit, howl. 'Drugs? Please! This is better than drugs! Better than sex!'

'How would you know, Miss Wynn Virgin Morgan?' She laughs at me again.

'Shut up, you pomegranate pusher!' I look at my hands. They're already stained. 'Just give me more!'

The Boy

Not only did I ask Edie out for New Year's two whopping months in advance, I told her we'd do whatever she wants. Whipped much? To my chagrin, she vetoes the Ramones tribute in favour of a Long Island house party. But wait, there's more. Apparently I deserve to be flogged for inviting one of my bandmates.

'A/B, how could you?' Edie's not pleased to learn Kendall's our third wheel.

This baffles me. After all, Edie made no bones about the fact that she wants me at this party to cement her status in a new social stratum. Logically I assume the only thing more ingratiating than one rock star is two rock stars. 'How could I what?'

Edie narrows green laser beams and performs heart surgery, sans anesthetic.

'It's not like we'll have to attend to her all night. People will be all over her, and Kendall loves that kind of attention. She's coming by car service; we won't have to chauffeur her around.' Edie's mouth is a thin pink line. I switch gears, go for her soft spot. 'Come on, the poor kid had nothing to do. How would you feel?'

Success!

'Why couldn't I have fallen for a cruel, heartless bastard?' Edie asks the ceiling. 'Why did I have to fall for a sweet mushy dumbass instead?'

I snatch her in my arms for a quick canoodle. 'Too bad for you,' I whisper into her clavicle. 'Sweet mushy dumbass – for ever.'

The party, while hardly a history-making rock-and-roll event, is off to a pleasant start. Not nearly as jappy as I feared. Edie lives in a modest middle-class town, but the soiree's a few notches up on the utsy scale. Every house is on the water, a boat in every backyard. But the dozen or so kids already assembled are low-key and friendly. There's a slight haze of cheeba, and no keg. Hummus and baba ghanoush. Kings of Leon and Bob Marley. Basically, a well-to-do neo-hippie gathering. I fit in fine.

Our hostess, the olive-skinned, hook-nosed Santhea, is the new friend of Edie's BFF Alexa. There's been some shuffling of late – Edie met me, Alexa met Santhea – this is really the first chance for everyone to get acquainted. I don't know a soul besides Edie, but hey, several months of celebrity and the rigors of touring have made me at ease anywhere, except maybe a Taliban hideout.

There's no hint the party will go out of bounds. Santhea's tolerant parents are on premises, amiably monitoring – they don't actually hit off the bong, but there's no need to be surreptitious about it. We're not big drinkers – most of us sip mineral water or soda, although champagne, uncorked as of yet, is on ice. As New Year's anticipation grows with the crowd, the vibe stays mellow, copacetic.

Then Kendall makes her entrance. And everything changes.

Not in a big way, though. It's subtle. A shift as opposed to a swing. Six months ago Kendall would have been invisible to these people. Her 'off-ness' would have gone unnoticed. Now her 'off-ness' has become the 'on-ness' of a rock diva. She walks in, her presence acknowledged with a buzzy effect.

Caftan flowing as she runs to the door, Santhea clasps Kendall's hands, takes her coat, leads her around. No introduction required. Everyone knows who she is.

Kendall doesn't beeline for Edie and me, standing near the fireplace, dipping pita triangles into Middle Eastern delights. She chats amiably with one cluster of admirers after another, her Southern accent sonic flower petals against the nasal 'oh-my-gawds!' of Nassau County. Then she waves, weaves our way. Edie stiffens. For no reason. No reason at all. Except that's how it is. Edie does not want Kendall here. And that's that.

But Edie's a cool person; she doesn't want to be a bitch. Plus, she likes herself, so she hates feeling threatened. Who can she blame for her current state of affairs? That would be me. Right about then Kendall ambles over. 'Hey, you guys! Happy Almost New Year!' The chummy three-way hug she goes for gets neatly cross-checked. 'Oh, Edie,' she says. 'Your friends are all real nice.'

'They're not my friends,' Edie says flatly. 'I don't even know these people.'

'Oh? Really? I thought – well, they're awful nice.' Then she turns to me. 'Hey, A/B! What's that you're munching on?'

'Ah, well, that's hummus – ground-up chickpeas. And baba ghanoush is—'

'Boboga . . . what?! Bless my soul!' Kendall swats my arm. 'You're joshing me – that's not even a real word. Edie, he must keep you in stitches.'

'Sure,' she seethes. 'Though sometimes I'd like to see *him* in stitches.'

Silence. Awkward silence. The mother of all awkward silences. At least for me. It's possible Edie enjoys her fury on some perversely justified level. And Kendall, I doubt she picks up any nuance of weirdness.

'You know, A/B, I bet we're in the worst trouble with Mr Wandweilder for skipping that Ramones thing,' she blathers on. 'Stella's the only one from the band going, as far as I know, but everyone who's anyone else is sure to be there.'

'You said she had nothing else to do.' Edie breathes the words at me.

Before I can begin to conjure an explanation, Kendall goes on: 'Well, I reckon we can always go late if this party gets dull. I have the driver all night. Gosh, all the traffic was going the other way – smooth sailing coming out here. That driver could not believe I was leaving the city for Long Island.'

That rips it for Edie. She ekes out an 'excuse me' and bolts. I ought to go racing after her, but what would I say?

'Is she . . . all right?' Concern creases Kendall's face.

'She – she's mad at me,' I manage, obliquely, lamely.

'Oh, gosh, A/B! It's not because I'm here, is it?'

The last thing I want is to make two women miserable! 'No,

Kendall. It's not you, it's me.' Yep, those words actually come out of my mouth. 'I'd better—'

'No, let *me* go. Girls know how to talk to each other.' She touches my arm comfortingly. 'Don't you worry, I'll just make chitchat, let her see how nice and regular I am. She doesn't know me the way *you* do.'

Makes sense. If Kendall intimidates Edie, only Kendall can make it right. Right? Sure! By the stroke of midnight it will be worked out, canned sitcom laughter in the background. So I let Kendall follow Edie while I wander in search of that bong. Several heady hits later, I am feeling no pain. Cloud-walking, my head and feet turned to sponge. Those three guys I'm smoking with – Sam, Dan, and . . . Wham, is it? Spam . . . ? They've got some good shit and are ridiculously generous.

So when an extra oomph of excitement stirs the atmosphere, it takes me a while to figure out what's up. Santhea's a burbling blur, passing out noisemakers and hats; her parents pop champagne corks and fill plastic glasses. Dan, Sam, and Spam float toward dates like astronauts in zero gravity. Santhea slaps a paper cone on my head, snaps the elastic under my chin. This shouldn't be funny but it is.

The countdown begins: 'Ten! . . . Nine! . . . Eight . . . !'

A whiff of perfume behind me . . .

'Seven! . . . Six! . . . Five! . . .'

A tender touch at my elbow . . .

'Four! . . . Three! . . . Two! . . .'

I turn woozily around.

'ONE!!!'

'Happy New Year, A/B!' The voice honey, the eyes stars.

'Happy New Year, Kendall . . .'

The room starts to spin. 'Auld Lang Syne' kicks in. Kendall and I ring in the new year like any boy and girl who find themselves facing each other at midnight. With a kiss.

The Voice

The whole way into Manhattan, A/B's in a pitiful state. Can I ever forgive Edie for getting him so upset? Hopefully, I won't have to; hopefully, she's out of the picture for good. When Edie discovers us, we are kissing, but that's only natural – you'd probably kiss Magilla Gorilla at the stroke of midnight on New Year's. It's not like we're making out, sloppy and drooly; we're simply holding hands, placing a small, tender kiss on each other's lips. Well, I won't repeat the curses that girl ranted, but this time I let A/B scramble after her. I treat myself to a glass of champagne and join that silly 'Auld Lang Syne' song. I sample some of the weird food but I don't like it one bit. By and by, I notice A/B roaming the house, dazed, hurt, helpless. You ever come upon a child's abandoned mitten on a cold winter sidewalk? That's how I feel for A/B right then. As far as what transpired between him and Edie, I don't ask. That's none of my beeswax.

'Hey,' I say quietly. 'Maybe we should leave. My driver can follow you home, then take us to Bowery Ballroom. I'm sure the tribute's still going on.' A/B perks up a mite at that idea, mumbles that they rode to the party with Alexa. Even better. I

149

steer him toward the Lincoln. He huddles against the door and scarcely says a word. I don't press him. Boys need to work things out for themselves. Besides, music has such healing power – he'll feel better once we get to the club. Trouble is, our names aren't on the list. Darn, I forgot to tell Mr Wandweilder we might come. But the bouncer shakes his head at the doorman. 'Man, don't you know anything? This is 6X!' he says. 'Half of them, anyway.' He opens the way, and we glide inside.

Wall-to-wall bodies, moshing, schmoozing, moving, and shaking. I clamp A/B's hand. The Snooks are onstage, delivering a slurry version of 'I Wanna Be Sedated' that sounds like they've already been sedated enough. Mr Wandweilder leaps to his feet when we approach his table. Stella's there; so is Wynn, with Malinka. I wave, happy to see them, and feel vindicated. I know I did the right thing. This is where we belong, A/B and I.

Also at the table are some grown-up industry types – lean men in suede blazers, women with sleek hair and chic clothes. But my eyes are drawn to four glamorous girls who look familiar. Are they on a TV show? Models, maybe? Before I can place them; Mr Wandweilder descends on A/B and me like a goofy dragon, draping one arm around each of us.

'You guys! You're here!' he booms. 'Now we're all together. Me and my band, the best band ever! 6X is in the house! Whoo!' Mr Wandweilder is always enthusiastic, but usually he has a bit more, well, decorum. I do believe he's drunk! I catch A/B's eye and know he agrees – he even manages a tiny smile. 'Now look, you guys, I've been working my *tuchas* off on this deal for weeks, and it's about to reach critical mass! So I want to introduce you to some people, and I want you to be nice –

150

but of course you will; you're the nicest kids I know! Just don't be *too* nice, OK? You got me?'

Again A/B and I trade bemused glances as Mr Wandweilder wheels us toward the four girls I vaguely recognise. He makes a comical bow before them and hollers: 'Kendall! A/B! I want you to meet the fabulous, beautiful, and above all, rockin', Touch of Stretch!'

The Boss

We're supposed to be finalising details on our next video, but we're so geeked about possibly going on tour with Touch of Stretch and Ayn Rand we can't contemplate anything else. Touch of Stretch, the progenitors of 'primp punk.' A gimmick, if you ask me – dressing old-school starlet, playing metal riffs, and snarling lyrics about sex, drugs, rock and roll, and more sex. But they make bank: *Wanton Soup*, their second album, is already platinum. So there's respect. When we met them at the Ramones tribute, they barely acknowledged us, but it was mobbed and earsplitting in there, not conducive to a Girl Scout wish circle. As to Ayn Rand? Look, I may have met my future husband, but if I got within two feet of frontgod Franklin K. I would come in my pants, all right.

'Focus, people!' Brian claps for attention in the WandWorld conference room.

'Wait, Brian, is it true Britt from TOS is doing Franklin K.?' I ask. 'And that he writes all their material?'

'You, Stella? Caught up in idle gossip?' Brian says with mock dismay. 'Come on, all of you. The tour isn't a done deal yet, but the video shoots Wednesday. This is your last chance to look over these storyboards. You see something you don't like, now's the time to speak up. Anyone? Wynn – this is your show.'

She blows her bangs, now long enough to tickle her nose. 'I'm just so glad I don't have to prance around in my bra, I'd skip rope in a purple dinosaur suit.'

I feel that. I'm down with doing 'Hello Kitty' instead of 'Lingerie Model.' The bonus? Gwen Stefani, who's a big 6X fan, convinced the Harajuku Girls to cameo in our 'Kitty' clip.

'Just get us the hookup with Ayn Rand,' I tell Brian. 'We'll handle the video.'

And we do. No tantrums, no tragedy, no muss, no fuss. I gotta give us props for being so professional. I also believe being home these last few weeks has been good for us. A post-road reality check. Speaking for myself, I feel balanced, centered, straight. Part of that has to do with me getting my mind right about Didion. Buying him a cell phone, what a flash of genius. Sometimes he forgets to turn it on, but I can still contact him whenever. And he's been calling. Not every day, no, but I don't want some clown who has to check in every five minutes to ask if it's all right to flush the toilet. I *like* wondering when I'm gonna hear from him.

Being in a healthy place in my relationship lets me be there for A/B when he hits me up for help with his. I'm expecting it. Him showing up on New Year's, no Edie in sight, and mimicking a beaten dog? You don't have to be Sister Stargazer to know something's sour. At the 'Kitty' shoot, while Kendall and Wynn do their scene with the Harajuku Girls, A/B corners me at craft service – aka the snack table. 'Stella, tell me: What do women want?'

I reach for a donut. 'You – clearly,' I say.

'No, come on, I'm serious.'

Damn, he looks beyond serious. He looks forlorn. He looks like Hansel after the birds ate all his freakin' bread crumbs. 'I *am* serious – or is it some other A/B Farrelberg with a fan club in Texas?'

'OK, let me rephrase: What does the woman *I* want want?'

I scope a spot where we can sit down undisturbed. 'All right, looks like we got a minute. What happened?'

He gives me the New Year's Eve blow-by-blow, yet still casts Kendall in a halfway-innocent light. Boy has brains like macaroni.

'All right, A/B, let me break it down for you. One) Kendall Taylor is crazy about you. Two) Kendall Taylor is crazy. How come you don't see that?'

'I—'

I cut him off. 'Rhetorical question, A/B. Because you *do* see it, you just don't wanna deal with it. And wait, hold up – I don't blame you. You don't wanna rock the boat because you know Kendall's the one most likely to drown. Now, Edie, I presume, is a rational human being. So your only option is to be straight with her.' He really should be taking notes, but he's definitely paying attention. 'Forget telling her there's nothing between you and Kendall; instead, explain that you wouldn't put it past the Southern belle from hell to boil a bunny on your stove, but it is what it is. She's the lead singer in your band and you're not about to walk away from 6X.' I finish my donut, lick my fingers.

154

'Then tell her you love her and leave the ball in her court. If she can work with that, great. If not, she's gonna have to break up with you.'

A/B looks about to dry-heave. He cracks his Gatorade and downs it. 'Oy vey,' he says. 'Any way I can convince *you* to talk to Edie? No, no – don't smack me. But if she dumps me? Then what? Will you stop me from strangling Kendall?'

'If I have to,' I say. 'What am I gonna do with a dead singer and a guitar player in lockdown? But, dude, have a little faith. If your girl's all that, she'll stay with you. And who knows, maybe you'll think up some way to make sure she does.'

The Boy

I don't think up a way to make sure Edie stays with me. My buddy Moth does. Now, Moth, of course, doesn't see my problem. Moth is of the mind-set that two girls is better than one, that three is better than two, et cetera exponentially. He sure as hell thinks Stella's advice to come clean with Edie is insane.

'You cannot be honest with women!' he cries. 'Observe!' A production assistant on our 'Hello Kitty' shoot, Moth juts his chin toward various female confabs on set. Stella and some wardrobe chicks; the Harajuku Girls; Kendall, Wynn, and the director, a tall, strident Irishwoman with a coppery braid. 'Cliquish by nature. Always talking. Whispering. Scheming. I tell you, my friend, they are devious. Devious!'

While I have seen evidence of female cunning, I refuse to malign the entire gender. By the same token I can't discount everything out of Moth's mouth that pertains to the fair sex. So I ask what he'd do to really prove his love to a girl. He strokes his stubble, then snaps his fingers. 'Ah, yes!'

His suggestion scares me shitless, but I get it done. That very evening. And later that very evening – which would make it that very night – I show up at Edie's unannounced. There's no other way, since she won't take my calls. Mrs Stern comes to the door in robe, slippers, and scowl. At the sound of my voice, little Lily and Roz bound down the stairs to stare. Mrs Stern shakes her head. 'Go tell your sister to get down here!' she commands. 'And get back in bed!'

Edie takes her time as I cool my heels on the sofa. I run a finger along the edge of the afghan. Oh, the times Edie and I snuggled under it – in case anyone walked in on us they couldn't see our hands. To think I might never snuggle 'neath that afghan again!

'Ahem!' Edie says.

I look up. She's wearing the ancient Nirvana tee she had on the first time I saw her. I'm sure it's no accident. I hear Moth in my head: 'Devious! Devious!' Next I hear John Cougar Mellencamp crooning: 'Hurts so good!' Me, I can't make a sound. The speech I based on Stella's counsel won't come out.

'Well . . . ?' Edie says, hip thrown out, arms crossed over her chest in a way that, wittingly or not ('Devious! Devious!'), makes her boobs swell and strain against the threadbare shirt.

I stand up. Verbalisation? Impossible! So I grab the corner of my own T-shirt, yank it up to expose my chest – left pectoral, to be precise – and stand there, eyes pleading, nipple bared. When she sees what I've done she begins to melt. She steps up to me before her legs turn completely to mush. With a finger she traces it, delicately, hesitant – it's still fresh. There, in a heart, inked to the skin above my own beating heart, the only thing I really came to say:

A/B LOVES E/D

The Body

Popular opinion has it that a tour with Ayn Rand and Touch of Stretch would be the best thing that could happen to 6X. Every baby band in the country is jostling for the slot. The two proven hit-makers sold out venues on the last leg of their American tour – that in an environment where poop-pop and crap-hop acts are cancelling dates – so the opportunity for the opener is enormous. And their fans, though compatible with ours, are perceived as 'hipper,' more 'influential,' so it would expose us to a new audience. When Brian interrupts our rehearsal to glowingly proclaim he's accomplished this coup, everyone roars approval. Everyone except me.

Well, I never was the popular girl, so why would I agree with popular opinion? My silence snags their attention, but before they can comment I give them the drum roll and cymbal crash they want. I smile. Go 'Whoo!' Telling them I've got a bad feeling – what purpose would that serve? None.

It's probably paranoia. Did I really believe doom-and-gloomism had vacated my psyche? Sorry, it was just on hiatus. Hanging with Malinka was so fun. She got up close to my flaws and foibles and didn't run screaming back to Orlando. Plus I had a genuinely pleasant visit with my real dad, and then my mom acted so adult upon her return, not pestering me to trash him once. Yet now the holidays are over, and typical Wynn weirdness resurfaces.

I keep it to myself. Before we hit the road, I spend the time between rehearsals alone, finishing the lyrics I started down South. 'Please Send Socks,' 'Not Quite Full,' 'Mae Verna,' and 'Las Vegas Meltdown' I'm pretty happy with. '(Stella Meets Her) Match' and 'Maybe, Malinka' – I'm still struggling with those, so I put them away. I stock up on composition notebooks and Uni-Ball pens to jot whatever occurs to me in the Midwest. I do some girly things, too. Get my hair cut, finally. A manicure. Let a sombre aesthetician get medieval on my blackheads. Buy underwear. But forget about shopping for anything else. The label thinks we need to amp up our stage-wear and hires professional help. A team of stylists rolls clothing racks into a Universe conference room – without even conferring with us first. If that sounds insulting, get this. Just as we begin garment perusal, Gini LaDuc from marketing enters shakily with a memo.

From: Gilded Lily Management
To: Universe Records, Wandweilder Worldwide, 6X
Re: 6X wardrobe concepts
Darlings –
This is to detail styling concepts to avoid, lest they echo those of our client Touch of Stretch. The following **cannot** be worn onstage by members of 6X:

- Anything Marc Jacobs
- Any vintage clothing from the period 1946–1964 (this includes accessories)
- Pencil skirts
- Poodle skirts
- Cardigan sweaters
- Marabou, ostrich, or feathers of any kind
- Fur (real or faux)
- Veils
- Opera-length gloves
- Spangles (sequins OK!)
- Charm bracelets

Furthermore, members of 6X must avoid the following cosmetic items:

- Bright red lipstick
- Bright red nail polish
- The perfumes Chanel No. 5 and Jungle Gardenia

Thanks in advance for keeping your styling choices in line. Touch of Stretch looks forward to seeing you in Pittsburgh!
XOXO
Gilded Lily Mgt.

Gini LaDuc reads the memo aloud. Her eyes blink a staccato as if she's got sand in her contact lenses. Then the memo gets passed around for each of us to review, in case we doubt its veracity.

A/B breaks the pall of quiet: 'Ooh, and I was so looking forward to those opera-length gloves! Not to mention the Jungle Gardenia!'

I keep my mouth shut. Dread feels like the onset of sore throat. I pick at my new manicure. I know I'm not paranoid. This is no consolation.

The Boy

Batmobile, Shmatmobile! When little boys quit fantasising about becoming the Caped Crusader and start on the far more attainable goal of rock stardom, this is the vehicle they imagine themselves tooling around in: the MondoCruiser 8000 Series. They thought of everything when they built this two-tonne turquoise phallic symbol, from the functional (two potties) to the frivolous (flip-down DVD players above every bunk). With sleeping accommos for twelve, lounges, a galley, and luggage/gear space, there's ample room for band, road manager, tutor, and crew (yes, we are with crew now, a crew of one – Benson Bennagin, the world's most experienced roadie – dude's been at it since Dylan went electric!). Even the occasional mom, dad, or significant other. It costs a fortune to rent and run the split-level diesel-guzzler, but we have no choice. The schedule's grueling – we'll drive by night and sleep en route.

Our parents all come to bid us *bon voyage*, which is touching in a mortifying way. My mom accepts a tissue from Mrs Taylor. My dad and Stella's calculate mileage. Wynn's mother inspects the quality of the linens. E-slash-D – yep, that's how my girl goes now – also attends the send–off, and I show her around the mighty Mondo. 'And here,' I gesture to the bunks upstairs, 'is where I won't be doing any groupies.'

She punches my arm. 'That's right, you won't.' Then her eyes get watery. 'As if groupies are what worry me.'

I climb into one of the bunks, try to pull E/D in beside me. 'Ach, this experiment proves there is not room for two!' It's my wacky professor voice. I'm trying to be jolly. To no avail. One fat, glossy tear pools in its duct and lands on E/D's cheek. 'Hey,' I say. I smooch it away, then fumble at her neckline. She smacks my hand. 'Come on,' I insist. 'Let me see it . . .'

Tauntingly, she peeks inside her T-shirt, then slowly reveals the tattoo on the rise of her left breast: E/D LOVES A/B. I kiss her there, but when I look up, another fat, glossy tear cascades.

'Sweetie, sweetie,' I say. 'We talked about this . . .'

'I know.' She sniffs. 'No crying.'

'No crying. Remember, if you think you're going to cry, say the magic word.'

E/D nods. 'Seattle.'

Seattle. Last night, we booked her ticket (with Mrs Stern's grudging agreement). E/D'll meet up with us in Washington, ride with the band to our Portland and San Francisco gigs, and we'll fly home together.

'Seattle,' I say, using the collar of my shirt to blot another stubborn tear.

From below, squealing, stomping, and squabbling – Stella, Wynn, and Kendall boarding the bus. E/D and I know it's time to say goodbye.

The Boss

You gotta draw the line from the start. I don't care who you think you are. My message? Do not mess. I make that clear when the Touch of Stretch rhythm section, twin sisters Romy and Relish Vallane, comes to our sound check in Pittsburgh. They cop squats third row centre, prop their feet up, and attempt to psyche us out. Like we don't have enough to contend with. Two months ago, we were bumping into each other, playing clubs the size of your kitchen, and now – Carnegie Centre. Crystal chandeliers, hundred-foot ceilings, gilt-encrusted everything. Seats, too – last place I performed that had theatre seating was the school auditorium in seventh grade. And the stage is huge, a basketball court. Yeah, it'll be great having room to strut around, only it's gonna take a minute, all right. It's an adjustment. The last thing I need is a pair of LA punk chicks in my face.

Emissaries, no doubt. Lead singer Britt Gustafson and guitarist Sue Veneer are too cool to check out the puny opening act but will want a full report from the field. One of the twins has a skirt on, and the way she's positioned her legs you can see right up it. That's my ammunition – if she starts up, I'll remark how classy it was to flash her coochie, then ask what she does for an encore.

But they don't start. Not really. They listen as we run through a few songs, and when A/B calls out to the soundboard regarding treble trouble, I move up the proscenium to stare them down. Romy or Relish sticks her tongue out at me, then elbows her sister and they both mug. I stick my tongue out and mug back. Maybe they'll be all right. I'd like that. Wynn and Kendall are fine, but they can both be kind of uptight. I get the impression my flow won't make these Vallane chicks clamp their hands over their ears.

It's on me to break the ice, so after sound check I step up. 'So how'm I gonna know who's who?' I study these duplicates for differences and find none. Shiny dark hair ripples from widow's peaks. Narrow, flickering eyes in wide, shallow faces. Plump lips, naturally rosy-pink. The kind of lips guys love.

'You want to quit staring?' says one, standing to go eye-to-eye. 'I'm Relish and she's my baby sister.'

Romy — younger by what, six minutes? — stands too and shuffles her feet. Fine, I get it. Personality will distinguish these two. Romy's the 'quiet' one while Relish will just trash you to your face.

'So what's up with your guitar player?' Relish asks. 'He's kind of sexy.'

'Nooooo,' whines Romy. 'I hate you, Relish! I already told you *I* like him!'

Relish shoves Romy, tells her to shut up. Unless these two have seriously short attention spans, A/B's gonna have his hands full. 'A/B's cool,' I say. 'Very funny. Very sweet.' Just talking about

165

a boy has the Vallanes licking their too-plump, too-pink lips in a predatory way. 'Very taken,' I finish.

'By who? By you?' says Relish, as if that would only make the game more fun.

'Me? Please,' I say. 'He's got a girlfriend in New York.'

Romy and Relish hoot in tandem. 'Girlfriend!' Then Relish gives me the same shove she gave her sister. 'We're not in New York,' she says with a flickery wink. I decide to take the shove as a friendly gesture. But I'm glad I'm over A/B. I wouldn't want to have to fight these two.

The Body

'**S**pace – the final frontier!'
That's what A/B says when he gets a look at the Carnegie Centre stage. I giggle, but get a twinge of envy too. I mean, yes, playing drums is physical – but you're stuck in one spot. Only during our set, I'm happy to live vicariously through my bandmates. At long last unchained, their opened-up moves – A/B's Chuck Berry duck walk, Stella's saunter, even Kendall's jigs – take our performance to new heights.

After our set, however, while watching Touch of Stretch from the wings, I make a huge mistake. I compare us to them. Stupid. 6X and TOS are so different. Technically speaking, they're not even good. Musically, I mean. Oh, Sue Veneer can really shred, but the Vallane sisters are certainly no better than Stella and I, and Britt Gustafson cannot sing. With my one-note range I know I shouldn't talk – but I'm sorry, she can't. She screams, she snarls – but she won't even attempt melody. So why do I feel threatened? Two reasons.

First, their songs. This is fundamental but also subtle. Touch of Stretch tweak the verse, chorus, verse, chorus, bridge formula in such a subversive, ingenious way – so it comes off catchy yet just unique enough to riddle you. Lyrically, too – they put a new spin on traditional bad-girl themes with wicked double entendres and offbeat metaphors. What I wouldn't give to be a fly on the wall of one of their songwriting sessions, if only to confirm that Franklin K. is the mastermind behind it all, that Touch of Stretch is merely an outlet for his anima. I swear, I'm obsessed with that gossip now – I really, really want it to be true.

Second, their . . . presence. TOS make kabuki seem colourless. They make soap opera plots feasible. They make a bullfight seem about as dangerous as walking a dachshund. Try as I might, I can't muster up real disdain for how punk it's *not* to spend hours primping before a gig. The hair, make-up, and styling combine to truly spell-binding effect. There's something desperate and doomed about their B-movie-queen image; they give off the vibe that each show is a pre-suicidal swan song. It's chilling, perverse, and desperate – very cool. And Britt, well, I don't know about a Grammy, but she deserves an Academy Award. When she lowers her veil for 'Stunning,' she weeps real tears.

To paraphrase Joan Jett, I hate myself for loving them. I can't even gauge my bandmates' reaction – I'm too busy being mesmerised. But as TOS hurtle into the wings to extend the ecstatic, torturous wait for an encore, I can't look at them any more. I slap my hands together till they hurt, then go numb, but my stare is fixed on a spot of stage rigging, not the panting, glistening girls a few yards away from me. Then I look at Stella, but she's a sphinx – she could be bored stiff, or simply wearing a game face. A/B's clapping, but at his core he's a regular guy, a good guy – I get the feeling he finds the over-the-top sexuality of Touch of Stretch a little icky.

Naturally I expect Kendall to be absolutely horrified. But what do I see when my gaze wanders her way? She's . . . enraptured. Cheeks flushed, eyes bright, she woo-hoos the band's praises and only stifles her applause to wave at them like they're all sorority sisters or something. Weirder still, once Touch of Stretch delivers a two-song encore and – blasé, victorious – drift toward their dressing room to clear the stage for Ayn Rand, Kendall follows several paces behind, a hypnotised handmaiden, a lobotomised lady-in-waiting.

The Voice

Just because I am a role model and a superstar doesn't mean I know everything. In fact, a girl like me – still so young, yet with such responsibility – I probably need a mentor more than the average going-on-sixteen-year-old. That's why I have high hopes about Touch of Stretch. No offence to Wynn and Stella, but I need exposure to worldly, sophisticated young women who've been in the business a while if I am to grow as an artist and a person. And I can't imagine anyone as cosmopolitan as Britt Gustafson.

But she's also just about the nicest person I've ever met. That's doubly wonderful since when you're beautiful you don't have to be nice. Platinum hair, sky-blue eyes, rosy cheeks, yet as friendly, helpful, and sweet as can be. Plus, her being twenty-one you wouldn't think she'd give me the time of day. But of course, I'm real mature for my age – and Britt can tell right away. The instant our eyes meet she understands – we both do – that we share something deep. Us both bearing the frontwoman's burden has a lot to do with it. It takes gallons of gumption to get up there and lead your band to glory.

'Britt! Britt!' Touch of Stretch and their entourage sweep

through the wings after their Carnegie Centre set. I rush to catch up – I simply must say something flattering to Britt. I call her name again and reach to tug the edge of her furry white capelet.

She stops, and her bandmates and hangers-on stop too. She turns, and they turn with her. As she looks at me, about a million emotions I cannot read scroll across the screen of her wide eyes. Finally she smiles, dimples on display. 'Hiiii, Kendall!' Her tone is flat, but softer than I would have thought, considering the racket she makes onstage. 'What's up, Special One?'

Her calling me 'Special One' – it's like she knows me already. 'Oh, Britt!'

'Oh, Kendall!' I notice that her make-up is runny and cracked. Tiny tentacles of red weave in the whites of her eyes. A testament to how hard she works.

'I just . . . I must . . .' Shoot, I hate it when words won't come. But my stammering and stumbling doesn't seem to bother Britt. In fact, it seems to move her.

'You want to tell me something, Special One?'

I bob my head.

'And I want to hear it, truly I do, but I could pee you a river right now.' She giggles. 'Ooh, "Pee You a River!" Someone, write that down – a song title if I ever heard one. Come on, Kendall, come to our dressing room before I do something unladylike.'

And just like that, lickety-split, I am part of her fold.

The Touch of Stretch dressing room is a dank, grey cement space not much bigger than 6X's dressing room. Yet it's

171

another world – a world from before I was born. So storybook, so fabulous – all done up in Touch of Stretch fashion. There's a fancy make-up table with tulle skirting and a curlicue chair. An etched-glass cocktail bar on wheels set with an ice bucket, crystal, and champagne. Black-and-white portraits of Touch of Stretch in ornate frames. There's even one girl costumed like a maid, with a uniform, cap, and stiff black apron; she walks around with a tray of chocolate truffles (which no one seems to sample but me). An older guy with a pencil-thin moustache and a satin jacket pops the champagne and fills flutes.

Britt, back from the bathroom, sits on the sofa and taps the cushion to invite me to sit beside her. She fits a cigarette into an ivory holder, spews a flume at me. I cough, but before I get embarrassed, Britt apologises and blows her next puff at someone else. We get on the subject of shoes as Sue Veneer, on the curlicue chair, begins to undo her T-straps.

'Somebody find my bunny slippers,' she demands, throwing in some blasphemy I won't repeat, and two girls scurry to obey. Another stream of blasphemy spews forth as she massages her feet. Why do people who refuse to praise the Lord then blame the Lord for their pain? I don't wonder that aloud, since I am a guest, but it sure does come to mind. Next thing I know it's like a podiatrist convention in there, everyone trading tales of woe about corns, calluses, bunions, and such. Sue tells Romy Vallane that her being pigeon-toed is a sign that she's frigid. Whatever that means, Romy doesn't like it. 'I hope you get foot fungus, Sue!'

'I hope you get crotch rot, Romy – oops, forgot, you already got it and gave it to the entire Eastern Seaboard on our last tour of duty.'

'I hope you get syphilis of the throat!' counters Romy.

They definitely seem to be getting off the subject, but Britt swings it back. 'What about you, Spesh?' She nudges my knee. 'Those are cute shoes. Do they kill?'

Everyone fixes on me. Of course. I appreciate Britt kindly drawing me into the discussion, but being put on the spot turns me into a worm on a hook. I am torn between being honest – admitting that my feet aren't suffering – and fabricating a story about a gigantic blister that busted and got infected and everything, just to fit in. Tussling with this internally, a third option comes to me – and it's just right. 'Gosh,' I say, 'the truth is I have a terrible confession to make. Even though I love high heels I don't think I walk in them too well. In fact, I can be about as clumsy as a blindfolded giraffe—'

'A blindfolded *drunk* giraffe,' snickers Sue.

'A blindfolded drunk giraffe on ice skates,' adds Relish.

'High-heeled ice skates,' finishes Romy.

I smile to show I can take a ribbing, then seize my opportunity to compliment Britt. 'Watching you onstage tonight, you're so graceful and poised,' I say. 'You walk in heels the way I can't even walk barefoot.'

Britt's eyes go bright. 'Come on,' she says. 'Let's see.'

Gosh, she can't expect me to parade around the dressing room!

'Up. Now!'

Apparently, she does. All Britt's features scrunch intensely to the middle of her face. I have no choice. I get up. Everyone steps back, giving me room. What have I gotten into? Biting the bullet, I make my way from the sofa to the bar to the tutu-flounced table.

'Tsk, of course you look like an oaf,' Britt says. 'You walk with your feet!' She crushes a cigarette in a large ashtray, waves her hand. 'You want to look sexy in heels, you don't walk with your feet. You walk with your ass.'

'Um . . .' I am bewildered. 'My . . . ?'

Britt stands up with a flourish. 'From here,' she says. Then she slaps me right on the butt! Really hard! In front of everyone! My face must look like a maraschino cherry. 'Allow me,' Britt says, ignoring my blush. She slinks around the room, legs criss-crossing, toes landing lightly, dainty yet indulgent, and I see what she means. Feet are simply the follow-through; the movement comes from a far more womanly place.

My butt still burns from where Britt spanked me, but I think about moving from an even more intimate area. The spot I touch when I get those surges. My you-know-what. I square my shoulders and slit my eyes, and what do you know if I don't sashay around like Miss USA and a runway model and a gypsy queen all rolled into one. My goodness! If I thought I loved high heels before, now that I know the secret – well, it's like the difference between pining for a boy from afar and kissing him on the lips.

The Body

I have become a researcher . . . no, an archivist . . . no, an archeologist. Yes, that's it – I'm digging in the dirt, digging *for* dirt, every vile stinky tawdry scrap and shard I can find to justify my loathing for Touch of Stretch. It's so not like me. Except for all the evil isms – racism, fascism, like that – I swear, I've never hated anyone or anything. I'm sure it's unhealthy. I'm hoping it burns out before it engulfs my positive passions. It's already given me this bizarre kind of writer's block. Whenever I put pen to paper, it's a TOS rant or an addition to the dossiers I'm compiling, based on what I learn online (at TOS fan sites and slam site touch ofcrap.com). Here, let me read from what I've found . . .

Dossier Subject: Sue Veneer. Real name: Susan Moskowitz. Age: 23. Piercings: four. Tattoos: seven. Plastic surgeries: one (nose). Hometown: Van Nuys, California. Celebrity hookups: Trey Chricton (*That Stupid Show*); Dmitri Stone (guitarist, the Dregs). Arrests: two (drunk and disorderly; aggravated assault – charges dropped). Bottom-out moment: the aggro assault – apparently Sue caught Dmitri in bed with her former Manicurists bandmate, singer Vanna Flange, and was compelled to beat Vanna with a Frye boot. That marked the end of the Manicurists and the genesis of TOS.

Dossier Subject: Relish Vallane. Age: 19. Piercings: two. Tattoos: three. Plastic surgeries: none. Hometown: Bel Air, California. Celebrity hookups: Trey Chricton (*That Stupid Show*); Lucas Kelly (MTV-VJ); Ran Martin (bassist, Die Fledermaus). Arrests: none. Bottom-out moment: *US* magazine's 'Worst Behaved Teen Star of the Week' (public urination).

Dossier Subject: Romy Vallane. See Relish Vallane for basic data (includes piercing/tattoos/surgeries). Celebrity hookups: Trey Chricton (*That Stupid Show*); Lucas Kelly (MTV-VJ); Forrest Crane (keyboardist, Die Fledermaus). Arrests: none. Bottom-out moment: totalled Mercedes SL, a high school graduation gift, on grad night.

Dossier Subject: Britt Gustafson. Age: 21. Piercings: one. Tattoos: none. Plastic surgeries: two (breast enlargement, chin excavation). Hometown: Malmö, Sweden; raised Huntington Beach, California. Celebrity hookups (random sample – too numerous to list all): Trey Chricton (*That Stupid Show*); Lucien Vickers (Churnsway); Joel Hoffner (*Yet Another Not Another Teen Movie*); Malik-Malik (MC, Urban Surrealist Squad); Franklin K. (frontman, Ayn Rand – undocumented, but please, Kendall says his valet knocks on the TOS dressing room door every night, fifteen minutes before Ayn Rand goes on, and squires Britt to an undisclosed location).

Phew. There you have it. It feels good to get this off my chest, even if only to the soulless unblinking lens of a camera. I can't talk to anyone else. Kendall's in la-la land, practically an honorary member of Touch of Stretch. A/B's a guy – he'd think I'm just being a catty chick. Stella, well, we do discuss TOS, sometimes sort of trash them, but she doesn't know the extent of my hatred. Plus she seems to actually like Romy and Relish. So nauseating. Do those wannabe tough girls truly believe hanging with a Brooklynite gives them cred by extension? Can't Stella see she's being used? Doesn't she find it disgusting how they trade guys? Ick. The way they paw at A/B, it seems he's their next victim.

The only person who might feel my torment is P. I haven't expressed it to her, but she's perceptive. We're shooting towards Chicago, waiting for Kendall to grumble awake so we can begin our lesson, when she engages me in an ominous yet hopeful conversation.

'Tell me, Wynn: Are you familiar with karma?'

I pick at a muffin top. 'Um – I think. "What comes around goes around . . ."?'

'That is the lay interpretation, yes.' Her gaze is unerring – and unnerving. It pokes at what burgeons inside me, taking my temperature, testing for emotional malignancy. 'Let me assure you it is not just a concept,' she goes on. 'But it has its own clock. Sometimes it feels like the karmic carousel is in slow motion—'

'Hey, Miss Peony. Hey, Wynn.' Kendall shuffles through the lounge toward the galley. 'There any muffins?'

Peony drops her voice. 'And sometimes it happens so fast it'll make your head spin!'

The Boss

Well, well – will wonders never cease? We're finally getting an audience with the elusive Ayn Rand. We've played four dates with them already yet haven't crossed paths. This is intentional – on their end. Their sound check? Closed! Plus they hole up in their dressing room till showtime, as if breathing the same air as the opening act could give them cooties. It's freakin' insulting, is what it is. But tonight all three bands will have dinner together – the brainchild of the Chicago promoter and the programme director of WDIK, the alt-rock station. Three fans win a place at the table to watch their favourite rock stars chow down. Any excitement I might have had about being in the same room as Franklin K. has gone down the sewer. The guy dissed me, all right. He can kiss my ass.

And then I meet him, face-to-face . . .

The Midwest is all about beef, so naturally the event takes place in a steakhouse. A lot of pewter, a lot of polished oak. Waiters about three hundred years old. It's four-thirty PM and the place is desolate – of course, who eats this early? We're led to a private room. To my astonishment, Touch of Stretch are already here – these girls like to make an entrance, so I don't know how their handlers conned them into arriving on time. Relish gives me the smoke sign – puffs an invisible blunt – and when I go to say hi to her and Romy I can tell how toasted they are.

'You guys take your glaucoma medicine?' I ask.

They crack up. 'Girl, you crazy if you think we could handle dinner with fans and radio people without the chronic,' says Relish.

I'm about to be mad at them – so annoying, when gated-community girls try to talk street – but Romy palms me half a squished fatty of what's probably grade-A ganja. Just then, the heavy wooden doors peel back and a procession begins. The radio DJ, the programme director, the promoter. Next, the lucky fans: a chunky guy with a Touch of Stretch baby tee tight across his man boobs. Two apoplectic females – shaking, frothing, practically in tears. Behind them, assorted jesters and henchmen for Ayn Rand, and then . . . ta-daaah! The men of the hour. The men of the freakin' decade. Sharp dark suits that barely contain their devil-may-care rock-and-roll souls. Stak Estervak, Eric Hall, Rocky Sandborn, and Franklin Kertavowski, better known simply, and for obvious reason, as Franklin K.

Suddenly the room is too small. The air gets thinner. Light-headed, I watch Ayn Rand make the rounds – accepting hefty cocktails, lighting cigars, saying hey to the photographers and journalists assembled as if they're all pals from back in the day. Even one of the ancient waiters steps forward, and Franklin K. slaps him amiably on the back.

Hmm. So. Franklin K. Oh yeah, he is all that. The sexiest ugly

179

man alive. Built like a linebacker. Immense. His head looks like it was carved out of granite in a hurry – hard, broad strokes of chin, jaw, brow. A boulder for a nose. His mouth is meaty, yet when he smiles – an easy boyish game set up between stubble-shadowed cheeks – you want to touch his face. And he smiles a lot. None of that pent-up high-strung intensity of your basic broody frontman. But it's hard for anyone else to be relaxed around Franklin K. He moves through the room with a brutish silkiness that makes you check yourself, simultaneously hoping he won't see you – and that he will.

He does. 'You guys must think I'm the biggest piece of shit.' He takes a gulp of brown booze, the ice in his glass not even daring to clink. Pushes at his mouth with the back of an enormous hand that seems to have five knuckles per finger. 'But, of course, I am.' He shrugs. And he smiles. And I want to touch his face.

Somehow A/B has wandered up and finds his voice. 'No-no-no!' he says. 'Please. You guys – we understand. We didn't even notice you were snubbing us. Well, of course we noticed. You're Ayn Rand. But we didn't think of it as snubbing, just that you're, well, you've got priorities. So no hard feelings, none at all, and—'

Franklin K. puts his beautiful, monstrous hand on my shoulder. You know how a cat will head-butt you when it wants to be stroked? That's how it feels. Then he leans over – it's a long way. His eyes are black pits, perimeters tinged with flame. He smells like aged whisky and good weed and the fine weave of his worsted suit. He nods once, toward A/B. 'Does that one ever shut up . . . ?'

180

The Body

I have been to hell, and it's a steakhouse in Chicago. Shall I enumerate the reasons?

1. P and Gaylord have been denied access. P's vegan and nothing would please Gaylord more than a few 6X-less hours, but to me it's wrong on principle. True, all the other crew members are also excluded, but I still think it's mean.

2. Seating arrangements are structured – band members strategically separated to spread our individual charm among the guests most effectively. I'm sandwiched between a balding Clear Channel executive and Ayn Rand's loose-limbed bass player, Stak Estervak, both of whom are speaking to other dinner companions, leaving me to chat up my menu.

3. All members of Touch of Stretch are within my line of vision – talk about an appetite suppressant. The Vallanes bicker over the bread basket. Sue Veneer stabs at a shrimp cocktail but doesn't seem to eat it. As far as I can tell, Sue doesn't bother much with food as that would interfere with

her drinking. Across the table sits Britt Gustafson, a drooling male fan, and next to him, Kendall.

4. Kendall is stymied by a steaming crock of French onion soup. With its mass of molten cheese and whiskery, slippery strands, French onion soup is not something you eat when you've got twenty strangers, including the hottest male star in rock and roll, seated around you.

5. I've figured out what would make Kendall – generally a fried mozzarella sticks sort of girl – order French onion soup. A self-satisfied smirk flits onto Britt's lips as Kendall struggles with spoon, breadstick, glops of melted Gruyère, and broth so hot it makes both nostrils run into her bowl.

Kendall's blissfully ignorant of the fiendish pleasure Britt takes in her sloppy soup. Not me. I squirm over my salad, Caesar dressing making sick, slick whitecaps on waves of romaine.

'I am in hell.'

'Do you realise you just said that out loud?' Stak Estervak asks.

I swear, I blush more deeply than his Shiraz. Stak laughs. Not a mean laugh. 'It's cool – I do it all the time,' he says. He taps the rim of his wineglass. His fingernails, like mine, are bitten, cuticles a wreck. 'Wait a sec – aren't you a little young to be working for The Dick?'

What? 'Oh . . . I don't work for the radio station.' He is utterly without an inkling. 'I'm Wynn . . . ?' Nothing. 'I'm in 6X . . . ? We're on tour with you . . . ?'

He lets this register for a beat. 'Oh,' he says. 'Well. See what I mean about foot-in-mouth disease?'

After that, Stak and I start talking. Really talking. Tour van breakdowns and bedbuggy motel stories; stalker fans and rival bands and more shocking, hilarious scandals and sagas in Ayn Rand's four-year climb from shitty Chi-town clubs to the top of the charts. I share the silly way 6X got started, my learn-by-doing approach to drums, how I think Stella's really the driving force of the band.

'Every band needs someone like that – musicians are notoriously flaky,' Stak agrees, adding that if it wasn't for the motivating behemoth of Franklin K., he'd probably be working in a slaughterhouse.

It's easy to talk to Stak. I like the way his hazel eyes change shade depending on how he feels about a subject. How his glossy brown hair resembles a plop of chocolate pudding. His ravaged nails, his snaggly smile. But when he asks why I believe hell is a steakhouse in Chicago I only tell him half the truth: that I'm uncomfortable at parties where I don't know anyone, leaving out the part about Britt Gustafson, the face of evil.

The Voice

Halfway through dessert – cheesecake, which I just couldn't resist, even though I'd already put away my steak, a baked potato, creamed spinach, and that messy onion soup – Britt leans over Tony, the biggest Touch of Stretch fan ever. 'Come on, Spesh, let's hit the little girls' room,' she says to me. I take another quick forkful and excuse myself.

'You amaze me, Kendall, really!' Britt carefully pats the curls that took her stylist all afternoon to arrange. 'Doesn't it bother you, pigging before gigging?'

Now this is a little confusing, since Britt was the one encouraging me to get the French onion soup and extra sour cream for my potato and all. But I sure don't want to make her feel bad about it. 'Well, I *am* about to pop,' I say.

'I would think so! But if it doesn't affect your performance, and you don't worry about getting fat, what can I say.'

Britt checks her teeth and relines her lips. I go into a stall and think on what she said. I wash my hands and gaze at her. She's so on top of everything. And she's my friend. I want her to be my friend forever. 'Well, honestly, Britt – lately I have been concerned about my weight . . .' Then my whole tale of woe spills out. I tell her how upset I was seeing myself in the Gap commercial, yet drowned my sorrows in candy. I even tell her about splitting my pants onstage in Vegas.

'Oh, Kendall, how awful!' Britt puts down her eye pencil and walks over to me and hugs me, right there in the bathroom. I hug her back. I'm so thankful I took the leap and shared my problems, because she is so wise and beautiful and not even judging me at all. 'But you know, honey, it's normal,' she says. 'We all eat too much sometimes. We all worry about how we look. It's part of being a woman. So you mustn't feel bad about it, Kendall, OK? You promise?' She picks up her eye pencil again.

'Thank you, Britt, thank you so, so, so much,' I say. 'That makes me feel better.'

'Besides,' she says. 'You can still get rid of it.'

What could she possibly mean by that? 'Get rid of it?'

Britt sighs as though I am the most ignorant rube she's ever met, but smiles to show she doesn't mind. 'You have a ten-minute window,' she says, and when she reads on my face that I haven't the faintest idea what she's talking about she lays it out, straight as a line of thumbtacks. 'After a binge, you have ten minutes – fifteen max – to get rid of it. Stick your finger down your throat. Make yourself throw up. Purge.'

She says it so matter-of-factly I don't want to doubt her. But what girl who ever picked up a copy of *Seventeen* magazine doesn't know the medical term for what Britt just described. 'Britt . . .' I say. 'I couldn't do that. That's . . . bulimia.' How could she not know this? 'It's an eating disorder,' I add.

'Kendall, don't be stupid. It's only a disorder if it controls you.' She regards me like a teacher passing out test papers. 'I thought you were a strong person.'

Her words make me feel wobbly inside. 'Oh, Britt, I am,' I tell her. 'You wouldn't say that if you only knew what I've been through!'

Warmly, she reaches for my hand. 'Spesh, I *do* know. Not the details maybe but in my heart I know how strong you are, what you're capable of. That's why I love you.' Then I feel a chill; she withdraws her hand. 'So to think you believe I would lead you astray . . .'

'No, Britt, that's not it! That's not it at all!' My hand grabs hers back. 'I can't tell you what your friendship has meant to me this tour!'

'Well, I thought so,' she says. 'I had hoped so.'

We look at each other for a meaningful moment, and then Britt squeezes my hand. 'Go on,' she says with soft impatience. 'The clock is ticking . . .'

The Boy

M an, E/D was right to say she wasn't worried about groupies. Of course, back then her main concern was Kendall. She hadn't met Romy or Relish Vallane. Those girls are dangerous squared. At least I can say nothing happened between the three of us. Um, no I can't. OK, I can say I didn't do anything but parry and deflect.

We're smoking a little weed — me, the Vallanes, Stella, and Flaco, this skinny guy in overalls, who seems to run things in the boiler room of Madison, Wisconsin's Cheddar Court Theater — when Stella says to Flaco, 'So, are you the master of all we survey?'

'Yeah, you know, part-time,' he says. 'I won't be a janitor all my life, but I get to see some killer shows. Plus,' he gives Stella a sly look, 'there are other fringe benefits.'

Yeah, like getting rock stars stoned — occasionally foxy female ones.

'Wanna show me around?' Stella asks, and Flaco flicks on like the Cheddar Court marquee. They scurry off, and I'm thinking, *Huh? Isn't Stella head over Docs for Didion Jones?* So why ask Flaco for a tour of his subterranean domain? I'm still mulling this over when I get attacked. Tigress on the left! Tigress on the right! Fortunately my opponents failed to solidify their tactics beforehand. They're dividing – but not conquering.

'Come on, A/B, don't you want to kiss me?' says Romy or Relish 'cause up close – and we are very up close! – the twins are even harder to tell apart.

'Uch, A/B, don't,' says Relish or Romy, swatting her twin. 'She doesn't know how to kiss. Kiss *me* . . .'

If the Vallanes had conferred and concurred to present a united front, a *Penthouse Forum* experience might be my fate. Instead I manage to fend them off. 'You guys, you guys! Romy! Relish! Come on!' I say. 'Stop that, I'm ticklish there! Ooh, there too – come on . . .' On one hand, yes, it's very arousing. They're beautiful, they're persistent, and they're twins for God's sake. And I can't fault a certain body part for . . . succumbing to a degree. But I am not ruled by any one particular body part; I am the sum of my parts, and some of those parts – heart, brain, integrity (which, OK, is not a limb or an organ, but cut me some slack) – don't like where this is going. Besides, those girls are treating me like the sale rack at H&M. The picking and pinching goes on until Stella and Flaco complete their circuit.

Flaco is floating. I seriously doubt he 'got' anything; having Stella pay attention to you for ten minutes is enough to make any guy walk on air. I want to pull her aside, ask how she could leave me alone with those two, but I know how wussy that would look – and I'm just so relieved she's back I let it go. As we all wind up the spiral stair to watch Ayn Rand do their thing, I congratulate myself on my narrow escape.

The Boss

Guilt is garbage, useless; I don't buy it. So I don't feel a shred over chilling alone with Flaco. All I let him do was turn me on to some mediocre weed. But yeah, there's a certain satisfaction in knowing a boy wants you and holding him at bay with your self-respect alone. When my thoughts flashed on Didion, I was like: recognise – treat me right or someone else will. And don't you know there was a message from him when I checked my cell? Now I'm juiced because he's in Minneapolis – and we're on our way there.

Catching the Didion Jones Show means cutting out before Touch of Stretch and Ayn Rand go on. Boo-hoo-hoo! Wynn and A/B come along; they've had enough kowtowing too. A/B suggests we all hit an IHOP after Didion's gig. As if a short stack is what I crave. One incredulous look from Wynn explains how dumb an idea *that* is.

Back at the hotel, I don't even try to be nonchalant. The mush in my murmur gives me away. 'Damn, Didion . . .' We lie facing each other on the king-size. 'I missed you like crazy.'

'Me too, Stella.' My name never sounded so good! 'You've taken up residence.'

He says this like he's not entirely pleased. That's OK. The boy's got abandonment issues, clearly and with cause: Mama the ho, Granddad the dearly departed. Didion became a midnight rambler and adopted the mantra: Don't get attached. It worked – till he met me. 'Stella, you are in my blood . . .'

It's all I could hope to hear before our tongues get too busy for words. Yet even though it's been so long, we're in no rush. We kiss for ever, and when we move on we draw out each tantalising step. Original, huh – a boy who doesn't try to play you like a video game, squeezing and shooting. Not that he's the toy, either. We're equals. That first time we were together it felt like Didion held all the power, but maybe I just wanted to give it up to him. Tonight we are matched. Perfectly, amazingly matched.

Next morning, Didion gets on board. He doesn't make a fuss about the bus, but after riding shotgun in semi cabs reeking of salami heros, polyester sweat, and Camel nonfilters, the lap of luxury can't suck too much. Sun streams through the windows. People in cars watch wistfully as we zoom by. Didion's presence feels natural. Everyone accepts him, and I'm magnanimous with my man. He talks Delta blues with Gaylord, swaps herbal recipes with Peony, jams with A/B.

Only Wynn and Kendall act a little funny. Solicitous but restrained. Then Kendall busts loose with an impromptu 'Go Down, Moses' and Didion joins in. Buttery baritone meets creamy soprano, putting the 'spell' in gospel and giving you that slap-yo-mama hush. The MC becomes, not a magic bus, but a seriously spiritual one.

Until Kendall throws her hands to heaven, crying, 'Didion, I bet we could cut a gospel record, you and I! Let's do "Do Lord"! Or "Let the Circle Be Unbroken" – oh, I love that one!'

Now, Didion's my man and I see no problem in their duet. But Wynn? Flips!

'Can't you ever keep your stupid mouth shut?' she mutters. That's the gist, anyway – Wynn's words are low, but the look she's giving Kendall is unmistakable. I've seen her hurl it at Touch of Stretch.

'Whuh . . . Wynn . . . what?' Kendall looks like she just got bounced around in the gear bin.

Wynn stares at Kendall like she's a two-tonne mosquito – a pest of stupendous proportions. 'Can't you *ever* keep your *stupid* mouth *shut*?' she enunciates. 'Or do you *always* have to *flaunt* yourself so *pathetically*?' Bananas – Wynn transforms into her mother's mini-me! Now, a verbal smack-down from an angry black woman is scalding, all right, but one courtesy of an Upper East Side blue blood? Like getting run over by a dry-ice truck. This is nothing like the beef Wynn and I had in Vegas – that shit was scorching, primeval. The way Wynn laces into Kendall now is ten degrees below zero.

'Why . . . wha . . . ?' Kendall's reduced to babble again.

'Oh, please.' Wynn's weary. 'You sucking up to Britt Gustafson is sickening enough, but fortunately you're out of our sight when that felching goes on.'

Did Wynn just say 'felching'? Oh no she didn't!

'But really, Kendall, *do* try to avoid performing that act on Didion while we're all locked up together,' she goes on. 'Perhaps you've forgotten he's with Stella, who I'm sure would remind you of that if she weren't so occupied basking in the afterglow.'

Wynn swings her slit gaze to me, then to A/B, then back to Kendall. 'But of course you never respect *anybody's* boyfriend, do you?'

The Body

Oh my god, I am such a bitch! Hormones? Hardly, though Kendall accepts the old PMS excuse. No, it's Touch of Stretch madness making me lash out at my own bandmates. Uch. Why can't I just let people be happy? If Kendall's blissed out under Britt's wing, what's it to me? Am I really such a petty, pernicious person? Maybe P has something in her herbal repertoire to tranquilise me.

I don't want to wait twenty minutes, when we're all supposed to meet in the hotel coffee shop for a preshow bite. I don't even bother with shoes, just pad down the hall to her room. Just as I'm about to knock, my fist freezes – I hear noises inside. It's evil to eavesdrop but I don't care. Long, low, wails. Quick, high yelps. Some yoga technique, like Breath of Fire? A Wiccan incantatory ritual? I think not! P's having sex in there – but with whom? If there's a resurfaced Nebraskan boyfriend from her past, she failed to mention him. So it must be someone on the tour. One of the roadies? Our bus driver?

I take off down the hallway, into the stairwell, down a flight to Stella's floor. Bang, bang, bang! No answer. Bang, bang, bang! 'Who?'

Finally! 'Me!'

'Wynn? Oh . . . chill a sec.'

Dreamy-eyed and tucked in a terry-cloth courtesy robe, Stella lets me in. Didion's in bed, leaning against the headboard, wearing nothing but his beat-up acoustic across his lap. 'Hey, Wynn . . .' he purrs over his strumming.

'Hey.' I clasp Stella's wrist. 'You're not going to believe this, but Peony Randolph is sleeping with someone on the tour!' This is huge news, great gossip, but Stella couldn't be less fazed. 'Sleeping with, as in the euphemism for screwing?'

'Yeah, well . . .' Every syllable wades through a haze of afterglow. 'That's nice. Peony's cool,' Stella says. 'She deserves a little action.' Then she giggles, and glances toward the bed.

This is too weird. Stella calling P cool? Stella *giggling*?!

'Wynn, do me a favour, will you?' she asks. 'We don't feel like going to dinner, and room service will take for ever. Order me a Tomato Surprise from the coffee shop . . . and, Didz, what do you want?'

'Nothing, cherie,' he says. 'I'm good.'

Stella moves toward the bed to confer with her man. 'Are you sure? You don't want anything? Grilled cheese maybe? Side of fries?'

Lean muscle stretches along Didion's back as he puts his guitar on the floor. He says something I can't quite grasp, then snatches Stella quick as a trap, flips her onto the bed. She squeals, bucks, and struggles with glee. Cement-footed, I inch toward the door. 'Wynn? OK?' Stella pants. 'Tomato Surprise . . . ?'

'Yes . . . OK,' I mumble.

I want to vomit. I stand in the hallway, feeling myself rattle and heave. Whatever gauzy rationale I once used to dupe myself that I meant something to Stella – that she cared about me – has been taken out by a marauding army of one: Didion Jones. And the worst part is, Didion's not my nemesis. He didn't set out to destroy anything between Stella and me. Never even thought about it. It's just a natural state of affairs, a side effect of his entering her life. He's here now, he's with her, he's unlocked the love she's kept in a vault and it's all his.

Let's recap. Stella has Didion. A/B has Edie – a strong-distance relationship. Kendall has newfound BFF Britt Gustafson, who seems to be diverting her from A/B for the moment, but knowing Kendall the way I do I'm sure she's arming herself with all the big boy-slaying guns in Britt's amorous arsenal. Kendall's a Chihuahua with a chewy when it comes to A/B; he's her imperative objective, her mission in life. And now even P's getting some!

That leaves me . . . alone. Oh, there's Stak. I'll turn a corner and there he'll be with his chatty detachment, then some minion will touch his shoulder and he'll be off. A momentary bright spot, Stak is – nothing more. And Malinka? As predicted she's over me; I've heard from her exactly once since the tour started. This should probably bug me but it doesn't, not really. Put it this way: I miss Stella more, and I still see Stella every single day.

The Boy

Flesh and bra. Travel with a bunch of chicks, you become inured to the sight of them in various stages of undress. So when the scantily clad female beside my bunk tries to yank me from a deep sleep, I am neither amused nor aroused. 'Leave me alone,' I grumble.

'Come.' Poke. 'On.' Poke. 'Get.' Poke. 'Up.' Poke.

I thrash around. I smell gin. I open my eyes. Sue Veneer? 'What's going on – what are you doing here?'

'What's going on is I was playing your SG and I broke a string . . . and when I couldn't find any in your guitar case, I didn't want to snoop around.'

What, her playing my axe without asking permission, that's *not* a violation?

'What I'm doing here is . . . shit, every now and then I need a break from that bitch.'

A bunk light flicks on. 'A/B?' It's Wynn. 'What's going on? Who is that?'

'Hey, got any guitar strings?' Sue calls out.

Wynn and I in stereo: 'Shhhh! You'll wake the whole bus!'

'No, no, no. Don't wanna do that. Just minding my business,

doing Sue Veneer Unplugged, when *thwaing-g-g-g!* Almost took my eye out . . .'

Wynn clambers out of her bunk, the Guided by Voices T-shirt she sleeps in grazing her thighs. 'Shh, Sue, come on. Let's go back to the lounge.'

I get out of bed too. 'Yes, and let's try not to make a ruckus, shall we?'

Sue snickers, does a decent Elmer Fudd: 'Be vewwy, vewwy quiet . . .'

Downstairs, Sue offers her bottle of Tanqueray. Wynn and I demur. Sue shrugs, swigs. 'You guys aren't mad, are you? It's just . . . Britt . . . sometimes she . . . urgh . . . !'

Man, does this get Wynn's attention. 'Um, Sue,' she says, 'you want to talk about it?'

Sue stretches and grunts. 'It's like this,' she says. 'I don't care what your damage is as long as you're up front about it. I'm Sue Veneer, I'm a brat, and I may actually have a teensy prinking droblem. Not that I'm proud of it, but it's me. I don't pretend to be a saint. Now, Britt Gustafson, in case you haven't noticed, has a barbecue pit for a heart. But does she cop to it? Nooooo. She prances around like she believes her own press clippings – that she represents some glamorous neo-feminist movement or is, you know, a decent human being.'

'Sue, I had no idea,' Wynn says. 'I mean, yes, I consider Britt to be a monster, but I thought you were all pretty horrible by affiliation. I judged you by the company you keep and . . . I – I'm sorry, Sue . . .'

'Yeah, well . . .' Shockingly, Sue begins to go weepy. 'I'm not Attila the Hun.'

'Oh, Sue, please don't cry. You don't have to act like Attila the Hun . . .'

Am I going to remind them Attila the Hun was a dude? Not on your life.

'But I think if you tapped into your strength and asserted yourself instead of knocking yourself senseless with a bottle every night you'd feel a lot better.' Wynn blows the bangs off her face. 'Not to mention,' she adds, 'how it would make Britt feel.'

Sue says nothing. She wipes her snot, then twists the broken D string into a garrote.

The Body

Word travels fast in a microcosm. So when we hear that Orpheum security is involved in a hostage situation with a crazed Ayn Rand fan, we rush from our dressing room to see the offence unfold. Of course, word gets warped in a microcosm too. It isn't a hostage situation at all, merely a misunderstanding. What the burly guard thinks is a deranged devotee of Franklin K. is actually more into . . . well, me. And she's not insane — just very enthusiastic, and sometimes her intent gets lost in translation.

'Oh God!' I gasp at first glimpse, trying to make my way through the throng before someone winds up in the hospital. 'Malinka! Let that man go!'

'Weeeen!' Malinka greets me, but still maintains a chin-lock submission hold on the guard foolish enough to deny her backstage privileges sans laminate.

'Excuse me . . .' I approach the facedown rent-a-cop carefully. 'Sorry . . . um, she's with me.' Tensions ease tangibly. Malinka stands up. Slowly and with difficulty, the security guard does too. The Brutal Butterfly does the funny flappy move that earned her nickname, and everyone cheers;

then Stak Estervak breaks through the hubbub.

'Holy Mother Mary Margaret! Malinka Kolakova!' Stak's so excited his voice is a good octave higher than usual. 'It's you! It's her! It's really her – you!' Boggle-eyed Stak's basically prostrating himself in front of my friend. So ironic – a member of cooler-than-thou Ayn Rand losing it like that. 'Come on, Wynn, introduce us! Please!'

'Yes, Ween, who is this person braying like farm animal in heat?' Malinka eyes Stak with an edge of suspicion.

The curious crowd will not disperse, and I'm starting to feel ridiculous. 'Malinka Kolakova, Stak Estervak,' I say quickly. 'Stak, Malinka.'

'I know!' Stak is ebullient, thrusting out his hand to pump Malinka's.

'This horny donkey boy is hanging with you – with Seeks–X?'

Is she from Russia – or Uranus? 'Malinka, he's *Stak Estervak!*' I hiss under my breath. 'He's in *Ayn Rand!*'

Still sceptical: 'You are sure he is not mealy-mouthed male groupie?'

If only a bolt of lightning would strike me now!

'Only for you, Ms Kolakova!' Stak is oblivious to insult. 'Or can I call you Malinka? Can I?'

As Stak leads us (all of us – Stella, Didion, Kendall, and A/B tag along) to the previously off-limits enclave of Ayn Rand's dressing room, Malinka explains her MIA status into my ear. She's been in Australia – where tennis season just terminated. At first she couldn't figure out when to call, due to the time difference, then she lost her cell, which had my digits in it.

200

Ultimately, she found a hard copy of our itinerary, jetting Stateside as soon as she won her last match. 'My plan was to see Seeks-X kick balls in Denver, but the second leg of my flight was delayed,' she says. 'But here I am now, free as a turd!'

I have to laugh. I have to hug her. She's such a blast! Plus, there's no denying the lustre of her appeal to Ayn Rand, who flutter and titter around Malinka like they're in a community theatre production of *The Mikado*. Even Mr Noblesse Oblige himself: Franklin K. In fact, when his manservant shepherds Britt into the dressing room to administer what I've concluded is Franklin's preshow blow job, he doesn't even nod in Britt's direction.

Oh, how the whole scene makes Britt burn! She was having a bad night to begin with – we all heard the fireworks between her and Sue. Besides, you could tell watching their dynamics onstage that Sue's had enough of Britt. The other night, when Sue unloaded on A/B and me, among her litany of complaints was Britt's insistence that she not take a solo during 'Bit Part,' their new single. Well, tonight Sue tore it up – fingers flying, stride wide, tongue wagging – as Britt stood at the mike in a snit. And now this: Britt struts in, expecting her regularly scheduled clandestine rendezvous with her DL BF only to find him offering his neck for Malinka to autograph!

'I have never before signed a boy's Adam's apple!' Malinka says. 'Is a little tricky, no?' She manages the feat and caps the pen. 'Oh, I almost forget – I have message for you,' she tells Franklin. 'In Australia, I met Crimson Snow – she is wrapping film in Brisbane. Nice girl for movie star. Big tennis fan. When I tell her I am soon to see Seeks-X, she gets all cutesy in the face and says, "Seeks-X is touring with Ayn Rand, aren't they?" and I say I do not know this but she is pretty sure it is fact. So she says to me, "When you see Franklin K, tell him Crimson has reconsidered."'

Franklin's response is just what you'd expect – laid back, laconic, delivered with a half shrug: 'Oh yeah? Well, what do you know.' His tone is cool, noncommittal. But Crimson's communiqué – cryptic to anyone but Franklin himself – certainly puts a new twist in his grin.

The Boy

It's getting to be a capacity crowd here in the MondoCruiser, with Didion and now Malinka riding with us. At least we got Sue Veneer to return to her own vehicle after one session of bus-seat psychoanalysis. Good thing – otherwise I don't know where we'd put E/D when she meets us in Seattle at the end of the week. Right now we're en route to Boise, and I am missing her so bad.

The so-soon-and-yet-so-far feeling is driving me bonkers. Plus, I am trying to negate the neurotic part of my nature that's none too thrilled with how E/D's been spending her leisure time lately. She's starting a band. With her new friend. Her new friend *Aaron*. Aaron plays guitar too. Aaron has killer taste in music. Aaron writes songs. Aaron's in her physics class. There is nothing physical between E/D and Aaron, of course; E/D hasn't assured me of this because the possibility of something physical between them has never come up in our conversations. I have to trust her. So I say 'uh-huh' and 'cool' a lot when she carries on about new friend Aaron. But when I hang up I fume – is it too much to ask that her new friend be an Emily or an Alison? I wouldn't say I'm tortured by this turn of events, but it has interfered with my nap schedule.

When I can't nap, I need distraction – desperately. Wynn and Kendall have their afternoon lesson with Peony. Malinka watches *Spinal Tap* on DVD like it's a real documentary – she doesn't get the joke. Didion and Stella cuddle on the couch – limbs over limbs, afros in fusion, looking all awww! (do people see me and E/D that way?). Our roadie, Benson, has his nose in a technical manual, and Gaylord's on the phone with the Boise promoter, haggling over some stipulation in our rider. 'It's right here in black-and-white!' Gaylord says. 'Page seven, paragraph twelve, point vii:' "Two pair white Adidas tube socks and six pair Gold Toe knee socks in black, red, or pink will be provided . . ."'

So I open my laptop and start surfing. Randomly! Innocently! Except this pop-up pops up and, well, come on . . . who can resist celebrity porn? Do I click here? I'm human – you bet I do. Do I click there, on 'for a snippet of our latest sizzling amateur superstar action'? Ditto.

And holy crap! It's only a smidgen of a snippet but more than enough to make countless horndogs plunk down $19.95 to see the whole thing. The latex bustier. The impressive endowments. The bad camera angle that verifies the amateurishness, adds that extra voyeuristic ooh-la-la. Go ahead, guys, pull out those credit cards. Me? No way, man. Sure, I'm a healthy red-blooded American male, but I can barely get through the nano-snippet. I don't think anyone wants to see someone they know – even if it's someone they don't especially like – starring in an amateur porn tape. So I am definitely in the minority of healthy red-blooded American males, not to mention European and Asian and African and South American and Australian and Antarctican males. I really, really, *really* don't want to watch Britt Gustafson get busy.

The Boss

Goddamnit! Didion's gone! He's there in the wings at the Boise gig, gives me a sweet kiss before we troop sweatily out for our encore, but when we come offstage he's not around. Not that I'm worried – it's just weird, all right. We've fallen into such a great groove; the last week has been paradise. Any doubts I had about him not liking our sound or thinking I'm a crap bass player? Forget about it. That first night he heard us play, I snuck him a glance mid-set and he was so digging us. Then, later, his comments . . . Didion's a *musician*, and he treats me like one, pointing out what I do well and where I can improve. I crave his criticism as much as his praise. It's a respect thing.

But that's love. Love equals respect, respect equals love – can't have one without the other. So it doesn't make sense that Didion's not in our dressing room. Like I said, we have this groove going, grooves within a groove. A series of tiny intimacies post-gig. We take a corner. Didion presses a towel to my forehead, my cleavage, the nape of my neck. He cracks me a Red Bull; I take a few gulps. We look at each other. He remarks on something I did onstage that was sassy or stupid or whatever. We look at each other some more. We touch. The dressing room is crowded and noisy but we don't notice – we're in a zone of our own.

Except tonight I get my own towel. I get my own Red Bull. I take a corner and pull out my earplugs, tucking them into their case, tucking the case back into my pocket. I watch my bandmates banter and stretch. I see friends, strangers. My brain rationalises that Didion's probably in the bathroom or getting something from the bus, but another part, more amorphous, less anatomical, denies this. Yet I'm cool, I'm chilling; I take a slice of ham from the deli platter and fold it over a slice of mini-loaf but I can't eat it because of the lump in my throat.

'Hey,' says Wynn.

'Huh?' I say.

'Nothing, just hey.' She surveys the cold cuts, drapes a gherkin in turkey, takes a bite. 'Fun tonight . . .'

Wynn looks distinct, but everyone else in the room is sort of soft-focus. I hear them fuzzily, like my earplugs are still in. Malinka cackles. Kendall accepts a compliment. A/B on his cell with Edie. 'Yeah . . .' I say.

Wynn licks her fingers. 'Where's Didion?' she asks.

No levels or layers or subtexts. It's a perfectly normal, neutral question, considering me and Didion have been joined at the loins since Minneapolis. I look at her, see that she's Wynn Morgan – my friend. 'I don't know,' I tell her. 'I don't know.'

Something wary in her eyes, just a flicker. 'Is that . . . all right?' she asks.

I tell her the truth: 'I don't know that, either.'

The Voice

The Lord works in mysterious ways. It's important to accept this, really take it to heart. That way, if life seems to go awry you will stay positive – you'll know it is part of God's plan. Alas, the people who need to understand this most are so resistant to it. Stella, for instance. The poor girl has been off her rocker since Didion Jones ran out on her – with no discussion, no goodbye, not even a 'Dear Jane' letter.

'Why?!' Stella's raving, ranting, showing the sofa cushions no mercy. A/B and Mr Gaylord have taken to their bunks, while us girls convene in the lounge. 'Why?! *Why?!*'

'Oh, Stella, there must be a reason,' Wynn says, hand over heart. 'I mean, I don't claim to comprehend guys—'

'Didion is not *guys!*' Stella lashes out – and here Wynn is only trying to comfort her. 'How dare you lump him in with the whole retarded male gender!'

'I know, I know, that was stupid – I'm sorry . . .'

Why does Wynn even bother? Stella's just the type to bite the hand that feeds her. I sit there with my mouth shut – lending moral support by just being there. I do feel for Stella, her all-too-common situation: A girl is in love and a boy does what a boy will do.

'I must have done something to piss him off . . . scare him off . . .' Stella flips through an internal inventory of potential slights, misread remarks, missed cues. 'Or maybe it was something I *didn't* do . . .'

'Oh no, Stella!' Miss Peony looks appalled. 'You of all people, blaming yourself for something *he* did? I find that inconceivable!'

Stella digs her fingers into the sofa like upholstery is her enemy. 'Peony, the last thing I need right now is a feminist lecture from you,' she says. 'What, you got laid in recent memory so now you think you're an authority?'

I suck in my breath – so Stella found out about Miss Peony and Mr Gaylord! Wynn sucks in same as me, so it seems she's in on it also. Malinka does it too – either she knows, or she's just playing along. But no one sucks in her breath more than Miss Peony, who realises her secret is out. 'I – I – Stella, what do you . . . how can you . . . ?' she sputters. 'I don't know what you mean!'

'Yeah, fine, Peony, whatever – just as long as you spare me, all right,' Stella says. 'In fact, if you can't say anything constructive, why don't you just leave me alone – all of you!' She buries her face in the cushion. Stella would rather suffocate than let us hear her sob.

The Boy

The proverbial shit hits the proverbial fan – does the timing suck or what? A Fallujahan theme park would be more fun, and my girlfriend's landing at Sea-Tac in an hour. Gaylord and Peony quietly but viciously freak out à deux. The Britt Gustafson scandal is at fever pitch, prompting brand-new bizarreness from Kendall. Most combustible, though, is Stella, who's completely unhinged over Didion's delinquency.

We're lounging around in the seats of the Hoffenpepper Concert Hall when Britt Gustafson arrives, flanked by the damage-control team of label publicist and Gilded Lily rep. Kendall leaps to her feet with a 'Hi, Britt!' but is blown off in a blind fling of fur-tipped shawl. High heels tap urgently across the stage; Britt demands a spotlight, squints at it, screams bloody murder into her mike – that's the extent of her sound check. She and her handlers move on to powwow elsewhere, still sorting out the media frenzy surrounding that dubious erotic debut.

The mission? Give the tawdry tape a rock 'n' rebel spin to stem the humiliation quotient. Upping the stakes is the rumor that Britt's been ostracised by the Ayn Rand camp. No word of an official dumping, since the affair with Franklin K. was never officially acknowledged, but everybody's buzzing that they're kaput. And if coolness kingpin Franklin K. is over Britt, how long till the rest of the world is too? Especially if there's truth to the theory that he's the brains behind TOS. Meanwhile, *Inside Britt Gustafson* is doing boffo online box office. It's also been seen in its entirety at least once by everyone on the tour with the exception of our own Kendall Taylor. Which all must add up to fiendish enjoyment for Sue Veneer.

You can tell she's loving it by the haughty way she strolls into the Hoffenpepper. But behind the cavalier nonchalance, Sue's got to be conniving to gain dominion over Touch of Stretch. Step one would involve winning the Vallanes to her side, but those two look pretty wonked-out stoned when they finally toddle up the Hoffenpepper aisle. The twins have been a somewhat reliable weed connection for those of us who indulge (to wit: me and Stella), and I guess Stella could use something to mellow her right about now. 'Yo, Romy!' she shouts out, gets up. 'Relish . . .'

The girls meet in the centre aisle. 'What's up?' Stella strives for a casual air. 'Hey, you guys got a joint you can spare?'

The twins look at each other, trade smirks. 'Sure, Stella,' says Relish.

'Yeah,' says Romy. 'You look like your glaucoma is acting up real bad.'

Neither girl seems in a hurry to rifle through their purses to pull out a stash. 'Real bad,' Relish agrees. 'What's the matter, Stella?' she asks, a goading touch of malice in her voice.

'Yeah, what's wrong, girl?' chimes in Romy. 'You having problems . . .'

'Man problems . . .'

'What's the matter, you lose something . . .'

'Like your boyfriend . . .'

'It must be tough, getting dumped like that, just split on . . .'

'Shit on . . .'

'Better check your gear, your iPod, your wallet. No telling what a guy like that might have run off with . . .'

Not the sharpest tacks, those Vallanes. Relish has just sealed their fate.

Stella, who's been letting their disses pile up into a nice set of seething, silent rage, makes like a heat-seeking missile. She grabs hefty fistfuls of twin ponytails and double-loops them, then whirls both Vallanes around by their hair in a diabolical dance move that would impress the Bolshoi Ballet *and* the WWF. Both Vallanes scream in unison.

Sue watches this plot twist with interest, shoulders raised and chin thrust, indicating she's prepared to leap into the fray if necessary. Wynn and Malinka leap to their feet, step up behind Stella; Kendall and I hang back. (Go ahead, call me a coward, but my fingers are my livelihood and I must avoid fisticuffs at all costs; besides, I couldn't hit a girl, even a girl who could whup my ass!)

'Ow!' moans Romy. 'Let go! Ow, Relish, make her stop!'

Relish uppercuts a push to Stella's shoulder. 'Don't be blaming us if you can't manage your man!'

Bad move, that push. The taunt doesn't work in their favour either.

212

'Don't *blame* you?' Stella's homicidal. 'I'm gonna kill you!'

Alas, with her hands occupied, Stella can't throw a punch. The Vallanes can't do much, either, since the slightest movement intensifies the scalping sensation. Quite a conundrum – till pugnacious inspiration strikes. Stella pulls up on the twins, then slams their foreheads together like a set of Viennese orchestra cymbals (the sound, of course, is more *clunk* than *clang*). Stella must find this satisfying – she releases the twins, who wobble like demented Weebles. If this were a cartoon, you'd see orbiting stars and birds. I watch the Vallanes run off, see Wynn's light touch on Stella's arm.

Stella sets her mouth in a line, puts hands to hips. I can only assume she doesn't chase them, but I don't get to watch for myself. I can't be late to the airport! I've got to be on time and smiling when Edie steps off the plane. Man oh man, exactly what this mix needs – more volcanic oestrogen!

The Body

Having Edie along is cool, in a best-behaviour-inducing way. And what a doll – she flew all the way with a hamper full of bagels. Must have something to do with the water or the altitude, but you simply can't get decent bagels outside the New York tri-state area. Three dozen crunchy-crusted delights, plus pounds of cream cheese and lovely lox. Yum!

Not that I can fully fixate on dinner. My gaze flits around, gauging everyone's mental state. Stella's taken over the whole tub of chive cream cheese; she's ripping apart her bagel and dunking chunks into green-flecked froth, which seems to calm her. It's Kendall I'm more apprehensive about. Not that she had a bad reaction to Britt's video – quite the opposite: She's in this state of blithe denial, pretending the tape is some kind of hoax, even coming up with excuses for the way Britt's been flouting her since the video ordeal began. Apparently Britt has lost interest in Kendall's self-destruction now that her own life and career are imploding.

Well, now Kendall will spend the remainder of the tour with A/B's girlfriend in tow. Kendall and Edie skirt each other carefully, courteously. Of course, Edie has nothing to worry about; A/B looks at her like she invented the atmosphere. Any wonder I expect Kendall to crack? Yet she ploughs through bagels like they're about to become illegal, then goes to the fridge for a pint of B&J's and plops in front of the TV with a spoon.

'That was a real treat, Edie, thank you!' says Gaylord, his joviality a bit forced. 'So, anyone up for a walk?'

Peony cuts her eyes at him in the oddest way. 'Fine!' she says shrilly. 'Go for a walk!' Rising theatrically, she moves toward the stove. 'Kendahl, I'm brewing your voice tea now. Please put away the ice cream – you know what dairy does to the vocal chords.'

'Mmm, no – s'OK, Peony,' Kendall mumbles through Chunky Monkey. 'I'll have my tea right before showtime. Will you fix a thermos? Thank you!'

With an uncharacteristic slam of the kettle, Peony charges from the galley and up towards the bunks. Claustrophobia sets in; I'm definitely into getting off this bus! Malinka puts her boots on. 'Um . . . Stella? Want to go outside a while?' I ask gingerly.

'Yeah, sure . . .' It's amazing how well she seems to be dealing with the Didion thing. Venting at the Vallanes must have been exceptionally therapeutic.

We head out and aim for the small park half a block from the Hoffenpepper. 'This is crazy; I'm so cold!' I'm complaining, and we've only gone about two yards.

'You Americans have no blood!' Malinka starts jogging in place. 'Come, I race you – that will bring the heat.'

'Race me?' I say. 'You're a lunatic! I'm going back for my hat – I'll just be a sec . . .'

I hurry towards the bus. But I don't find my hat. I don't even look for it. That noise – that awful noise. It paralyses me. Until I figure out what it is. And where it's coming from. And who's making it.

Kendall.

The bathroom.

The horrible, purposeful, pathetic sound of retching.

The Boss

Heartbreak is for other people. Weak, stupid heifers. Soap opera characters. Not me, right? Yeah, well, ha! Just call me Little Miss Meltdown. The hardest part? Since heartbreak is not in my job description, I gotta make like I'm fine. My game face? Photoshopped. My posture? Erect. My playing? On point. Self-recriminations rage in my head: I'm ugly, I'm stupid, I'm ass on bass; I did it with him too soon; I suck at sex. Speak them aloud for just one second and what do I get? Peony or somebody reminding me that I'm Stella Anjenue Simone Saunders, I'm above that. Please!

Capping the Vallanes didn't really help; it's just part of the facade. Truth? They're right: It's not their fault if Didion decided to play me. I'm not calling him again – I'm done. All I can do is lick my wounds. Watching A/B and Edie all cute kills me. Even worse is Wynn and Malinka. There's this ease between them, but a ticklish tension too, an edge to the way they laugh and talk and hang on each other. Malinka's like Xena, Warrior Princess, transported to twenty-first-century America to forge an alliance with an MTV goddess. Except it's not fantasy; it's real. Their bond is another relentless elbow in my mosh pit of pain, since Wynn's the only person on the planet I could possibly talk to about what's going on inside me and she's all BFF'd up.

So it's too freakin' cold when she texts me to meet up in her hotel room after the Seattle gig because *she* needs to talk to *me*.

'Hey.' Wynn is grim.

I walk in and there's Malinka, of course. It's an upgraded room, of course. But Peony's present too. What kind of twisted Tupperware party is this gonna be? I go directly to the minibar and forage. 'You mind?' I toss over my shoulder at Malinka, who's no doubt responsible for the upgrade, and footing the bill.

'Oh, is no problem, Stella,' she says. 'Our minibar is your minibar!'

I help myself to Stoli, Red Bull, and what the hell, a stupid expensive jar of macadamia nuts. The female forum waits on me as I mix my poison in a water glass, then sit at the desk and take a healthy swig. 'Well?' I say. 'What up?'

'It's Kendall.' Wynn's on the bed in a lotus, a pillow in her puzzle of lap. 'I think there's something wrong with her . . .'

'Ooh, shocker!' Mean, maybe, but I've got my own shit to shovel.

'It's serious – or, it could be, I don't know.'

Peony leans restlessly against a bureau, blinks her saucer eyes. She's been a bundle of bad vibes ever since I called her out about getting some. 'Wynn, get to the point.'

She goes for it, without a breath. 'OK, tonight, our preshow walk? I have to come back for my hat. Peony, you're upstairs, and Kendall – she's in the bathroom throwing up. And the thing is, I don't ask if she's all right because I know – I just know – she's not sick.

'I mean, I never told you guys the stuff I saw last tour. Like one night, I forget what town, but she's sitting alone by the pool at three in the morning cramming candy bars. And then, Vegas, remember that stunt she pulled, running off before we finished the set? Well, she split her pants. Only now, I swear, I hadn't thought about it, but she still eats like a horse, yet she lost whatever weight she gained, and . . . isn't it obvious? Kendall's bulimic or she's getting there and we have to do something!'

Uch. Kendall puking her guts out on purpose – not a pretty picture. Makes me put down the macadamias, all right. If Wynn's right, Kendall doing herself damage is serious– for Kendall, and for 6X. Of course, it makes sense – from what I know about eating disorders, Kendall fits the profile: a perfectionist in a high-pressure career where looks count big-time. When a girl like that can't control her world, the only thing she feels she does have dominion over is her weight, so it's easy to fall into the trap. On a positive tip, though, it kicks me into problem-solving mode, gets my mind off Didion. Only I can't think of a quick fix; all I can do is shoot down that-won't-work proposals.

'We must call her mother at once,' says Peony.

'Mrs Taylor?' I counter. 'No good. She wouldn't cop to her darling daughter having an eating disorder, and even if she did, that woman's mind-set is so smalltown backwoods, she'd wanna lock Kendall in a shed with a Bible and pray the bulimia out of her!'

Wynn nods in agreement. 'It's true, Peony. You know Mrs Taylor. Telling her would only mean the end of 6X.'

'Why not just go tell Kendall: "OK, Kendall, you are puking! Puking is bad! You must stop!"?'

I try not to roll my eyes, but I wonder if Malinka ever took steroids and if they had a reverse effect on her brain. 'Because she'd deny it,' I explain. 'Look, like Wynn says, maybe she doesn't have it full blown yet. Maybe it's temporary, something she picked up on tour.'

Icy anger does a *coup d'etat* across Wynn's face. 'And I know who she picked it up from!'

We look at her expectantly.

'Oh, come on!' she says. 'Who does Kendall mimic like a myna bird? Who taught her to draw on a mole with an eyebrow pencil? Who's her role model from hell?'

Malinka's too new to our crew, and Peony's had her head up her ass, but of course I get Wynn right away. 'That bitch!' I say.

'Exactly,' Wynn intones.

We both turn to stare at the negligent Peony. 'Oh my stars!' she says. 'You mean Britt Gustafson, don't you?'

This time I permit my eyeballs to complete their circuit. 'Well, nice to see you back in the zone, Peony. Look, I know you're not her babysitter. I'm just saying—'

'No, Stella!' Eggplant tresses rustle. 'I am aghast. I am more than Kendahl's tutor. I care about her, have worked diligently to steer her toward enlightenment – to think of her abusing her system like that! But I've been, well, I've . . . well, you're all aware that Gaylord and I . . .'

'*GAYLORD?!*' Me and Wynn shriek the name.

Damn, if only I could freeze-frame the moment – it it feels like me and Wynn from way back. Peony turns pink – extreme embarrassment. 'Oh. So you *didn't* know.'

'We knew you hooked up with someone . . .' I start.

'But *GAYLORD*?!' Wynn and I finish together.

Peony gives us a baleful stare. We shut up. 'Regardless,' she says. 'We aren't here to discuss my romantic misconduct. We're here about Kendahl's predicament.'

'Well,' I say, 'now that we're pretty sure we know the cause, I don't see what else we can do except ride out this tour and hope Kendall gets it together once Britt's out of the picture.' Meeting adjourned: They know I'm right.

The Voice

Poor, poor Britt! If only she'd let me see her, she could lay her burdens down. Of course I know why she's avoiding me — she's embarrassed. Purity can be a problem — people think I'm so naïve. Well, I may be unsullied but I'm not stupid. I'm well aware that Britt has sex. Gosh, she's got just swarms of boys, and she isn't saved, so I'm not even shocked. As far as this videotape folderol goes, if it really is Britt in it then someone is taking advantage of her, and it's that person who should be punished. Instead it's Britt, poor Britt, who's being treated cruelly. By everyone — from *The Star* magazine to members of her own band.

But this — this has to be the be-all, end-all indignity!

It's the last night of the tour, and the mood is like a carnival whip — every which way, happy yet sad and a whole tumble of emotions in between. All three bands give it their all, but I'm especially proud of Britt. Considering the circumstances — the bad press, her feuding with Sue — you'd think she'd want to curl up in a ball and die. Not Britt. She takes the stage on a cloud of Chanel No. 5. Her bouffant enormous, her snug suit pearly white, her pumps pointy with daggers for heels. Audience

222

reaction is mixed – the devotional screams are tainted with catcalls and boos. All Britt's turmoil turns white hot with passion, and she ignites her band into a fireball. By the end of the set, the true Touch of Stretch fans drown out the naysayers.

Britt ought to be feeling much better after her magnificent performance, and I so want to share this moment with her – surely I'm the one who best understands her glory and her pain – yet she glides past me, unseeing, to barricade herself in her dressing room. Oh, how my heart aches for her! Will she stay there all night – or is she merely freshening up for the big closing-night party backstage? Even Ayn Rand, who haven't been the friendliest bunch – in fact, they're the snootiest boys I've ever met – will be present.

It's all very whoop-de-do. For one thing, it's as if rock-and-roll fairies went around sprinkling tinsel all over everything – yes, tinsel, like at Christmas, but black tinsel, if you can imagine. There are flowers, huge arrangements. Extra fancy catering, too – goodness I'm so het up, just a mongoose and a snake of feelings inside me, I can't tell how many times I fill my plate. I run to the bathroom (the one in the theatre, not our dressing room; I've got to be real careful, since my slimming regimen is none of my bandmates' beeswax!). And when I come back? Yay! There's Britt!

I feel a guilty little twinge, like maybe I'm neglecting my public, people who want to be close to me, but I need to be near Britt. This is my last chance to reconnect with her before the end of the tour, keep our friendship going. But I don't want to burst in on her like some goggle-eyed fan either, so I sort of hang around in her vicinity. She's strolling slowly, almost stalking the area, surrounded by her publicist, a lady from her management company, and a photographer. Britt lets her silver fox stole drag on the floor – she doesn't give a fig how expensive it is – as she makes her way to Franklin K. See, I figured out that those two have a secret romance. But now that the tour is over there's no need to be hush-hush any more. I'm glad. Surely with Franklin K. at her side, Britt can handle any mean thing being said about her.

Britt sidles up to him, links her arm through his and plants a kiss, leaving a bright red mark on his cheek. The photographer captures this in a series of flashbulb pops. Franklin K. smiles big and wide – he's a sort of hulking, prizefighter-looking person, but his smile is so charismatic. I push my way a bit closer; maybe I can be in a picture with them: the three lead singers, smiling victorious together.

Franklin K. runs sausage fingers over Britt's fur. 'Hey, Britt, nice dead animal,' he says. 'I'm glad you came over; I've been meaning to introduce you to someone.'

Britt licks her lips to shine them up for another photo op. 'Oh, really?'

He steers her deeper into his entourage. Britt's people follow, and so do I. Then – dear Lord! – he throws his beefy arms around another girl! I only see her from the rear: petite figure, shiny waves of red-gold hair.

'Ack! Help!' she mock-screams. 'Grizzly attack!' Franklin spins her around, grabs her again, and – oh my gosh! – it's Crimson Snow. She's wearing faded jeans and not a stitch of make-up, but of course I'd recognise her anywhere. The way she's snuggled up against Franklin K., she is quite obviously staking claim. And they both seem awfully delighted. The whole world freezes up for a second, then the photographer begins shooting off frame after frame of the happy couple. Britt's publicist punches him in the arm, hissing, 'Hey, A-hole – you work for me!'

And Britt? She really looks like a mannequin now; she's paralysed.

'Come on, Crimmie, I want you to meet Britt,' says Franklin K., a mean twist to his mouth. 'Apparently Britt's quite a spectacle on film too . . .'

Crimson Snow makes a disapproving face. 'Frank, cut it out – don't be like that.' And Britt begins backing away – walking with her feet, not her bottom, walking clumsily – until she's swallowed up by the partying throng.

PART FOUR
Jet

'I thought the only lonely place was on the moon . . .'

— *Paul McCartney*

The Boss

Brooklyn. Springtime. Beautiful. Blue jays taunt the sulky stray cats in the backyard. Lilac bush emits more perfume than the ground floor of Macy's. Out on the block, stoop inspectors and baby strollers, delivery trucks and the ice-cream man. I pound out my independent study in the AM, and after that the world is mine. Sometimes I hang at home, eating my mom's lasagna or penne, leftover, cold – the best! – or walk around the 'hood. Or if I get a bored with domestic bliss? Just jump on the N train, roll into Manhattan.

Whenever I do that, I always seem to wind up at WandWorld. I'm like the unofficial intern – except no one dares ask me to make coffee. It's cool, gives me instant access to all 6X business. Like at the moment, we're weighing options. Ayn Rand actually asked us to go out on their next leg as second headliners – killer, right? – but we haven't committed yet since *Bliss de la Mess* is about to drop internationally. We want a sense of how the record's gonna do overseas. Maybe a European tour, or at least some promotional appearances across the pond. Plus, I'm really learning the management thing – how you deal with labels and booking agents, develop talent and forge relationships. Who knows, if I decide to get out of performing when I'm older, me and Brian, we could be partners.

Me. Brian. Partners. Ha! What a pair!

For all that wining and dining and flying and fawning, Cara Lee Ballantine opted to sign with a Nashville-based firm, which had to hurt. Professionally – for damn sure. Personally – maybe. I don't want details about potential quiet storming between those two. All I know is it's how many months later and here's me and him, single in the city. And the banter, the sideways looks, the uncanny way we're both in the mood for the same sandwich or the same tunes, it's all just like back in the day.

'Hey, Stella, come here a sec,' Brian hollers from his office. 'Look sharp!' I catch the CD he tosses. A demo. Some band called Boy King. 'Give it a listen, tell me what you think.'

'Can I test drive it in here?' His system is soooo good.

'Sure, but if that schmuck from Sony returns my call and I start talking like a brown-nosing dickwad, I don't want you giving me grief about it.'

I pop in the disc; crank it. Not bad, Boy King – crunchy but lazy. I skip to the next track. Now they're sounding derivative. 'Spawn of the Snooks and Ayn Rand,' I offer.

Brian nods. 'Not a bad thing, though.'

'No,' I say. 'There's worse people to copy. They videogenic?'

He laughs. 'What are you, a manager?'

'You mean a brown-nosing dickwad? Uh, no, Brian – that would be you.'

Just then, Susan buzzes: 'Eberlee from Sony returning.'

Brian picks up the handset. 'Get outta my office! Go make yourself useful.'

I press eject, take the CD and hip-sway out the door.

'Hey!' he covers the receiver, mimes drinking. 'Go make coffee . . .'

He's got me grinning. Like always. This feels right – I'm not itching for the road again, not yet. I'm comfortable. Copacetic. In a good place.

Goddamn if it doesn't take one phone call to jack my peace of mind and turn my life into carnival spin art.

The Body

When Stella calls, I'm just leaving the Teen Towers – our last lesson there with Peony before Kendall's vacation. It's gorgeous out, and I'm hoping Stella's in the area. Life on tour is a constant wade against the tide of humanity – so coming home, having my own time and space again, it feels odd, empty. Especially with Malinka back on the tennis circuit. (I swear, Sergei, her muscle-bound troll of a trainer, he was so mad the way she played hooky with 6X!) So if Stella's around we can meet at St Marks, goof around.

'Hey! Where are you?'

'Just leaving WandWorld. Wynn, look, you gotta come to Brooklyn with me!'

Ooh, cool. Except for an interminable dinner with my mom and stepdad at the River Café, I've never actually been to Brooklyn. Never seen Stella's house, her room. Never sat on her bed watching videos and eating Oreos. 'I can meet you at Union Square in ten.'

'Good,' she says.

I'm already walking fast – something tight in her tone. 'You OK?'

'No,' she huffs into the phone. I can almost feel her shudder. 'I'm not.'

Sandal straps agonise every toe as I hurry crosstown. Stella's waiting at the subway entrance. Ashen and sweaty and scared and mad. And all at once I know.

Him.

I clutch her arm, search her face. 'He called you.'

Stella nods, then shakes her head.

I'm confused. 'He didn't call . . . ?'

She digs her fingers into her 'fro. 'Yeah,' she says. 'He called all right. But it's not like he just called. Wynn, he's here.'

'Here?! Where here?!'

'In New York! In freakin' Brooklyn. I'm like "Where are you?" and he's like "You know La Fête?" and I'm thinking *what*? He's talking another language; he's not making sense. La Fête, La Fête, what the hell is La Fête? So he's like, "You don't know it, little Haitian joint?" And I'm all holy shit! La Fête! *My* La Fête! It's two freakin' blocks from my house. So I make up some bullshit, I'm with the band, we're in the city, a meeting, blah-blah-blah. But he says no problem, he'll try the *tassot*. Can you believe?'

She's pulling me down the subway steps. We slide our MetroCards, slam through the turnstile. Now Stella's pacing the platform and when the local comes she hops on, then off, and I'm not sure what I should say or even what I'm doing there. I mean, Didion's *her* errant boyfriend. I'm sure the two of them have plenty to discuss. Am I supposed to be the interpreter? The referee? The trusty scribe and documentarian? The express roars in, and I sit there reading ads for beer and plastic surgeons and

233

how impotency doesn't have to ruin your sex life. Then we're going over the Manhattan Bridge and I can see the gang graffiti of Chinatown and then the East River, flinging the sun back at the sky in glinty shards, and the skyline so stable and stoic and hard and real. Once we're in the tunnel again, I know we're getting close because Stella speaks: she asks what she should do.

'I don't know,' I say.

'Rhetorical question!' she snaps, then softens. 'Godamnit, Wynn, I'm sorry. Just . . . I don't wanna walk in there myself. He – Didion makes me weak. Physically weak. Mentally . . . freakin' worthless. The second I think I'm over him, *bam*!'

La Fête is a small place with zero decor, a smattering of tables, a Formica counter with six stools. Percussive music barely noticeable. A clingy mélange of garlic and cloves. It's a weird time of day – too late for lunch, too early for dinner – but most of the tables are occupied by dark men in shirtsleeves. They hover possessively around coffee cups, but each one glances up at the sight of me. God, I am *so* white. A large woman in a gaudy dress leans over a back table, laughing with spicy hunger. The tone of her laugh, flirty and familiar – she must be chatting with a regular. So where's Didion? I take another scan until the woman wags her finger, sidestepping away from the table in mock shock. Stella clutches my arm. 'He's a freakin' shinehead . . .' she breathes.

What? Who? Oh. Wow. Didion. His head shaved, his flawless bone structure all the more prominent, his smile the span of the Brooklyn Bridge and as bright as the glints off the water. We edge toward the table like sleepwalkers. And Didion's smile goes wider and brighter. I doubt Stella's made eye contact yet. I know I can't.

'Oh, hoo, Missy,' the waitress-owner-whoever says to Stella.

'Marvette,' Stella mumbles without looking at her. She places one hand on Didion's table. I glance at Marvette, who seems about to unload another chuckle but checks it. Then she gives me a look, like, 'I believe you have outlived your usefulness here,' and I shrug back, 'You are so right.' I spare Didion a negligible wave; he flicks his eyes, shows me his palm. Slowly Stella lifts her head. I hear him say her name. I watch her sit down. Marvette moves to the counter and I follow, sitting on a stool. She pours me coffee like liquid licorice, then leans her arms on the Formica and stares off into space.

The Voice

When my mom suggests a vacation, I figure hum-de-hum, it's off to Frog Level, since that's the only place we ever go. So I just look at her agape when she tells me we'll be celebrating my sweet sixteen in the Caribbean! An island called Martinique! With all the travelling I've done as a rock star, nothing has been quite so glamorous as a tropical paradise. Goodness knows I need to wind down from the tour, and also deal with my heartbreak over Britt. Losing a dear friend has got to be as bad, if not worse, than breaking up with some boy.

The only trouble I have with our trip is that it's a Club Med. I've heard of Club Meds. They're real popular, and what if the whole place is crawling with people who know who I am and I don't get a moment's peace? Honestly, if my mom wanted to take me somewhere special you'd think she'd pick a more exclusive resort, which gives you an idea how much my mom understands my world. But what the heck – sometimes a girl is just too exhausted to explain.

Besides, shopping for swimming costumes is a treat. I buy seven – we're in Martinique for a whole week, and I refuse to appear at the pool in the same costume twice – and guess what?

They are all bikinis! Not skimpy or anything with your butt all hanging out, but I've never felt slim enough for a two-piece before. Now I wouldn't say I'm a hundred per cent happy with my body – I'm very big on self-improvement. But these days at least my bust sticks out more than my gut. My mom is impressed too.

'Kendall, I am so proud of you!' she gushes as we sit under an umbrella sipping virgin piña coladas. 'I was awful worried about you going on tour and being away such a long time, but you showed me, didn't you? You worked real hard, not just onstage but in your studies – Peony says so – and, well, honey, just *look* at you!'

I cross my ankles and arch my back, a position I learned watching Britt. Then I tilt my head over my shoulder. 'You really think I look good?'

My mom grabs my hand. 'You really have blossomed,' she says. 'And you carry yourself with such poise, like someone who was raised up right. Your talent . . . your values . . . and now you've shed your ugly duckling feathers and emerged a swan!'

That ugly duckling comment? It rankles me slightly but I choose to let it go. 'Thanks, Mom,' I say.

'Of course . . .' My mom takes a thoughtful sip from her curvy glass. 'Now that you've had this . . . well, there's no other word but *transformation* – you'll have to be even more vigilant. About your honour, your reputation. Between your fame and your figure, boys will be coming out of the woodwork. Older boys, too, most likely.' My mom smiles. 'And that Gap ad was just the beginning in terms of opportunities. Modelling. Movie scripts. Maybe your own TV show . . .'

I fiddle with my straw. Modelling? Gosh, could I ever get skinny enough? And acting – it sounds wonderful, but I have trouble just memorising song lyrics!

'So I've been thinking . . . and making some decisions,' she says.

And I think: *Uh-oh* . . .

'Now I always believed it was crucial for me to have a career separate from yours. And I do love what I do – but I love you more. Of course Mr Wandweilder is fine at handling your music affairs, the band and all. But honey, you are Kendall Taylor; you are bigger than 6X and you need someone you can trust taking care of your interests. Plus . . . I just . . . I *miss* you, honey. I want to be with you more, while you're still a teen, before you up and get married and have children of your own.

'So here's what I'm thinking, you tell me what you think: We sell the house and buy a big airy condo in Manhattan. High ceilings! Tons of closets! A nice terrace so we can have some greenery around. And you and I will live together as a real family again.'

Boy, oh boy! She *has* been thinking! Leaving me simply speechless. I need to absorb this. It makes sense for her to manage me full-time. Only . . . give up my Teen Towers place – my privacy – to invest in a bigger apartment? I just don't know; this was supposed to be my vacation, and now I've got more pressure. So I say: 'Mom, I think . . . I think the lunch buffet is starting.' I gulp the rest of my coconutty concoction. 'I think we ought to get in line.'

The Boy

The Sterns don't have a swimming pool. They don't have a sailboat or a hot tub or any of the utsier suburban accoutrements. But they do have a gas grill that's been collecting cobwebs since Mr Stern, in a fit of midlife crisis madness, left his family to 'find himself' (last known whereabouts: the fjords of Finland). So I've taken it upon myself to dust off and crank up this fine appliance. As man of the house, the chore is encrypted in my DNA.

Not that I've officially moved in – my mom would guilt me into an early grave if I didn't come home occasionally – but I do spend a preponderant number of hours at my girlfriend's house. Funny, E/D's mother *has* to know we're having sex. After all, she took E/D to the chick-doc and personally conducted a lesson in condom usage on a hapless cucumber. Mrs Stern is a cool mom – but not too cool. She wants her daughter safe and she likes me, so she basically condones what we do as long as I'm sacked out on the living-room sofa when she heads off to work in the morning.

(Hey, you like how I slipped that in? How I omitted describing the most awesome night of my personal life to the prying Cyclops eye of this camera? At one point I might have blurted out every graphic detail, but the Britt Gustafson scandal inspires discretion.)

Anyway, who knew I had a flair for propane? E/D and her mom tend to the fixin's while I go alpha male at the grill. I ease into it, starting small, with hot dogs, graduate to burgers and corn on the cob *en* husk. This afternoon I'm feeling my inner Iron Chef and decide to go all out: barbecued chicken plus veggie kebabs. Lily and Roz sit rapt on the patio asking me questions more suited to Yoda:

'A/B, what's in barbecue sauce?'

'A/B, how come they call chicken legs drumsticks?'

'A/B, how come chickens have wings if they don't fly?'

'A/B, how do you tell if a chicken is a chicken or a rooster?'

They make me smile. They drive me crazy – but they make me smile. E/D is in and out of the kitchen, hauling lemonade and bean dip and coleslaw. She pours me a glass and tells me I look cute in my Kiss the Cook apron. Her mom emerges with seven different degrees of sunscreen and insists we all slather up even though it's practically four PM already.

Talk about an idyllic scene. Straight out of a Disney movie. Birds chirping – and sizzling. Lawn mowers purring. My 'good vibes' iPod playlist pouring aural ecstasy from the speaker dock. Ah, but what's a Disney movie without a villain? And up he shows. Unannounced. Uninvited. Aaron.

'Hey!' This guy in a baseball cap peeks over the picket fence. And all the ladies Stern shout: 'Aaron!' Lily and Roz run to let him in. Traitors! E/D doesn't run but flip-flops over leisurely, and for a split second I think she's going to plant a peck.

Suddenly, the strings of my apron chafe, but she grabs his wrist instead and drags him in my direction. 'Dude, cool, you can meet A/B.' Then she yanks me away from the Weber. 'Sweetie, this is Aaron, remember, I told you? The guy I play with?'

Strange how she hasn't uttered a peep about Aaron since Seattle. Now he's strolling into her backyard. Presumptuous bastard, wouldn't you say? I hope he has the good sense not to mess with a man holding barbecue tongs. I put them aside; remove my patchwork mitt. 'Hey, good to meet you,' I lie through my teeth and size him up. He's got a few inches on me and looks like he plays one of those erudite sports, lacrosse or something. Is he the kind of guy girls think is hot? He's blond under the cap – do chicks like blonds?

'Yeah, man, you too,' Aaron says. We shake. 'It's not often we get a celebrity in our midst.'

Is that a dig? Aaron grins, as if to say I shouldn't take it that way.

'Really,' he says. 'You're the shit.' He adds something about my solo on 'Hello Kitty,' a turn of musical phrase I am rather proud of, so I say thanks.

'Aaron, are you going to eat something?' Mrs Stern's got an annoying little smile going, like she's thinking: *Isn't it cute, two boys competing for my daughter.* Whose side is she on anyway?! 'We've got plenty.'

Of course she's got plenty! What is a Jewish mother if not a cornucopia with a manicure! But Aaron splits his gaze between E/D and me. And E/D looks at me – like it's my call. But it's not – these are not my chicken parts – so I lift my eyebrows to lob the ball back in her court.

'Sure, Aaron, you should eat,' she says, then squeezes my arm. 'A/B's an awesome cook, among his many talents.'

'Yeah? Cool!' Aaron sits at the picnic table. E/D sits too. The two of them commiserate about some insane physics teacher as I hurl hunks of fowl onto a platter. But I manage to mellow out enough to chow. Aaron doesn't seem like a complete asshole. We keep the conversation benign, general – the weather, movies, et cetera. By the time Lily and Roz clear our paper plates and Mrs Stern brings out thick slabs of watermelon, Aaron mentions that he's got his guitar in the car and suggests we jam. I'm thinking: *You are so on, dude – there is no way you're going to out-wank me.* 'Good idea,' I say. I keep my trusty Martin at E/D's, so I go inside to fetch it, and E/D's acoustic too.

'Edie, take a blanket!' Mrs Stern says as we settle onto the dandelion-ridden lawn. 'It rained yesterday – the ground's still wet—'

'Ugh! Ma!' E/D moans. 'We're not going to catch pneumonia from damp grass!'

Me and Aaron stifle our snickers, and it feels up to me to kick things off, so I go into the intro of Floyd's 'Wish You Were Here.' E/D knows the chords because I taught her. And Aaron, well, he should or shame on him – but he obviously doesn't; he struggles to follow along and keeps screwing up, so I benevolently tell him to play something. He starts that Churnsway song that was everywhere you went last summer; I don't remember the name. I pick it up no problem.

'Sing,' E/D tells Aaron.

'No, you,' he counters.

'No – I don't know the words.'

'Shut up, yes you do.'

I noodle the lead notes over their strumming.

'OK,' E/D says. She's got an appealing, husky alto, and she's clever, making up lyrics when she forgets. We all join in on the choruses, and I show off a bit on the bridge.

'Man, that is so cool, I could never do that,' Aaron gushes over my fretwork.

Tut, tut! I think. 'Sure you could,' I say. 'You just have to practise. The more you play the better you get.'

He shrugs. 'I guess . . . but I'm not really interested. I just . . . for me, the guitar is a tool, a vehicle. E/D's going to be the flashy lead—'

'Ha!' she snorts.

'—guitarist in our band,' Aaron says. 'No, really. I just need to be good enough to get my songs across . . .' And then he looks away. Wistfully. Waiting.

I take the bait – what can I say, I'm curious. 'Oh, yeah, I heard you write songs,' I say, nodding encouragement. 'Come on, play something you wrote.'

He starts hemming and hawing. We start begging and pleading.

'Well . . . will you let me check out your Martin?' he says.

A slight agony of hesitation before I hand over my mahogany baby. And then Aaron starts to fingerpick clumsily and sing this song about a girl and a dog and a rowboat and, I swear to God, a lily pad. His voice is reedy but strong, and he mugs a little when he sings, half closing his eyes and sort of puffing out his lips like he's watched a lot of emo videos. The performance walks the line between precious and painful, but maybe I'm not

the one to judge, maybe it's just not my thing. So I glance at
E/D. And her eyes are half closed. And she knows these words
about the girl and the dog and the lily pad – she's mouthing
them silently with her lips sort of puffed out.

The Body

Science is not my forte, but if my hypothesis proves correct, spores can grow roots. Casting about aimlessly one minute, digging in the next. Subject of study: Didion Jones. This time, he's settling down, burrowing deep. Or so he'd like us to believe. And my, hasn't Didion been industrious! Step 1: an apartment right in Stella's neighbourhood (rooming with two seniors from the Pratt Institute). Step 2: re-establishing ties with his uncle – the doctor uncle, the oncologist uncle, the uncle on faculty at Mount Sinai who knows everybody old and powerful and rich, which leads us to Step 3: voilà, Didion's the new sous-chef at Rhomboid, a four-star restaurant so chi-chi it wows even my mom. Step 4: charming the guy who books Walk Don't Walk, the current 'it' café of the Lower East Side, and landing himself a steady Thursday-night gig (major, since Thursday's the new Friday).

'God, Didion – entrenched much?' Yes, I'm that snarky when he greets us before his WDW debut. He shrugs me off, but Stella insists on defending his disappearing act and explaining to me why 'everything's different' now.

'He just couldn't stand it, us on the road – the nice hotels,

245

the MondoCruiser.' She must be quoting him verbatim. 'Didion's a *man*, not a mooch. But at the same time, seeing us, all we've achieved, it motivated him to get his. Enough hitchhiking troubadour, black Jack Kerouac boolshit. No, he is serious.' Stella sips her drink thoughtfully. 'Besides,' she says, 'you don't have to be Sigmund Freud to recognise the boy had major abandonment issues. He bounced because he was scared of commitment.' She can't wipe the grin off her face. 'Then he realised he couldn't live without me.'

Let's hope so, I think, and try to change the subject. But Stella stays in her lane. 'Listen,' she says, toning down her voice as if she's about to impart classified data. 'I'm gonna get Brian to take him on . . .'

How did Stella develop such an insatiable appetite for self-destruction? Of course, if they were all robots, her plan would be foolproof. Didion has talent, Brian sells talent – *basta!* But last I checked, the elements involved were all quite human. So . . . take the guy you've been crushing on for more than a year and team him up with the guy you're madly in love with now – yah, mm-hmm, that makes sense. Naturally, this being Stella, there's no way to dissuade her. The only prayer we have is Paris.

The city, not the heiress.

Bliss came out in Europe and Japan last week, both singles – 'Oliver' and 'Kitty' – going to radio and MTV Europe/Asia simultaneously. The response has been . . . interesting. England? Not so much as a ripple yet. It's only been ten days, but I'm worried – I heard the British either pounce or pass. Over in Germany and Holland, 'Oliver' is doing OK, and it's a smash hit in France. Which is creepy. I mean, the French? They have taste in clothes and food, but music? Any love is good love, I guess, but the dotage of the French feels like a bitchy review in *Entertainment Weekly*.

Wait — weirder, the Japanese are going crazy over 'Kitty.' It's like civil war. A lot of the population hates it; there've been public outcries and protests, because here we are condemning this huge national icon. But then there are pockets of insurgents who love it; they're customizing Kitty tees with drawn-on bloody wounds, and I hear there's even an underground club in Osaka called Uch! Scat! Shoo! (Uch! Scat! Shoo! — that's a line from the song). All I intended to do was trash an annoying two-dimensional character, not polarise a superpower. But Brian and the international division of Universe say there's no such thing as bad publicity (although I bet Britt Gustafson would beg to differ — they split up, Touch of Stretch, you know . . .). Anyway, we should find out fairly soon if we're going over there or not, and I hope we do, because if Didion Jones has planted himself in New York City, I think it's best if an ocean inserts itself between him and Stella.

The Boy

The 'burbs, where I'm from, is car culture, but New York City is power to the pedestrian. Even death cabs and maniac bicycle messengers yield to the intrepidly on foot. It helps if you *like* to walk, which I do, so when Kendall asks if I'll 'see her home' after Didion's early set at WDW, my first reaction is sure. But before it comes out of my mouth I look down. You know Kendall's penchant for high heels – if I'm going to catch the 10:47 train to Long Island, we'll need to maintain a brisk pace. Hmm, she's wearing those cork-bottomed shoes I think are called wedges. E/D has a pair, and she manages to keep up with me.

So I decide: 'Sure, definitely – let's just say goodbye.' I slap Didion on the back, tell him great set, say it's good to see him, and leave it at that. No: 'What happened to you, man?' Of course I don't condone his Houdini routine wreaking havoc with Stella's sanity, but that's one place my nose does not belong. That being said, the main reason I prefer walking Kendall home to putting her in a taxi is to poke around re: Danny Sloane, who we ran into at the club. I know Danny from the open-mike scene, but he's graduated to bona fide gigs now

– has a bit of a following, too. He works that alt-country thing, and he's not bad, especially when you consider he's from wealthy Westport, Connecticut, so his truck-stop shtick isn't even remotely authentic. But he delivers the material earnestly enough, and as far as I can tell he's a decent guy. Except he's got to be at least twenty-three, and it seemed to me he was hitting on Kendall.

'So . . . Danny Sloane.' I'm casual as can be as Kendall and I start up Avenue A.

'Gosh, A/B, he's awful nice; such good manners – is he from the South?'

Did he ply her with fake twang? What a dog! 'Right – southern Connecticut!' I say. 'You didn't . . . he didn't ask you out, did he?'

A pack of drunken frat boys pass in the other direction; Kendall comes close and takes my arm for protection. 'Well,' she says, 'he did ask me to come see him play.'

Phew, I think. Can't blame a fella for a little self-promotion.

'And he did ask how he could get in touch, to let me know when his gig is.'

Now wait a second. What kind of self-promoter doesn't carry flyers in his knapsack? Besides, WDW was plastered with flyers hyping Sloane's show next week.

'So what did you give him? Your e-mail? Your number?' I must ask this with unwitting emphasis, because Kendall grips my forearm, snuggling closer.

'Abraham Benjamin Farrelberg, I do believe you're jealous!' she says with a happy hoot. 'For your information I gave him both my number and my e-mail.'

I stop Kendall on the corner and turn her to face me. 'Kendall – look . . .' How can I say this? 'I am not jealous. You *should* go out with guys. Just not Danny Sloane.'

Hands on hips, head cocked in this coy-yet-challenging way, she goes: 'And what's wrong with Danny Sloane?'

'Nothing – everything – Kendall, come on. You don't even know him – yet you give him your number. That's proof you shouldn't go out with him!' OK, not even the CIA could decipher intelligence in what I just said.

Kendall swats my arm, then grabs it again and starts walking. 'Don't worry, A/B,' she says. 'I'm not going to date Danny Sloane. My mom would about have kittens, and besides – *I* know he's too old for me.' She's quiet a minute. People breeze past us, slapping our faces with snippets of conversation.

Then Kendall gets deep on me: 'You know, A/B, sometimes I think you think I don't have a brain in my head. But then I realise it's not that.' She sniffs. 'You know full well I'm no fool. In fact, you probably have a better idea what kind of girl I truly am than anyone. Trouble is, you don't *want* to know. The more you know, the more you'll think about me . . . and I reckon you have your reasons for not wanting to think about Miss Kendall Taylor.'

Silence again. What I expect they mean when they put 'meaningful' before 'silence.' 'It's OK, you know.' She pats my arm. 'You work it on out. I'll be right here when you do.'

She means that. Literally. We have reached the Teen Towers. 'Ooh! A/B! You have got to come up a minute!'

Whoa, her mood changes faster than a channel surfer with

ADHD. I don't wear a watch, but I bet I'll have to book it to catch my train. 'I can't, Kendall.'

'No, no, I have to show you something,' she insists. 'I promise it won't take long. I bought myself a birthday present – and you're going to love it! You have to see it, A/B, really. Just take a gander and then I'll shoo you out.'

Sometimes it's easier to acquiesce than argue with a woman. So up we go. The apartment is strewn with magazines and clothes, and the Murphy bed is down, unmade, instead of hidden up in the wall where it should be whenever Kendall has gentlemen callers. I sit on a stool – a nice, safe stool – in the kitchen nook as she bustles around her closet. Then out she comes, toting a brand-new pale yellow Epiphone Wildkat – two pickups, chrome hardware, and a flame maple top. Sweeeeet!

The Voice

Boys can be so single-minded! I'm counting on that when I show A/B my guitar. I figure he won't be able to resist it. Well, of course he misses his old 10:47 by a mile; he even completely forgets about it. I sit quietly and watch – I'm not joking, A/B plays so good, it's a wonderment not just to listen but to behold. I think that's what really gets girls about guitar players – you fix on his hands, his fingers, and think about what it would be like if he were playing *you*. Oh, I can't believe I just said that! But it's true. Anyhoo, once his guitar high tapers off, he asks what I'm doing with the darned thing.

'Goodness, A/B, what do you think? I want to use it as a hat rack?' Gosh, he can be so dumb!

'I don't know,' he says. 'You don't . . . play guitar. Do you?'

This makes me smile. 'No, I don't . . . not yet.' I consider reaching for it but change my mind. It's a pretty thing, but cumbersome; maybe I should have gone with a smaller, girlier style. I leave it on his lap, wishing I could confess the purpose behind my impulse purchase. The truth is, I know the trend for stars today is to do it all. Yet when I think about the future, acting, modelling – that just feels wrong somehow. Phoney.

Now my mom would disagree; she believes I should branch out. But my soul says no. My soul says music is a gift from Jesus, and that other stuff – well, the money's good and I want to be rich, but it doesn't make me *feel* rich, it makes me feel the opposite. And I don't want to be cheap. I want to be real. Coming off the madness of the road has helped me reconnect with simple values. I want to be real in my career, and in my personal life – have a real relationship with the boy I love. That's when it occurred to me: a way to kill two birds with one stone – a guitar!

Of course I couldn't say that to A/B; I keep it mysterious (per Britt, boys love that!) and simply tell him, fluttering my eyes, that I had a guitar epiphany. He beams at me like I have just recited scripture. He doesn't say a word, though, simply hands over the Epiphone. Trouble is, I'm afraid to touch it.

'Kendall,' A/B says in the kindest voice. 'This is your guitar. Take it.'

So I slide off the stool, and A/B arranges the strap around my neck.

'Come on, hold it. Hold your guitar.'

I stand up straighter and shake my hair back. I put my left hand on the neck part and my right over the strings.

'Mm-hm, mm-hm,' A/B says sort of to himself. He adjusts my left wrist, placing it the proper way. Inserts his foot between mine, parting my legs a bit, giving me a comfortable stance. He appraises me anew, then folds my knuckles, positioning my fingertips onto two of the strings. All the while he's murmuring, 'OK, OK, got to love the E minor, here, like this . . .' He gazes into my eyes. 'Press, Kendall. Press hard.'

I press.

'OK . . . give it a strum.'

'A/B!' I whine, suddenly silly. 'I . . . no . . .'

Oh, the look he gives me! I've never seen his eyes so penetrating, or such a scowl on his mouth. It's absolute. Downright demanding. Makes me all shivery.

'Wait, wait!' he says. 'Don't move.' He fishes in his pocket, pulls out a pick.

Now I feel equipped. A/B stands back, crosses his arms. He's still giving me the look, that don't-look-back-just-jump look.

'Go, Kendall.' His whisper has an edge. 'Hit it!'

The Boss

The slurry moan of slide guitar, it gets you all loose and wild and lazy, like you could start a fire if only you had the energy to strike the match. That's how it makes me feel, anyway, half-naked and lolling on Didion's mattress while he idly strokes a bottleneck across the strings. It's late Sunday or early Monday, depending on how you look at it, and Didion's back from Rhomboid, smelling of butter and wine . . . and me. What we do is, I come over while he's at the restaurant, and he wakes me when he gets home. Wakes me gentle. Wakes me rough. Wakes me with a nuzzle or a tickle or a slap on the ass, and I sprawl all over him. Then we either go to sleep or lie around – talk, play, cuddle. Eventually we shrug on clothes and roll over to my house – Didz's roommates are total slobs; we go someplace sanitary to make food. Traditional breakfast or whatever Didion conjures up. He's a maestro in the kitchen. Shocker, right? A little etouffee, cherie? Yeah, that'd be cool . . .

I'm in this haze. Oh, don't worry, I do what I have to do. Pound it out at practice. Waltz around WandWorld. Ace the ACT and SATs – my GED is a fait accompli. But it's all become secondary, interludes to fill the hours I'm not with my man. My parents don't say shit. Because Didion has them eating out of his hand (not just figuratively – his culinary skills keep all the Saunders well fed!). Because they trust me not to get pregnant or diseased. Because I'm more than meeting their expectations. And because, basically, they're realists – they could yell and scream and I'd just be like: 'Stella, out!' After all, now that the album's recouped everything Universe laid out, I'm starting to see real money and can support myself, thank you very much.

So anyway, back to the bedroom. 'You know why I shaved?'

It's like a line in an impromptu blues number. *Ba-bah-de-dah-dum: You know why I shaved?* I'm glad he brings it up, since I do not question him. I refuse to be one of those 'where are you, what you doing, who you with?' females. The kind I pity.

'You want me to know, tell me . . .' I rub the nubs on top of his head.

'It was to mark my determination,' he says. 'So the day I left y'all, I went to a gas station minimart outside Duluth and bought a pack of razors. The clerk did not look pleased. I was in that bathroom for ever. No hot water either. Check it out – I got scars?'

I rake his pate in the gaining light. 'None that I can see. But you bled?' I prod his shoulder with the heel of my hand. 'Good!' Just my subtle way of demonstrating that I'm giving him a free pass for his sudden split. We sit for a minute, then I say: 'There's hot water here . . .'

'Naw, I'm letting it grow back,' he says.

'I don't mean for you.'

Didion lifts an eyebrow. 'You'd be a beautiful cue-ball, cherie. You want to do it?'

I smile. 'No,' I say. 'I want you to do it to me.'

Later, we walk into WandWorld together for a meeting with Brian – who was blown away by the Didion Jones Show last week; we're here to strategise – and it's pure pandemonium.

'Stella!' Susan leaps from her desk. 'You . . . what have you – oh God!'

I make a face, but I'm not really irritated. I'm happy, freed up, without all that hair. Yeah, my 'fro was such a part of me for so long, an emblem of my spirit, my defiance. But being bald is a bold statement too. And the feeling? Freakin' amazing. The sun on it, the air, Didion's kiss – my whole head is a new zone of sensation.

'Gaylord! Brian!' Susan hollers. 'Stella – uhhh, Stella's here!'

They come out, stand there gob-smacked, while me and Didion try to keep our faces straight. 'Wow, Stella,' Brian says when his faculties return. 'You look great.' He chuckles. 'Very Josephine Baker.'

'Who?' I ask.

Didion loops his arm in mine. 'Not to fret, cherie,' he says. 'It's a compliment.'

'Jazz singer from the Twenties – she was huge!' Brian reminds me.

Of course. Fabulously talented. Drop-dead gorgeous. Way too much sexy black woman for the American public – had to jet to France to earn the raves she deserved.

'Talk about perfect timing,' Brian says. 'Stella, you're going to bring them to their knees in Paris!'

The Voice

Can you believe it – no French onion soup in France? At least not in the bistros we've been to so far. I check, first thing, and think of Britt. I don't dwell on her much any more, but in Paris I can't help it. She'd adore it here! Everyone's so sophisticated, having wine at lunch and all. But no French onion soup. They do have French fries, though – they're called *frites* and they're almost as good as McDonald's. Cheese is big, too, and ooh, the pastry. I reckon Frenchwomen invented the trick, because I haven't seen a single fat one.

We're on a promo tour, which means playing a little but doing tons of interviews and autograph signings and whatnot, the way we did when *Bliss de la Mess* debuted in America. Our first day is a shoot for *Guillaume*, a men's magazine – and I sure hope no one back home ever sees it! Oh, the first setup is fine, just us in jeans and T-shirts, but then A/B is banned from the premises, and it's me and Stella and Wynn in our underwear, hugging all over each other. The photographer keeps coaxing us: 'Touch her brrrreast, like so . . .' and 'Lift her panties so I can see her derrierrrrre.' It stirs up a whole hornets' nest of feelings, but I push them down: This is the order of the day, so I must be professional. Stella's a good sport about it too, but Wynn gets uppity – she's such a pesky feminist about not being portrayed as 'an object.' Jeepers, I am none too keen on posing in skivvies, but it's just us girls, so I frankly don't see what's so sexy or se*xist* about it. Besides, we get to keep the lingerie, which is fabulously expensive.

One of the nice things about Parisians is, unlike New Yorkers, they are not in a rush. What we'd cram into a day and a half in NYC will take nearly a week here, and we get plenty of downtime. For me, that means shopping. One afternoon on the Champs-Elysées I drop a good gazillion euros. All that silk and suede, the logos and labels – it's enough to make my head swim! The truth is, I need new clothes, the way my body is changing (and of course new shoes to go with them). But I also think, shoot, if my mom is serious about quitting her job and buying a condo in Manhattan, I better spend some money before she gets her paws on it.

Of course, the trip is not all Gucci and Chanel; Miss Peony's along, and that means lessons. But instead of hum-de-hum books and stuff, she's trotting me and Wynn to museums, historical sites, and architectural landmarks. We see the Mona Lisa (honestly, I don't get what all the hoop-de-hoo is about; she's awful small) and the Cathedral of Notre Damn (beautiful, I admit, but I can't imagine Jesus approves of the word 'damn'). A/B and Stella join us on these jaunts, which is nice – makes it feel less like schooling. When he's not too busy with our agenda, even Mr Gaylord comes. Him and Miss Peony are totally unabashed about being a couple now, holding hands and even smooching out in the open. Well, they say Paris is the most romantic city. Maybe something amorous will happen between me and you-know-who.

We came awful close that night of my first guitar lesson in New York. Then *she* had to call.

'Oh! Hey! You won't believe this Epiphone Kendall's got! I . . .'

Gosh, did she ever have a bee in her bonnet! She cut him off, and he kept going 'but Edie . . . but Edie . . . but Edie . . .' about a dozen times. I just sat there sweetly, practising my E minor, and when he finally got a word in he promised to be on the next train. Then he gave me a shrug and tore out.

That's all right. I meant what I said about letting him think through his feelings. With boys you have to use psychology. Just be as alluring as possible, stay in his line of vision, and let him come to you. That's why I flirted with Danny Sloane. And it's true that I want to learn guitar – it's just a bonus that it makes me more attractive to A/B. Plus, not to be crude, but it sure does help to look hot. Now that I'm getting skinny, he's got to notice.

It's a good thing I don't live in France! A girl would have to purge three times a day to keep her figure. (Maybe it's acceptable here – land sakes, they have two toilets, one for flushing and one just to wash out your down-there! – but for me it's a real cat-and-mouse game to avoid nosybodies.) Gosh, tonight we have the most amazing dinner yet, thanks to Mr Morgan, Wynn's real dad. He lives in a place called Prague, just like in our song, but he does lots of business in Paris. He even has an apartment in the fanciest district. Not that I've seen it, but Wynn's staying there instead of our hotel. Wynn and Stella – she begged Stella to stay with her. Sort of rude, I think, not to ask me too, but you know how Wynn's always jumping hoops for Stella. Anyhoo, Wynn's real dad is treating all of us to dinner – the band, Miss Peony, Mr Gaylord, plus a client and the client's daughters, who are huge 6X fans.

Now I know where Wynn gets her height from: Mr Morgan's awful tall too, and worldly, his accent a mix of foreign places. He's being real jolly and generous, but the more effort he makes, the more Wynn seems to withdraw. Well, that's her affair – family trials can be so complicated. The client's daughters, Solange and Claudine, are around our age, and their English is OK. They ask a lot about other rock stars and movie stars – as if all famous people belong to the same club. So naïve! But they're friendly little chatterboxes with excellent manners, except for a tendency to lapse into their own language – they'll ask a question, and I'll answer and they'll go: 'Ahh!' and start gabbing away in français. They must be so excited to be in our presence, they can't even eat. A few bites, then pat-pat-pat with the napkin like they're stuffed to the gills.

'Kendahl?' All French people pronounce my name like Miss Peony does. This is Claudine talking. 'You would like the rest of my tart?' She nudges her plate towards me.

'Oh, yes, Kendahl, please, have mine.' Solange has barely sampled this chocolate cake that makes Claudine's fruit tart look like health food. Well, I am pretty happy about the situation, having finished my crème brûlée – until Wynn wakes up. Miss Sulky hasn't even ordered a dessert of her own, but now she actually lifts off her seat and reaches across the table to take a huge forkful of cake. 'Oh my God! That is so good!' She plunks back down in her chair. 'How's that other thing?' she asks, repeating her act, attacking the tart. 'You better watch it, Kendall, before I steal them both.'

'Not unless I do,' Stella says, moving in to infringe upon my sweets.

'You going to make me fight you, Stella? You think you can pull off a coup de tart?' Wynn aims her fork like a catapult.

'Ha, ha, very funny,' Stella says. 'I dare you, bitch.'

Now if you didn't know these two you might think they're actually mad, but I'm sure they're funning because I've seen them feud. However, they're being so, so, so obnoxious, and that's unusual. Wynn's silver-spoon behaviour is bred in the bone, and Stella prides herself on knowing how to act in high-class circumstances. Seated between them are Wynn's dad, Miss Peony, and Mr Gaylord, who all wear expressions of horror.

'Oh really?' taunts Wynn. 'Do you double-dare me?'

'You know I do!' Stella forms a fork catapult of her own.

'*En garde!*' challenges Wynn. '*Advance!*'

Stella grits her teeth. 'Ready, aim, FIRE!'

Well, the next thing you know calories are soaring, Wynn and Stella are shrieking, Solange and Claudine are cowering, and the adults are stricken. Neither Wynn nor Stella is a very good shot. They miss each other completely, Stella's forkful splashing into the client's wine glass and Wynn's winging Claudine's nose and landing in her hair.

'Oh my God, I am so sorry, Claudine!' Wynn flails her napkin like a flag of surrender. 'I swear, I really am.' She cannot look at Stella – they'd both dissolve into giggles again if they latched eyes. 'I don't know what's wrong with me. I guess . . . I guess I must be terribly, incurably American!'

The Body

If you've never had a food fight, I highly recommend it. So gooey. So . . . liberating. Especially when the witnesses to your escapade are perfect strangers (bonus points for being French) and the distant parent you don't feel like faking affection for at the moment. So sorry, but I am a big fat brat in Paris.

Blame Daddy, or blame jet lag, or blame the chauvinist's delight of a photo shoot. Blame the fact that Malinka's in town for the French Open but her handlers have her on such a short leash we can't even hang. Blame whatever.

Uch. So bogus. *Whatever.* The ubiquitous, banal placeholder. The perennial all-purpose cop-out. The handy, universal Get Out of Jail Free card. We Homosapiens have this tacit agreement with each other that it's cool to whip out whatever when there are issues we don't want to face, feelings we don't want to stir, sore spots we don't want to poke at. How convenient – resilient, reliable whatever. Something ugly? Just drape a pashmina whatever over it. Wallpaper the world with whatever. Except lately whatever feels, flimsy to me, perilous even, like a car made of aluminium foil. One day I'll have to deal with the whatevers, all of them — face, stir, and poke at all that subcutaneous stuff.

Of course, I don't arrive at this conclusion flinging *gateau chocolat* in Paris. I reach it in Amsterdam, courtesy of a loaded brownie.

Amsterdam is cooler than Paris, more laid back, and has the extra benefit of being Daddy-free. Plus, it's storybook beautiful — we come by train, passing through tulip plantations dotted with windmills. The city itself is slanted and enchanted: skinny, sloped buildings, narrow cobblestone streets, syrupy canals, and everybody on bicycles. The heart of Amsterdam, right outside Central Station, reminds me of Astor Place in New York, all young people hanging out and goofing off, only the coffee shops don't belong to a conglomerate franchise. They do, however, boast a veritable menu of marijuana and hashish.

6X does a live set in Vondel Park, very pretty, and we're swarmed, but it's an amiable swarm, not scarymanic like it gets in the States sometimes. All the Dutch boys are supercute — rosy cheeks and mussy blond hair, very young Beck — but the girls totally surpass them, hot factor-wise: all these Karen Mulders and Brenda Noorts walking around. Believe it or not, the supermodel-quality people we meet are incredibly nice and attitude-free, and they all want to get us high.

That's an occupational hazard on tour — wherever you go fans are effusive about turning you on to whatever hallucinogen or opiate is regionally abundant. Mostly I demur — drugs scare me. I've just said no to oxycontin in Mississippi and heroin in Seattle, but I don't think a trip to Amsterdam would be complete without sampling one of the softer staples. Besides, when these kids we meet at our poster giveaway make a gregarious offer, not even Kendall can refuse (although quite possibly her willingness is another attempt to impress A/B).

Our sojourn takes us off the beaten path. Instead of hitting a shop on the main drag, we're invited to visit Dirk, a celebrated 'bush doctor,' or botanist – a grow guy. Neetlje, one of our new fan-friends, is related to him somehow. He's around my real dad's age, this Dirk, rotund and smiley with a handlebar mustache. There's an indoor farm on the top floor of his house. He lives in the middle with a wife and toddler son and on the bottom operates a private coffee shop/bakery. Farm? Correction: It's a rain forest up there. Where are the spider monkeys, the machetes? The smell is so heady I'm losing brain cells treading among the cultivated rows of industrial-strength plant life.

A/B looks like he's achieved nirvana, but it's not till we return to Dirk's cosy café that he demonstrates an appetite akin to a sumo wrestler at a sushi bar. Dirk dispenses a full assortment, not just his own crop – legendary 'brands' like Blueberry, Bubblegum, and Super Skunk. Of course, he has a vaporiser, and lightweight that I am, I suck on that with Neetlje and Johanna. But A/B and Stella are old-school – they prefer joints, which Heni, Neetlje's boyfriend, rolls with one-handed prowess.

Despite her earlier open-mindedness, Kendall hasn't taken a single toke. Then Neetlje requests that Dirk bring out the baked goods.

'Does it taste like marijuana?' Kendall sniffs her brownie.

'No, Kendall, it tastes like Duncan Hines,' says Stella, which we all find incredibly amusing for no apparent reason.

'Duncan Hines!' I bellow, crumbs falling from my lips to my lap.

'Pardon me, have you any Duncan Hines?' A/B apes the voice-over from the Grey Poupon commercial, making us all double over in hysterics, even the Dutch kids, who never heard of Duncan Hines or Grey Poupon. We're all on such a different planet from Kendall – I guess she'd rather catch up than feel left out, as she gobbles her buzz biscuit in three bites. 'Wow, it doesn't taste druggy at all,' she comments.

We're all having a blast, and within twenty minutes the brownie I ingest starts to affect me (the process accelerated, I'm sure, by those few hits on the vaporiser). It's good. Very good. Initially, anyway. We're laughing our heads off and somehow get on the subject of the golden age of American reality TV, much of which is currently being aired in Holland: 'Remember the time Ashton punked Justin?' 'Remember the time Sharon Osbourne punted that roast beef?' 'It wasn't a roast beef, it was a baked ham!' 'Remember when Johnny Knoxville fisted the cow?' 'That wasn't Johnny Knoxville, that was Nicole Richie.' 'No, I think they both fisted cows.' That kind of thing. No one notices Kendall reach for a second brownie – until she's just about done.

'Kendall, am I hallucinating or did you already eat one of those?' A/B asks.

Kendall, embarrassed: 'Don't you have better things to do than monitor how many brownies I eat?'

Once we recover from the inexplicable hilarity of 'brownie monitor,' Heni says: 'Oh, it is not an insult, Kendall. But Dirk's

brownies are powerful. Sometimes they take a while to hit you
– you don't want to overdo it.'

Right around then, my high shifts to another plane. What sets
it off, I don't know – a comment, a snicker, a change in the late
afternoon light. With a whoosh I go from shallow giddy to
tunnel deep. I don't want to be around people; I want to crawl
inside myself. Party girl morphs into paranoid girl. 'Stella!' I
snatch her sleeve. 'Stella, I want to leave.'

'What – already?' She's knee-jerk irritated, but her
beneficent mood is stuck. 'All right. Yo, Heni – how do we get
back?'

It feels like it takes another half hour, or half day, to get our
route straight – time is kind of runny and streaky, like it's been
left out in the rain – but finally we're ready to go. We stand up.
And that's when Kendall's double brownie delight decides to
come on. She's never been high before – and she's getting off
to a very strong start. Dancing in the street. Tossing tulips to
strangers. Serenading prostitutes. Then the munchies kick in
and she has to pit-stop at not one but two waffle kiosks.

I am starting to lose it. 'Kendall, come on!' It's dusk, and dusk
looks ominous to me. The twisty streets seem endless. And do I
hear fish murmuring to me from the canals? 'I really need to get
back to the hotel.'

Finally, we do. I hurl myself onto the bed, taking hungry
gasps, then remember a breathing technique Peony taught me,
and that helps me calm down. Calm down, not come down. I'm
still high as an escaped helium balloon, but no longer about to
hyperventilate.

That's when all my best whatevers begin to erode around me

like a fortress made of sand. Which isn't to say I spend the next few hours parcelling out my psyche into neat, organised little boxes. Not even close. I'd need about ten years for that. All I do is spend the next few hours copping to the fact that my whatevers exist. Acknowledging that there is something about me – *me*, not my mother or my father, not my bandmates, not my situation – that I need to face and stir and poke.

The Boy

This is where it all began. Sure, some would cite St Louis with Chuck Berry or Tupelo with Elvis, or elsewhere, even earlier, that noisy hooptie crash between blues and country on some nameless crossroads out in the boondocks. But I say no. I say here. For that particular thing we do – us, 6X – that rock meets pop thing, that switchblade with sugar on top, this is the starting point. Hamburg, Germany. This is where a bunch of Liverpool lads assembled to get their shit together in tawdry basement clubs – this is where the Beatles *became* the Beatles.

And I'm here, with my band, playing my heart out and bonding with me mates and causing a commotion, just like the Beatles did in 1960. Could life get more perfect?

Only if I could clone myself. For one night at least. Because tonight I'm hanging in Hamburg, and in Long Island my girlfriend will be heading to her senior prom with some wussy singer-songwriter named Aaron.

Not that I want to take E/D to her prom. Personally I'd prefer a blow to the head with a blunt instrument – a clarinet, perhaps. But I understand how important prom is to the ladies.

The only reason I went to mine was Kendall; she was about to start tutoring and wouldn't have a prom of her own. Looking back, I remember how excited she was. How she glowed. The way she fingered her orchid corsage to convince herself it was real. The touch of her hands on my shoulders as we swayed around in our lame excuse for dancing that somehow, remarkably, was not cheesy.

So I know what prom means to girls, and I would give all the knockwurst in Germany to be with my girl at hers. Except I wouldn't, really, would I?

'I'm dying here,' I moan aloud after signing what I hope is my final autograph of the day.

'Yeah, I know.' Stella stretches. 'Writer's cramp. I've never been so sick of my own damn name.'

I emit a big, gushy, 'help-me' sigh.

Stella picks up on it, sucking her teeth. 'All right, what's your problem?'

Wynn looks on, half-interested in my plight, half-interested in a ragged cuticle, while Kendall nods and smiles, pen in hand, still working the promo thing to straggling German fans.

'I'm just – look, I know you guys couldn't care less about prom—'

'Prom! Oh, please!' cracks Stella.

' but you are a rare breed of female. So cut me some slack. Because in a few hours a limo will be pulling up to E/D's house, and her escort is some character in a rented tux who sings about lily pads.'

'Shut up!' Stella in disbelief.

'Really, lily pads?' says Wynn. 'That's . . . um . . .'

'The corniest shit I ever heard in my life, all right,' Stella finishes Wynn's thought. 'Dude, trust: You have nothing to worry about.'

A last-minute Gretel comes up – pug-nosed, pigtailed, bubbly yet shy – to thrust a poster at me. I take up my Sharpie. 'Hi. *Wie heiβen du?*' I ask. Translation: What's your name?

She giggles. 'Gretel.'

'Gretel? No shit . . .' I mumble to myself, scribbling: To Gretel, Love A/B. Love. Ever notice how we throw the word around? 'I love that song.' 'I love cheeseburgers.' Wynn and Stella sign Gretel's souvenir, and she continues down the line for Kendall.

'I have nothing to worry about,' I repeat, returning the focus to me, my issue. 'I know I don't . . . probably. It's just, this is it, isn't it – until we retire to the old rocker folks' home. Always leaving the ones we love, flying in and out of their lives between tours, hoping they'll be there when we get back but knowing it's not fair to ask.'

Now it's Stella's turn for static frustration. '*Pfff* – don't get me started,' she says. 'I am having Didion withdrawal bad. And it doesn't get better with time, it gets worse.' She runs a palm across her stubbly scalp. 'But what are we gonna do? Pass on world domination?'

'Didion's different,' I counter. 'Didion knows the score.'

Wynn gives a huff. 'That's for sure.'

'What's that supposed to mean?' Stella goes guard dog.

'Nothing, Stella, God – it's not a dis,' Wynn says. 'It's just that gallivanting is Didion's modus operandi . . .'

Hot-potato looks lob back and forth between Stella and

Wynn. *Bang!* – I'm now a bystander to the conversation I initiated; it's become one of those weird intra-chick communications where what's not spoken is as important as what is. 'It's cool,' Stella says finally. 'You just can't relate. Wait till you fall in love – maybe then you'll get it.'

At which point Wynn gets weird. At first she doesn't react at all. Then her face goes rubbery – she's offended and fierce and confused all at once. She opens her mouth to say something, then shuts it like a trap, gives Stella a stiletto stare, and stalks off.

The Boss

A/B's right about Didion knowing the score, but Wynn's way off. Didion's on track now. He's making a demo for Brian to shop – three songs: 'Lust,' 'Wired,' and 'Sweet.' This is what keeps me sane while we're over here; I got my eyes on the prize. If everything goes right, Didion will have a deal and be busy on his first album by the time 6X starts recording our sophomore effort. Fast-forward to next year, we'll be on the road again, only no separation anxiety, no wondering what your other half is doing in the middle of the night – we'll be headlining, with the incomparable Didion Jones opening.

So I am supremely confident my man will be in New York, right where I left him, when we finish this promo spin. How dare Wynn infer otherwise? I told her on the low that Brian was paying for Didz's demo – if she's my friend, shouldn't she be cheerleading instead of dispensing her annoying negativity? Yeah, well, that's Wynn. Goes to show you looks and money don't mean shit. Some cashmere-clad skeletons in that closet, for damn sure. Or if she's just jealous I have a boyfriend, why doesn't she go find one her damn self? Or, please, do the world a favour and have a freakin' fling.

Not for lack of guys trying, lemme tell you. What about Kieran Dennis? What about Stak Estervak? Or two nights ago, we're hanging at this beer garden (yeah, the Germans are progressive about teens and beer, like the French are with kids and wine), and these American exchange students are all jockeying for position. One, Jonathan, he's perfect for her – a junior at Dalton, arts editor for the school paper, acerbic with a sweet side, looks like he walked straight out of a Ralph Lauren ad, and manages to direct his gaze in Wynn's eyes and not at her boobs. But would she give him the time of day? No.

Whatever. I'm not getting caught up in her shit. We're in Tokyo now, and I intend to make the most. This place, it's unreal. A futuristic theme park – neon, glass, shiny steel alongside shrines and gardens. It's like being inside a video game.

First we do a press conference for national television. Like what are we, politicians or something? That's the impact of 'Kitty' here – it hit Japan like an eight-point-fiver on the Richter scale, so all these journalists need to throw questions at us on the air. We handle it; just keep pushing our agenda, like we learned in media training, talking about how all we wanna do is rock out and have fun and meet our Japanese fans. And that's exactly what we do after the media circus. Go down to the Harajuku district – Tokyo's teen central, the hood where Gwen Stefani's fashionista friends got their name – for a free concert to countless screaming kids. Then, this being Japan, they have to return the favour and put on a show in our honour.

It's not a band, though, which is a relief (there hasn't been an interesting Japanese rock act since Guitar Wolf). No; it's the

Potent Chiyoda. Think David Blaine, version Far East, this magician whose trippy tricks and dry humour have invaded the trend-thirsty citizenry like a flesh-eating virus. An antidote to the keyed-up emcees that rule Japanese TV, his approach is deliberately slow and monotone. No cape or tux, he dresses kind of hip-hop, sweat suits and shit. His hair is the colour of transmission fluid.

Of course he has to make us part of the act – and I'm his first victim. He cuts me in half – the long way – with this guillotine contraption, then commands my two profiles to race into each other on Vespa scooters, and following a loud, smoky, flash-pot collision I'm back whole again. Next he sets A/B's SG on fire – you should have seen the boy sweat! – and puts out the flames with his tongue. When it's Kendall's turn, he has her jump up and down on this miniature trampoline and keeps telling her 'Higher! Higher!' until she turns into a dove. She flies around loose, then lands on his shoulder and sings – in Kendall's own voice. To turn her back, he puts the bird on a swing perch inside a giant gilt birdcage, sweeps a kimono-type thing over the cage, and – *shazam!* – there's Kendall.

Now it's time to do Wynn, and Chiyoda jokes that he's tired, that it's hard coming up with all these crazy new gags, so he's going to do something very traditional with Wynn. He is going to make her disappear.

'Wynn Morgan, are you afraid of the dark?' he asks.

'Um . . . yes . . . a little,' Wynn confesses.

'Ah, that is too bad . . .' Out comes this red origami contraption about the size of a Porta Potti. Chiyoda opens it, guides Wynn inside.

'Do you have any last requests?' Chiyoda asks, and just as Wynn begins to say something he slams the door. Then he launches into this monologue that makes absolutely no sense, glances at his watch, and opens the box. Predictably, Wynn's gone.

What's unpredictable, though, is Chiyoda cannot bring her back. Naturally we all think this is part of the act. Until it's obvious that it's not. Until police are called to take Chiyoda into custody. Until we're all backstage freaking out and Gaylord is on the phone to the States.

'Brian? Uhhh, Brian – Gaylord. Uhhh, listen, I don't have too many details yet and I don't really understand how this happened – even though it happened right in front of my eyes . . . but, uhhh, Brian? Uhh, it looks like, uhh, it seems as though, uhh, apparently Wynn has been kidnapped.'

The Body (Televised Address)

Please accept apologies if this message is of disturbance to your busy day. I speak to you as the most recent loyal member of the Heightened Intelligent People's Ministry of Anti-Commercialism and Conspicuous Consumerism. And I speak to you about a matter of most urgency, please excuse.

Although HIPMACCC is an underground organisation founded in Japan, our message and our goals are universal. HIPMACCC is comprised of young people unhappy with being used as market research guinea pigs. We are sad with adults watching our every move, charting our every conversation and cataloguing our every purchase. We are equally unhappy and sad with being force-fed new products and concepts and then coerced into determining whether they are very cool, sort of cool, or not cool at all.

Yes, it is true, when industries and advertisers first sought our opinions we were complimented, because young people have been cultural outcasts since the dawn of civilisation. It was always elders this and elders that. Then, most suddenly, our tastes and preferences mattered. Intoxicated by our newfound 'power' we did not realise we were being enslaved by your demands on our decisions. Flat or carbonated? Pink or green? Matte or glossy? Chunky or smooth? Such immense tonnage on our teenage shoulders. It is a very stressful time to be the young generation. Yet being taken seriously became a drug to us. We taste-test. We text-message. We buy and use with abandon.

It was only recently, when the youth of Japan became exposed to the poignant, plaintive song 'Hello Kitty Creeps Me Out' by the American rock and roll band 6X, that the blinders fell from our eyes. This song – a brutal assault on the supreme emblem of the corporation – has shown us that unbridled commercialism and conspicuous consumerism are deadly to the human spirit. Hello Kitty's unparallelled popularity represents all that is deviant about the global economy. Hello Kitty must be stopped! Or she must be given a mouth – for perhaps, sadly, Hello Kitty is a slave herself.

My name is Wynn Morgan, and I wrote 'Hello Kitty Creeps Me Out,' which HIPMACCC has taken for its manifesto. Since arriving at HIPMACCC headquarters I have come to understand the organisation's philosophy, and am eager to announce my alliance with HIPMACCC – even though I am now reading a prepared statement, as opposed to spouting my own spontaneous words. Also I want to say that I have not been mistreated by my comrades in HIPMACCC and have been given ample soup and Kellogg's Apple Jacks Cereal, as well as lavatory privileges.

Youth of Japan! Youth of America! Youth of the world! I urge you to please join HIPMACCC today! Tell your elders – your parents, the company: No, I will not be a pawn of the product!

End the scourge of commercialism and conspicuous consumerism! Throttle Hello Kitty with ungloved fists and stomp her corpse in triumph!

Thank you very much and have a nice day.

The Voice

It's so, so, so important to thank the Lord for all His blessings. I try my best, I really do, but I'm sure things slip through the cracks. Like did I shout out a hosanna when hotel housekeeping placed a mint on my pillow? And while I said grace over my room-service breakfast, did I make it a special point to thank God that the eggs were not rubbery, which they have been every other morning in this country where people eat their fish raw but seem stone set on cooking eggs till they bounce? The point is, when we forget to send praise and appreciation for His bounty, we risk losing what He has granted. It's right there in the Book of Job: The Lord giveth, and the Lord taketh away.

And now it seems that He hath taketh away Wynn.

Well, not Him personally, but He in His infinite wisdom has allowed her to fall prey to terrorists. The last two days have been real scary; that's how long it's been since the Potent Chiyoda failed to make Wynn reappear. As far as we know – we being me, A/B, and Stella – the magician is no longer a suspect. Trouble is, all our information comes from the TV news; it's not like we're privy to any inside info. That's so, so unfair – Wynn's

281

our bandmate, *our* friend, yet Mr and Mrs Joe Average Japan know as much about her abduction as we do.

Oh, I'm sure we're being kept in the dark for our own protection. That's what Mr Wandweilder says, anyway. He's here now, and Wynn's mom and real dad and stepdad, too. Naturally all our public appearances in Tokyo have been cancelled, and our Osaka engagements next week are up in the air. Plus, it's not even safe for us to go outside – paparazzi are staking us out, but the greater concern is that HIPMACCC might try to ambush the rest of us. Nobody knows much about the group – seizing Wynn is their first overt move to . . . well, they're out to accomplish something, I reckon, but I can't quite understand what. Based on Wynn's televised statement, it seems that they're unhappy with the way young folks get treated here now – as 'market research guinea pigs' – but they also weren't happy with how they were treated before, as 'cultural outcasts.'

Personally, if I was a regular girl and not a rock star, and major manufacturers wanted me to road-test their stuff, I'd be pleased as punch. But economics and socio-political philosophy aren't really my thing. All I know is me and Stella and A/B are cooped up here in the hotel – mostly we hang out together in the anteroom of this conference centre the hotel donated to the investigation. They've stocked it with snacks for us, but the Japanese idea of candy is just jellies and gummies and dried-up old peas with some kind of hot sauce baked in, which don't do a thing for me. So we're climbing the walls and can get to bickering, which makes me feel bad, considering how poor Wynn is heaven-knows-where.

I'm ashamed at how easy it is to take people for granted. Me

– the most grateful person I know. Yet when was the last time I told Wynn how smart she is, or gave her credit for her great lyrics, or said how much I care about her? I can't even remember.

The Boy

So have you heard about the 6X side project? A sad little adjunct to the seven dwarves: Whiny, Growly, and Hapless. Care to guess who's who?

Growly (pacing): I can't take this, stuck here doing nothing!

Whiny: Well then, why *don't* we do something?

Growly: Like what? Huh? What would you suggest?

Whiny: Um, gosh . . . we could go back to the Harajuku district. I bet kids would be inclined to tell us things they wouldn't dare say to the police.

Growly (to Hapless): You hear this?

Hapless (shrugs)

Growly (to Whiny): You think this is some kind of Scooby-Doo episode — we defeat the bad guy ghouls and save our friend while hilarity ensues? Get real, all right. A) We're practically prisoners ourselves here. B) If we did sneak out, the press would be all over us. And C) You want to make more trouble? Our parents are already screaming bloody murder for Brian to send us home stat.

Whiny: Fine then! Fine! I hear you! You don't have to jump

all over me . . .

Growly: I'm not jumping all over you. I am simply trying to point out the salient facts in clear and simple terms even you would understand.

Whiny: Now, that's what I mean – everything you say to me is so mean and patronising, and I just want you to know I am sick of it! Sick to death!

Growly (mimicking): Sick to death!

Whiny (to Hapless): Listen to her! Why does she treat me so bad? Why? What did I ever do to her?

Hapless (shrugs)

You get the idea. I play with my Game Boy; I play guitar; I go up to my room and escape into sleep. But whenever I look up or come back it's the same tape loop going round and round. Eventually, though, old Hapless hits the ceiling. When Growly starts giving Whiny shit about eating all the gummi beetles, down goes Grand Theft Auto. 'OK, Stella, enough!'

'Excuse me?' She's giving me that tough-on-wry tone, but I won't back down. Perhaps the world's most aggro video game has given me an extra edge.

'Look, just leave her alone . . .'

Kendall comes trotting to the futon where I've been schlumped, throws her arms around my neck, and starts blubbering. 'Oh, thank you, A/B! Thank you! You have no idea how difficult it is – she is just so, so cruel . . .'

I'm starting to weigh how much of this effluvium is genuine visceral content and how much is schmaltzy Southern belle syndrome when, much to my surprise, Stella, dragging her feet, head hung down, plunks on my other side. She sighs with a weighty, otherworldly softness. 'You're right – Kendal's right. I'm a witch . . . and I'm just, I'm exhausted, I'm worried, I'm upset. But it's no excuse . . .' She drapes her arm across me and reaches for Kendall, so now I've got two warm, weary, freaked-out female barnacles on my hull that I don't know what to do with. My own arms are pretty much pinned to my sides, so such comforting gestures as strokes to the hair aren't feasible. Stella takes a deep hard breath, flinching like it hurts her ribs, her heart. Exhales slow and hot against my neck. Grips Kendall's arm more desperately. And Kendall hangs on to Stella, too, with hushes and coos.

'It's OK, Stella,' she says.

Despite this reassurance, Stella does the oddest thing. She weeps. I know she weeps, because I feel the tension contract her body as it's smacked by wave after inner wave. I feel the wet through my T-shirt. But she does not make a single sound. I didn't know it was possible for a person to sob so violently yet so silently, and the impact of that knowledge – what can I say, it makes me cry too.

So we're huddled here, the three of us, on a sea-foam futon, in a nondescript hotel conference centre anteroom, halfway around the world from home, clutching one another: whimpering, orphaned puppies in the rain. Then someone says:

'I'm sorry.'

'Me too.'

'I love you.'

'I love you too.'

'I love you both.'

286

'I love Wynn!'

'I know! I know! Me too!'

'I love *us*. I love 6X.'

'Me too – I love us. I really, really do.'

'I believe in us.'

'We'll be OK.'

'Wynn will be OK.'

'We'll all be OK.'

'Are you sure?'

'I am . . .'

'I'm sure . . .'

'I promise . . .'

'I swear . . .'

The Boss

It's 3:24 AM Tokyo time when the phone beside my hotel bed slaps me awake.

'Please may I speak with Stella Angenue Simone Saunders, bass player of 6X?'

'Who the hell is this?!'

'Please excuse. Who I am is nonimportant.' The voice is female, chirpy. 'I call on behalf of Wynn Morgan, drummer and lyricist of 6X.'

I am ice-water-brain-bath awake. 'You're – what? Godamnit, who is this! This better not be a joke!' Is this actually me spitting such bad movie dialogue?

'No, this is not a prank call or humorous in any way. I call you because you are Wynn Morgan's emergency contact.'

Worst-possible scenarios infiltrate the base of my skull, skitter down my spinal cord, spider-spin out to my extremities. I squeeze my eyes tight. An amorphous prayer in my head: Please . . . God . . .

'Hello . . . ?' That flutter in my ear.

'Yes! Hello! I'm here . . .'

'I call to tell you where to find her.'

Find her? Oh, God! Find her *what?* The soundtrack to worst-possible scenarios fills in the word 'body,' so I squeeze my eyes again till firework sparks blaze up and blot out the images – strangled, mangled, drawn and quartered, shot . . . 'Find her . . .' I say.

'*Hai!* She will be waiting for you at the main entrance to Tokyo Disney at opening time, exactly eight AM. Thank you very much.'

No, I think. *Thank you.* And: *Please be telling the truth.* And: *Wynn's alive.*

Did I really entertain the notion she was dead? Damn, what *didn't* I try on for size over the last four frantic days? I even wrestled with the idea that Wynn was in on the whole thing, hooked up with HIPMACCC – not so far-fetched, if you know Wynn who, forget all her money, sticks with the same old-school composition notebooks and the same lineup of trashed band T-shirts and basically doesn't have a trendoid conspicuous consumer cell in her entire self. Then I thought, no – 6X is lifeblood to Wynn: It's her outlet, her passion, her purpose. Kendall is the voice of 6X, A/B is the fingers, I'm the brains, but Wynn is more than the body, the image – she is the heart and the soul of this band, and she'd eat her kit before she'd bail.

But it's fine, it's cool, she's all right. I stare at the clock: 3:52. Four more hours. Give or take. So what do I do? If HIPMACCC ass is gonna get busted for this, I rouse Brian and the cops ASAP. But if Wynn really *does* sympathise with her captors, maybe what she wants is for me to chill till just before her ETA at Tokyo Disney. Or is this is some kind of ploy –

Wynn will be one-eighty away from the main gate, and HIPMACCC *expects* me to alert the authorities now, so everyone will be looking the wrong way while they unleash phase two of whatever wacky shit is next on their agenda. ARRRGH! Struggling internally is not working for me.

So down the hall I go. I wake A/B. He gargles alternatives around for a while. But all we can decide is to tell Kendall – because what was up with that tearful group hug the other day if not to weave together the frayed ends and make us tight again? Then, as Kendall weighs the pros and cons, oops, what do you know, the whole crazy thing takes its toll and we all pass out in her room until the sun comes through a crack in the drapes. At which point we alert Barney-san.

Sirens blaring, lights flashing, Tokyo's finest sets out for the Far East version of the Mouse House, and there's Wynn in the unwashed outfit the Potent Chiyoda poofed her off in. Back at the hotel the reunion is subdued, which fits, since so much was at stake – you don't want a parade with confetti and trombones. Of course Wynn's family rushes up, and there are all these cops, statements to be taken and whatnot. Me and A/B and Kendall have no choice but to hang back, feeling like bystanders, Gaylord and Peony clucking around, surrogate-parenting us.

But the second she gets free, Wynn finds her way over to me, and I break off from the others, not much, a few steps, a few million miles. I look at her like I'm afraid to look. I smile like I'm afraid to smile, and she smiles back the same way.

'Dude . . .' What can I say? That's what I say. Her eyes don't move from me.

'I know,' she says.

'Holy shit!'

'I know,' she repeats.

'You all right or what?'

She blows at her bangs. 'You know . . . I don't know . . . I mean . . . I guess.'

Then we are hugging, and damn if I'm not digging my fingers into her back and rocking her back and forth, and she's digging and rocking on me, like we're never going to let go.

The Body

What happened in Tokyo stays in Tokyo. For the most part, at least. If something has to go down on record, here's the official story, the one I told the police. Bear in mind, I'm not much of a liar − it's not like I *fabricated* for the authorities. At the same time, I don't especially disagree with the tenets of HIPMACCC and wouldn't want them sent to jail for what they did to me.

Basically, I disappear. The bottom drops out of the Potent Chiyoda's red paper capsule, and down the rabbit hole I go. A chute, a slide, and then I'm . . . not backstage, *under*stage. It's murky but not pitch-black and smells like an indoor swimming pool. I assume I should stick close so the PC can bring me back, yet when this voice − girlish and excited, but authoritative too − calls out of the dim: 'Hello, Wynn Morgan! Please to follow me?' I obey.

She's in costume, like a mascot from a ball team or some such. I don't recognise the character or even what kind of animal it is, and while it does seem vaguely Hello Kittyish − dummy me, I don't put it together. She's not wearing the paw part of the costume, and her hand reaches for mine − curiouser and curiouser, right? A long corridor, then bright sunlight. An SUV with the driver and another passenger in back also wearing plushie suits. About then I start wondering if maybe this isn't *too* weird. The back door opens, and my escort – a fawn, I realise, with dilated pupils like Bambi on heroin – makes a little bow and gestures towards the interior. By this point I have to say something: 'Um, excuse me – this isn't part of the act, is it?'

'Excuse me, no, it isn't . . .'

'I don't think I should—' The forest creature draws a shiny metal object from a hidden pocket. 'Are you going to hurt me?' I ask.

'That would be a most unfortunate occurrence,' she says.

So I get in, next to what could be a dog or could be a chipmunk, who asks me politely to please allow for a blindfold. I laugh out loud – because it's funny, because it's freaking me out . . . felt animals with automatic weapons.

Maybe I get brainwashed; I don't know. They do talk to me about their message, their . . . objectives. How many? Um, Purin, Chococat, Deery Lou, the evil chickeny-looking thing, the monkey, some other kind of canine, Hello Kitty herself – about six, seven. I do read the statement written for me. They let me use the bathroom whenever I need to (but there's no shower – that's kind of gross). Yes, I'm fed miso soup and Apple Jacks. No, I never see anyone unplushied. Yes, they are male and female. No, I never see another gun.

I adjust to sleeping on a tatami with this little foam brick pillow. I think a lot – about who I would miss most if I never got away, and how I'd feel if I couldn't play drums again; I even start sorting out my assorted aforementioned whatevers. Then four, maybe five days later I'm instructed to put on the blindfold and – whisk! – it's off to Tokyo Disney, and that's pretty much the extent of it. No ransom or anything – they just want to get their point across in a splashy way, so that's me.

Now I'm back, and everyone's fussing and sniping over me. My mom looks like she aged ten years – an indication, I suppose, of her love. She's giving me these little pats and pinches to make sure I'm real, then rails at the detectives for incompetence. I assume she'll calm down soon enough and start researching Asian rejuvenation spas; my mom's got a sixth sense for people who do wonderful things with oyster flesh and seaweed. Still, I don't want to be snide – it was nice of her and my stepdad to drop everything and come all this way. My real dad too.

Only, talk about feeling the love in this room – it's all about the band. It's like one of those bizarre dreams where you're trying to go from point A to point B but there's all this crap in your way. I have to deal with the cops and my parents and Brian, too, who's holding off the press, but all I really want to do is get over to those guys. And I mean, I swear, the looks on their faces! Relief, of course. Like everyone else, they're glad I wasn't killed or maimed or whatever. But in their eyes is something else, this . . . unconditionality. This no-matter-whatness. This respect. Like, sure, they're dying to know what happened, but if I don't tell them that'll be cool too. I don't have to explain or expound, because they know I spent the last four or five days being me, and they're fine with that.

Or I don't know – I could be totally wrong and they're all

judging me, thinking I handled myself like a moron and they're embarrassed to be in a band with me. But when I finally wade through the muck and Stella and I are holding on to each other, I don't feel judged and I don't feel stupid and I don't feel like I need to apologise . . . for anything, ever again.

The Boss

Nothing like a good kidnapping to keep you in the public eye! No, come on, no one was more freaked out than me – I was bawling, all right, scared shitless. I'm glad my girl came through unscathed and blah-blah-blah. Only if as a bonus *Bliss de la Mess* sales spike like crazy and finally even the snooty UK is getting with the programme – I'm not mad at that. We reschedule the Osaka itinerary, but it's total insanity wherever we go; a riot at the venue when demand for tickets seriously exceeds supply. We've become that Godzillan in Japan and have to add two more shows.

The timing works anyway, because now we're on the bill at Glastonbury, this massive music festival in the English countryside. But first it's a week in London for gigs, press, and this-just-added: an appearance on *The New Ones*. This is big. *The New Ones* is a limited-edition six-episode remake of *The Young Ones*, this hit Eighties sitcom about four male college roommates. The musical segment always kicks off the same way: One of the guys has a problem, and how do typical guys, English or otherwise, deal with drama? They get shit-faced. So the famous line in *The Young Ones* and now

The New Ones is some variation on 'Let's go down to the pub . . .' and ta-da, the musical guest is playing there. Thing of it is, we're bumping off Alien Baby – they're not that popular in the States yet, but they're huge here, and they were originally scheduled. Only the plot happens to revolve around Nicky, the neurotic, anal-retentive anarchist character, faking his own kidnapping to get some girl's attention, and in light of recent events, Wynn-wise . . . well, buh-bye Alien Baby!

What's hilarious – cheeky as the Brits say – not to mention controversial, is the way Wynn's been written into the script, even though she doesn't exactly have a line. The pub scene is also supposed to take place inside Nicky's brain as he contemplates his caper. Wynn walks in, leans over his table, and whispers into his ear. Then he snaps his fingers and says: 'I'll do it!' as Wynn sits to count off 'Hello Kitty.'

The whole experience is killer from the jump-off, since the cast makes us feel welcome and wanted. We're there early so we can watch some filming, get into *The New Ones* mind-set. I gotta cop to having pre-conceived notions of the English as uptight and prissy, but the vibe on set is the opposite. Damn, the adlibs surpass the script, and the bloopers are even better – these guys are freakin' hilarious. The day is going so well, I don't expect anything or anyone to jack my mood. Then along comes Kendall. She's fine all morning, but once they start rehearsing Wynn's walk-on she slips into ofay mode.

Ask me? She can't deal with the extra attention heaped on Wynn since Tokyo, though of course she can't complain outright. The girl was abducted at freakin' gunpoint, all right? Even Kendall must realise it wouldn't 'sit right' to pull a flamboyant diva act, like demand screen time of her own, or go passive-aggressive and 'accidentally' screw up her marks or cues during our performance.

No, her whackosity is more subtle. I probably wouldn't even notice myself, except, be real, it's no fun for me watching *The New Ones* cast worship at the altar of Wynn Morgan either. So my eyes wander, la-la-la, what else is going on – and I see Kendall stuffing her greedy tube like there's no tomorrow. If it was once or twice, a second scone at craft service or whatever, I'd be like, no biggie, but she is going at it two-fisted. By the lunch break, forget about it – look, I can eat, we all can, but the more the English boys ooze over Wynn, the more Kendall piles on her plate. Wynn's too busy fending off actors to pick up on it, and A/B, too, is otherwise occupied. That English model, Cate Fern? She has a cameo as the object of Nicky's desire, and she's here peeling grapes and chatting up A/B, which no doubt adds fuel to Kendall's frustration.

So I watch her, Little Miss Train Wreck, until some mechanism inside her switches off, and she stops, practically mid-bite, and mumbles, 'Excuse me.' And I have got to know, all right? The subject of Kendall's eating disorder never came up again after Seattle – as if the absence of Britt Gustafson somehow cured her. But I can't kid myself any more. I've gotta suss it out. It's not just morbid fascination, either. It hurts to think of Kendall doing this to herself. Must be related to being in love – all these hidden resources of humanity or whatever popping up in me. Because all that touchy-feely nonsense we had back in Tokyo when Wynn was AWOL, well, it wasn't nonsense, all right. So I follow Kendall on the low to the loo, and I hear for myself.

The Boy

Ooh, the colours! I am *not* tripping my brains out as we approach the festival site and the landscape transforms from verdant variations to full-on rainbow, hillside after rolling hillside in tribute to Roy G. Biv. We all go whoa, and it takes a minute to register that what we're seeing is acres and acres of tightly pitched tents. Apparently British rock fans, as well as the other music lovers from throughout Europe converging on Glastonbury, aren't averse to camping.

We, of course, the talent, enjoy loftier accommodations. Our hired coach is the state-of-the-art UK cousin of the MondoCruiser. And the VIP area's a veritable who's who. Except for Coldplay, who'll arrive by helicopter for their set and whirlybird out immediately after, everyone you ever read about in the *NME* is milling around. I get a little – OK, a lot – starstruck, but it's a rock-and-roll smorgasbord out there. Look, it's Gorillaz! It's Franz Ferdinand! It's the Streets! It's the Darkness! It's the one-armed dinosaur drummer from Def Leppard! It's Kylie Minogue mugging with an ex-Spice Girl. Oy vey, it's John Lydon, please-sir-may-I-kiss-the-hem-of-thy-garment-sir. Duck! It's Alien Baby – no use running into them in case they're still mad about the *New Ones* thing. We're not the only Americans, either — the Snooks and Kings of Leon and Churnsway and White Stripes are proudly representing. As are techno bands from Belgium, black metal combos from Sweden, Moroccan and Malaysian and Ghanaian artists. Plus a plethora of posses and plus-ones — models and heiresses and lesser royals, fashion designers and magazine publishers and professional gamblers. Bodyguards, of course. And tons of little kids, nannies, and dogs.

I have to blink five times to ensure I'm not hallucinating Joss Stone, Joan Osbourne, and Joni Mitchell all gabbing away. Three generations of female vocal euphoria! Then Joss spies Kendall and waves her over. With a toss of hair, Kendall grabs my hand, hauling me with her. Somehow one foot follows the other, and I stand in the presence of greatness, the embodiment of beauty. If the four of them decided to free-jam, I'd drop dead from an aneurism of sonic joy. A massive white awning flutters in the breeze, the sky is a blown-glass bowl of blue, and the sun is the best friend I've ever had, so if I did drop dead I'd already be in heaven.

Naturally I can barely speak, and while Joss and Joan and Joni are benevolently tolerant towards me, they don't care if I utter a syllable or not — they want to talk with one of their own. A super-siren. The kind of girl who can make walls fall, who can lullaby the lion lying down with the lamb, who can give peace not just a chance but a decided advantage — simply by opening her mouth.

Kendall. Kendall Taylor. Miss Kendall Taylor. *The* Kendall Taylor.

How could I have thought of her as just Kendall, clueless Kendall, sometimes silly Kendall, even kind of annoying Kendall? I'm seeing her for the first time, seeing her for who she really is. One of this queenly quartet makes an amusing observation, and they laugh – in perfect-pitch four-part harmony. Their faces lift toward the open sky, and their throats, white birds rustling in a mountainside aerie, set loose this careless, incredible crystalline purity. A server strolls by with a tray of champagne. Nah, I think I'll pass. I'm already intoxicated.

The Voice

Is it a miracle? A natural course of events? I just thank Jesus! Finally, finally, finally – A/B comes to me.

I sense a change in him during our Glastonbury set. Something in the way he moves around me – he's suddenly shy yet inquisitive, an unbroken colt, and little old me holding out an apple. When he stands close to share a mike for harmonies, bless my soul, he blushes, then lopes off to the other side of the stage, head bent, mop of curls bouncing as his fingers blur on guitar. Of course, the teensy part in me of little faith tries to deny this is even happening, but the larger part, the part that knows A/B and I are meant to be, crushes it like the forceful, white-crested surf of glory. The sun is going down when we start our show, and by the end the evening star is gleaming at me, surely the eye of God. My voice – well, I don't want to be all conceited, but my voice amazes even me. It is new, exultant like never before, and the victory in my voice ignites my body, propels me with the freedom and grace of a real dancer. And, well, goodness, I have brought down the house before, but this crashing crescendo of applause makes the hills quake and the skies rumble. Yet I am completely at peace with the furor I create.

After, in the dressing room, I bask in the veneration as easily as I'd stand in a spray of warm summer rain. Wynn and Stella are the first to rush me.

'Girl, you were on fire! I'm talking first-degree burns! So serious it's fatal!'

'God, Kendall, really, I swear, you are sooooo incredible! Feel my arm – feel the goose bumps!'

They're both hugging me and I am hugging them back. Such a wonderful feeling. I've always known Stella and Wynn respect my talent, but tonight it's not merely surface praise, it confirms me on the inside too. And I need that. It's the oddest thing, but the more fame I get, the more I fear it all being taken away from me. So I detach from my girls so I can attend to the other well-wishers forming an unruly cluster around me in the open backstage party area. It's a fairy tale; I am the princess holding court, my heart swelled with kindness and charity and just about every noble Christian quality you can think of.

And yet . . . and yet . . . where is my valiant knight? I find him idling against a tree, staring at me. Wherever I may roam backstage, there he is – sometimes by himself, sometimes the centre of his own circle – he's within a few feet, near, yet not. His eyes never leave me until he sees me glance his way. Then he quickly looks away. It becomes a game I play while half listening to my devotees – the point is to get A/B to hold my eyes, yet I flush with sweet, sweet pleasure every time he drops his gaze. Finally, as the crowd begins to thin, his eyes take mine for a few seconds of aching intensity. There is a smoulder, a dark, pulsing gleam I remember from the time he first challenged me to hit an E minor – yet it's straining, as if A/B's afraid to release it.

Suddenly I feel almost sorry for him. A/B has had a revelation, and now he's unsure how to deal with it. And oh how I want to rush to him, tell him it's all right, comfort him. But no. A/B has to come to me. So I invite him with my smile – tender, knowing, patient – then turn to another fan, another air kiss, another accolade . . . until there he is.

'Kendall . . .' His lips are full and red, as if he's been biting them. His eyes can't control that smoulder. 'You . . . wow . . . tonight . . .' Ohhh, he is not the most articulate knight in the kingdom!

'Yes . . . ?' Shoot, I can't help it – I want to make it easy on him. 'It was a great show.'

'Sure, but . . . not just the show, I don't know.' He looks around – who's here, who's eavesdropping, who cares? 'Kendall, look, I just want you to know . . . maybe I don't show it, but I am aware . . . fully aware . . . I know how amazing you are.'

My fingertips flutter to my mouth, but all I say is, 'Thank you, A/B.'

'I don't know why, all this time . . .' he trails off.

'All this time?'

'All this time I've been such an idiot, but now, it's impossible, I can't . . .'

I smile. 'A/B, please – don't you dare say impossible. I know a thing or two about you too. I know how amazing *you* are. I always have, from the second you walked into that smelly old rehearsal space. You are Abraham Benjamin Farrelberg, and you can do anything.' I barely breathe this last thing: 'You . . . can do anything . . . you want.'

Now he smiles, but just a little. This is momentous, as we both know. 'I can?' he asks for permission, but before I grant it his fingers are already squeezing mine.

'Yes,' I tell him, beckon him, assure him.

Then I tilt my chin, close my eyes, and receive his kiss.

PART FIVE
An American Band

'We're comin' to your town, we'll help you party it down . . .'

— Grand Funk Railroad

WANDWEILDER WORLDWIDE
The Petri Dish for Talent

To: Keith Leider/Universe Music
From: Brian Wandweilder
CC: Tryst Freed
Re: 6X, etc...

Keith —

Thanks for the Cubans, man! Yep, our kids have taken the East and the Continent; it'll be good having them back on American soil.

We're in negotiations for various potential midsummer tours, but we gotta talk re: next single/video - Bliss has looong legs, my friend. Time for a ballad? 'Real Dad'? What think?

Other news: Two new acts under the WandWorld wing - I'm tipping you off first. Demos enclosed. You're gonna wanna send out the A&R

troops *en* force – we'll have showcases set up
for both next week. The band's a no-brainer,
a slam dunk – Snooks meet Ayn Rand with a dash
of the Damned. As to the solo artist, be
afraid...be very afraid. This young man is the
future. Come on, Keef, show me what a
tastemaker you really are!

Talk soon—

Brian Wandweilder, Esq.
BW/sc

620 Avenue of the Americas Suite 2003
NY NY 10011

The Boss

Just when you think it's safe to go back to Brooklyn, huh? After a soft-porn photo shoot, Dutch chocolate space cakes, terrorist abduction, eating disorder documentation, and hysteria-sized overseas success, all I want is home, sweet home. Gimme Coney Island and Gino's Pizza and the mattress on the floor of my man's flat and I'm mm-mm good. I earned that. Do I get that? Hell, no!

It's not like I anticipate full-frontal stress lobotomy. You know me – type A all the way. While the band was traipsing through foreign lands, our able-bodied manager was casting nets and stirring pots. And I'm more than ready to sift through the offers – tours, endorsements, whatever. Not to mention apply my skills as required re: Didion's career. No doubt everything's going according to plan, but there's nothing wrong with showing up and throwing a little weight around. Work that great-woman-behind-every-great-man thing. Also on the agenda, a delicate – yet disgusting – matter has gotta be dealt with, and no time like the present. Even at 35,000 feet.

'Yo.' I tap my swizzle stick against my seatmate's book. 'Any good?'

Wynn looks up, gives a quick quack of giggle.

'Oh . . . you know. Haiku is kind of cheesy, but beautiful at the same time, the simple symmetry of the form and—'

As if I wanna engage in a debate on Basho! 'Look, there's something we gotta talk about . . . I just need to make sure, considering everything, you're up to it. You're not just fronting you're OK. No residual kidnap nightmares?'

She raises her hand, Scout's-honour style. 'I hereby attest to my mental health . . . or at least no post-abduction deterioration in my mental health.'

I try to stare right through her.

'Stop it, Stella, I'm fine,' she insists. 'You can't tease me like that, anyway. So please say what you have to say. Did I do something stupid?'

'It's not you. Look, I'm just gonna say it.' I lower my voice – snoop insurance. 'Remember Kendall's problem? The one we hoped would magically go away once we got her out of Britt Gustafson's clutches? Yeah, well, guess who I heard puking her guts up in a BBC studio bathroom stall.'

Wynn gulps, blinks, blows the hair from her face. 'Shit.'

'Exactly,' I agree.

'So we're back to square one,' Wynn says morosely.

'I don't know, I guess I really wanted to believe her new proportions were just a natural shedding of baby fat.'

'Nothing natural about it,' I say. 'And it's got to stop. Not to be cold, but this isn't just Kendall's problem; this could have serious ramifications for the band. So we've got to move. There's treatment for this, right? Some twelve-step or whatever.'

'Of course there is, Stella – but how are we going to get Kendall into a programme? Convince her the clinic's a Jimmy Choo warehouse sale?'

'Yeah, I didn't get that far. Sticky emotional wickets are your area of expertise.'

Wynn nods. 'OK . . . well . . . I think we need to fill Peony in . . . and possibly – probably, by now – Kendall's mother.'

I don't say 'uch,' but I must think it loud enough.

'Don't worry, I'll talk to P,' Wynn says. 'And if we have to address the issue with Mrs Taylor, we can let her do that . . .'

Up the aisle she goes to peel Peony off of Gaylord. Good thing I know how to delegate. I settle in with my iPod and veg till we start our descent into Kennedy. Didion's waiting at baggage claim. I throw myself into his arms, and he swings me around like some corny down-market cologne ad, but I don't care. He's covering me in kisses and basso sweet talk, a crazy delicious Creole-English gibberish. Ultimately, though, he goes back to words I understand . . . but would rather not.

'I need you to meet someone, cherie,' he says.

And there's this girl. This blonde. This dreadlocked blonde, all right. Sunglasses on inside the terminal, but she takes them off when she sees us looking her way and slips them into her bag, a bag that looks like next year's bag, a bag that cost more than two months of Didion's rent.

'Stella, this is Tryst Freed . . .'

Bitch must be strong – how else can she hold out a hand with that much platinum?

'. . . my new manager.'

The Voice

Pancakes . . . pancakes . . . pancakes . . .

My mom is gibber-jawing about real estate – condos versus co-ops, and square footage and river views, and I am interested, I truly am. She is going after this like gangbusters – a major change in our lives involving lots of money. Except I can barely follow her. I'm not sure when this nagging little voice moved into my head, but it sure is insistent. All it can go on about is food – eating food, and getting rid of food. I try to swat it like some buzzy fly, but this fly is stuck in syrup . . .

Syrup . . . syrup . . . syrup . . .

Darn it! I am Kendall Taylor; I am a star with important matters to think on, like my career and my investments and the sweet, sweet boy who is finally, finally ready to bring me his love. So really, who's in charge here? Why can't I seem to prioritise?

Pancakes . . . pancakes . . . pancakes . . .

Now, my mom *is* actually making pancakes at the time. We're in our Jersey house; I'm leaning on the kitchen island in my robe, a little jet-lagged but positive about how we conquered Europe and Japan and especially Glastonbury. The English countryside is so pretty. Maybe one day, A/B and I can drive through it, just us in a Jaguar on the wrong side of the road. Maybe – dare I say it? – on our honeymoon. That's a long way off, but it's in my mind, clamouring to be heard above the murmuring undercurrent of . . .

Sausages . . . sausages . . . sausages . . .

Ugh! Concentrate, Kendall! I tell myself. Yes, marrying A/B is a long way off, and we have many hurdles to leap. Glastonbury means so much to both of us, but A/B and I haven't discussed what, exactly. Are we boyfriend and girlfriend now? When will he break up with Edie? Because he must – it wouldn't be right to up and never call her again. And when will we speak about Jesus? Because we can only have so much of a future until A/B accepts Him.

I don't bring up any of that on the plane ride home; I'm happy just to sit next to him, arms occasionally brushing, mushy grins occasionally exchanged. Watching the movie . . . well, I watch the movie while A/B conks out – he's so cute when he's sleeping! Trying to nap beside him is fruitless – the thought of it has me so excited I can only shut my eyes and pretend, then give up and quietly devour all the chocolate in my bag before heading for the lavatory.

We've been back a few days now, and I'm sitting tight – patience is a virtue! Tomorrow we have a band meeting and then A/B's giving me a guitar lesson and . . . who can tell? Oh, you may think I'm hankering for a real date, but I've come to understand such quaint notions are for ordinary people – rock-and-roll people, we're more spontaneous.

My mom slides some sausage links next to a stack of

pancakes. 'Honey, you sure you don't want any eggs?' she asks.

Eggs! Eggs! Eggs!

I shall defy you, little voice! I insist to myself. 'No, Mom, this is great,' I say aloud.

Butter . . . butter . . . butter . . . Syrup . . . syrup . . . syrup.

I clump and pour, and begin gobbling, mumbling thanks with my mouth full.

'LuAnn Kendall Taylor!' my mom cries. 'What has gotten into you?'

Uh-oh. Forgot to say grace. 'Sorry, Mom – it's just they're so good; I—'

'Is that what you learned on the road? How to act ungrateful?' Tsking, she sits across from me with her own food.

'No, ma'am, not at all! I always say the blessing – only this morning, I think the time change is catching up to me and I'm all disorientated. Plus,' I beam at her, 'you know you make the best pancakes in the world!'

Now she *hmpfs*, bows her head in hasty prayer. 'I bet you didn't eat a bite over there,' she says. 'What is a Japanese breakfast anyway? I can't imagine. Dollars to donuts you dropped another five pounds over there.'

More like seven. But I just mmm-hmm her.

'Well, that's two more good reasons for me to take charge of your affairs – make sure you give thanks and eat right when you travel,' she rambles on. 'I really ought to talk to Peony about that. Of course, you look wonderful, honey, but you don't want to lose too much weight. Running around onstage like you do, you need your energy.'

Grits? Grits? Grits?

316

'Did you make grits?' The little voice is right. Nothing balances out a mess of sweets and grease like something salty.

My mom gets up with a sigh. 'It'll have to be the quick-cook kind unless you're prepared to wait twenty minutes.' She bustles to the cupboard and gets the grits going, then ladles another round of batter onto the griddle. I clean my plate, then get a tad impatient. So I tap the butter to get a little on my finger, pour some syrup on top and lick it off. This makes me snicker; it's wicked in a way – such horrendous manners! – and I'm not sure why I do it, yet there's something pleasant about it, like being in a trance.

My mom hands me seconds, and I go for the gusto. Funny, I never actually feel full any more. It's not my belly that tells me to stop – my brain does. Goodness, I'll just eat and eat until: *ding!* Then I wait for the coast to clear – just bide my time, la-di-da. I give my mom a hug and a thank-you. Clear the table. Glance at the clock while my mom yammers a few more things at me. Stretch, yawn, and idly say it's time for a shower. Meander down the hall to the bathroom, singing. All the time my heart pounding and my head hollering:

Get rid of it! Get rid of it! Get rid of it!

Run the water loud. Kneel on the tile. Hold back my hair. Hurry!

Phew! Much better. But soon as I'm done, guess who's back? That taunting, unrelenting refrain!

What's next . . . ? Taco Bell? Oreos? Frosted Flakes? What?!

The Boy

How do old sayings get stuck in the vernacular when no one knows what they really mean? A stitch in time saves nine. Hope springs eternal. What the hell is that?! A foolish consistency is the hobgoblin of small minds. Who writes this stuff?! Here's one for you: The third time's the charm. Oh ho, not so, my good adage-man. I have kissed Kendall Taylor three times now, and I don't feel charmed – I feel cursed.

This time when I kiss Kendall, it's not an accident. She doesn't hoodwink me into it – I can't even blame it on cheeba! This time I kiss her because I want to; I want *her*. I've been watching her all night, and now she's mine. The air is chilly but my skin feels hot; the stars counsel *go! go! go!* I take her hand and I take her mouth, I kiss her and she kisses me back, and let me just say she may not have a lot of experience but she knows how to kiss – she knows how to kiss *me*. Not hard, not soft, but . . . yielding to me. Opening to me. And opening and opening and opening.

Our proximity to this enormous tree with violet flowers works in my favour – it offers semi-seclusion so our PDA is not overly P; plus, as the kiss gets more vehement, I press her against the trunk and she lets me, and I'm very close to grinding when one of the wiser stars above must bring me to my senses, reminding me one does not *grind* Kendall Taylor. Then, as I draw back, a gust of wind rustles the tree to make about a billion blossoms cascade down on us like silken purple snowflakes. Kendall's eyes are shining as she plucks a petal from my hair, and I think I could quite possibly pass out.

OK, here's another one for you: Hindsight is perfect. Hah! Or more like: har-har-*har*-de-har-har. Hindsight is anything but. Hindsight has indigestion. Hindsight has the hiccups. Hindsight needs therapy; hindsight needs Librium – megadoses, man. Because I have hindsight now – I am not in the open backstage space of a rock fest in the English countryside but the picket-fenced backyard of my girlfriend's house in Oceanside – and I would like very much to shoot myself in the head. I join the ranks of Jonathan Richman and Vinnie Barbarino as inwardly I wail: I'm so confused.

Because I love E/D. I do. She's smart and spunky and laughs at me at the appropriate moments. We have stuff in common, basic stuff – she's a member of the tribe, so there's the Jewish thing, and there's the whole rejection of the snotty suburbs but having it ingrained in you too, etched onto you like . . . like a tattoo. Aww, shit! A tattoo. I have E/D on me and she has me on her. So I love her, I have to love her, right? She possesses all the attributes I just listed and more – green eyes and integrity and freckles and talent . . . well, sort of.

Yes! No! Yes! E/D has talent. But Kendall . . . Kendall has **TALENT!!** Could be the crux of this whole curse. Could be the thing about Kendall I really need to kiss and hold and touch. Artist types are drawn to other artist types. And if her brand of artistry eludes you . . . sure, I can manage a doo-doo-doo here and a la-la-la there, but I'm no singer, so it's pure instinct to sniff it out, hunt it down, eat it up alive. Particularly when her brand of artistry complements yours — shows it off, helps it shine, dares it to top itself. Talent, the ultimate enticement.

OK, OK. So me kissing Kendall has nothing to do with her long dark hair or her high-heeled shoes or her sweet Southern accent or the way she's been buying these incredible clothes that would make your high school principal look hot.

And me kissing Kendall has nothing to do with these other changes, the not-physical ones, her morphing from a simple sunny day to a decidedly more turbulent, complicated, and unpredictable weather pattern.

My kissing Kendall has nothing to do with the fact that me kissing E/D is just too damned easy.

My kissing Kendall has nothing to do with me deciding, on some deep-seated insane level, to seek out that bad-idea treasure known as female trouble . . .

The Body

It's a slumber party! It's an intervention! It's a slumber party and an intervention! Actually I'm saying slumber party as subterfuge to guarantee attendance by the guest of honour – the, I don't know, interventionee? I'm having a hard time since one of my main allies – the one who put me in 'must do something' mode – has her own problems. Stella will play along, but thanks to the Tryst Freed situation, she's not much help in the planning department.

Tryst Freed, the newest employee of Wandweilder Worldwide. A real hotshot. Apparently, while we were in England, Tryst tried to steal Didion from Brian, so Brian stole Tryst from Magnitude Management, her former firm. Set her up with a nicer office, a nicer salary, a nicer expense account – and the client she was attempting to poach. Nice for Tryst. Nice for Brian, too, since around the time he took on Didion he also brought Boy King into the fold. And Boy King will be an easy sell; Didion, well, he's a genius and a complete original – in other words, a tough sell. Tryst will do Didion full-time; marketing him is her challenge, and she seems like a woman who meets her challenges. So, nice for Didion. Nice for everyone except Stella, who doesn't trust Tryst, hates everything Tryst has done on Didion's behalf so far – like get him to retire granddad's suits and slip into a whole new custom-tailored wardrobe. Why Stella'd bitch about that is a mystery to me – her thrift-shop yin has innate bourgeois status-conscious yang.

'Hey, you guys? You free Friday?' We're packing up after rehearsal, having slipped back into our groove of bi-weekly practices, and I'm laying my trap. I hope I'm stealth enough.

'Whatever it is, I can't – I've got a thing, a family thing, with my family!' A/B is such a Nervous Nelly lately.

'Actually, A/B, sorry but you're not invited. It's girls only.'

Stella zips up her bass case smoothly. 'Yeah? What kind of girl thing?' She ad libs her lines like milk.

'A Malinka girl thing.' This part is all true, so I don't stress. 'You know she's in New York for that big tournament, Forest Hills. I'm going to her match tomorrow.'

'Yeah, she's winning, right? I heard it on the news,' Stella says.

'Oh, she's unstoppable. But it sucks to be her in a way – when she's actively competing she's not allowed an extra breath mint; she can't stay up to watch Conan. I swear her coach is related to Stalin. But after Forest Hills she's done for a while – so we aim to party. My house – a sleepover.'

Now we have to bait the hook.

'A sleepover?' says Stella. 'What are we, twelve?'

Kendall agrees. 'Gosh, Wynn, that does seem childish. Besides, if we go out on the town A/B can come . . .'

'No, I can't; I told you I have this thing—'

'Well, if we have a sleepover you'll be doing my mother a

huge favour – and do my mother a huge favour, I'm for ever in your debt.'

'What are you talking about?' Stella says, on cue.

'She – my mother – she's running this fund-raiser next month at our house, and she's losing her mind; she hasn't hired a caterer yet. So she wants us as guinea pigs.'

'Your mother's gonna *cater* your slumber party?' Stella consults the ceiling. 'Damn, the rich really are different.'

'Oh, shut up,' I say. 'Didion's cooking spoiled you so bad you're going to turn down five-star cuisine? Not to mention the two pastry chefs my mom is making go *mano a mano*.'

Stella *pffffs*. 'Whatever. I am so irritated with Didion right now I could use a girls' night in. Forget that – I won't even tell him where I'm going; I'll just be out.'

'Not too passive-aggressive . . .'

'You know what, Wynn, if I want relationship advice I'll ask someone who's actually been in a relationship.'

'Hey now, now,' Kendall mediates, 'you don't want to be in a fight before what sounds like a real fun party.'

Inside I go: *Yes!*

The Boy

Me, a snaky, scummy player? No way! I'm just wondering if it's strictly mandatory to break up with E/D. Wait, wait – hear me out. It's true, I have feelings for Kendall, but that doesn't mean my feelings for E/D have gone up in smoke. And while Kendall and I did kiss, does a kiss constitute cheating? After all, in terms of physical intimacy, Kendall promises to be a teacup ride – the whole Christian virginity doctrine. So if E/D's the only girl I'm having actual sex with, am I hurting anyone by simply permitting emotional photosynthesis to occur with Kendall? Why instigate a big scene when in time everything might figure itself out? Because time is definitely a factor here – summer tour options are definitely pending; E/D is definitely starting New Paltz in the fall – where, by the way, her good buddy Aaron, that lily-pad poseur, is also definitely due to enroll.

Help, please, somebody! Either a push in the noble direction or a detour to get me irrevocably lost. The question is, who do I call? Moth will justify any and all reasons not to dump E/D while letting the Kendall thing brew. Without prompting he will cite the same precepts I just did, plus add a few less savoury notions of his own – like the fact that I'm an eighteen-year-old rock star and ought to start behaving like one, as well as infamous French wisdom. I can hear him already: 'Do you know what zay call a queer in France? A man who makes love to his wife more zan his mistress!'

Or I could hit Stella. This would require a certain amount of self-abasement. I'd have to come clean that my 'someone else' is Kendall – then I'd have to wait for her to stop laughing. But once she did, she'd screw my head on straight. What the hell: Heads, Stella; tails, Moth. It's heads.

'Heyyy, where are you? Are you in the city?'

'As a matter of fact, yeah,' Stella says. 'I'm laying out in Madison Park – you know, by the Flatiron Building.'

Stella – voluntarily immobile? Hmm, that's not her MO.

'Yat?'

For 'Where you at?' New Orleans slang she adopted up from Didion. Stella's like that with language – one week in England and she's 'sussing it out' and 'having a row' and 'taking the piss' out of you. 'I just got out of Guitar Centre; needed strings,' I tell her. 'I'm nearby – you want to get coffee?'

'Yeah . . . no. I'm comatose. Bring me an iced cappuccino – I'm near the clock.'

You want Stella, you play by Stella's rules. I get two to go and find her before the ice melts. A lawn angel in cut-offs and tank top, vintage Ray-Bans. She sits up when I sit down, and I'm hoping she'll take one look at me and ask, 'So what's wrong?' Instead she broods over her beverage, her eyes invisible behind the black shades.

'A/B, I gotta problem . . .'

Huh? That's a switch. 'You . . . have a—'

'Yeah, you know – Didion, Brian . . . *Tryst*,' she begins. 'The whole thing is a hot mess to me, but I seem to be the only one aware of it, so maybe I'm the *stunnade* . . .' She plucks at a clump of grass, musing. 'It's like, I know Didion loves me – but he . . . his definition of love . . . I never went into it with you, A/B, but if they gave a prize for dysfunctional upbringing that boy would win, no contest.

'And I know Brian wants the best for us – but all of us: 6X, Didion, now Boy King, so it's not like my wishes, my needs, are number one on his list. We're all just balls he's got in the air. Then this Tryst. Her track record's impressive, all right, I feel that. But the niche she's carving for Didz . . . Of course, nobody's said anything to me – why should they? I'm only the person who brought Didion to WandWorld – but I'm getting the vibe that they're positioning him to a different audience, as in not our audience. Some older boho-urban crowd. Now, A) I deserve to be consulted! My whole vision was Didion and 6X together. And B) Why take the obvious approach? It's like Didion's black and plays acoustic guitar, so he fits this slot, and then they lump us in with Boy King, since they're pop-rock or rock-pop or whatever, and we are too. That . . . *devalues* us, all of us, the listening public included. What, Brian and Tryst and them just wanna spoon-feed the world what it already knows instead of daring to educate? Not that there's anything wrong with Boy King. The demo's cool; they have potential. But goddammit, A/B, if anyone's gonna ride 6X's coattails it's gonna be Didion Jones!'

Finally she pauses for breath, plucks at the grass. 'You know what it's like, A/B, being in love,' she says. 'You ever feel that the world wants to eat your love alive?'

The Boss

Spinning my wheels and going nowhere fast – talk about motion sickness. Paralysed. Impotent. I can't fix this. Maybe it's not even broke. But I'm done, all right, I quit. Sort of. Because you know how you can think and think and still come up brain-dead, but then you stop and suddenly, eureka? That's what I'm counting on. That's why I change lanes and apply myself to this other crisis situation we got going on.

'This place sounds horrible!' It's Wynn, me, Malinka, and Peony sitting on the terrace of Wynn's townhouse, Central Park a big green blanket below. Gourmet temptation is at our disposal, but under the circumstances – too ironic – we just say no. (Well, not Malinka. Girl gave a proper beatdown at Forest Hills and has embarked on a post-tourney self-indulgence spree – she polishes off the caviar in seconds flat.) Wynn fans herself with one of the clinic descriptions she printed out off the Net. 'It's bulimia boot camp . . . no, worse, prison. Eat a Twinkie, spend a night in the box.'

'Yeah, like that'll work on Kendall,' I say. 'Freak Show needs kid gloves and feather pillows.'

'I disagree,' says Peony. 'I don't think coddling Kendahl is the way to go.'

'So you vote for Cracker Jack Jail?' I'm stunned. 'Potato Chip Penitentiary?'

'No.' Peony sighs. 'That won't do either.'

'Anyway,' Wynn interjects, 'all these places are inpatient—'

'Oh, you must be patient with people who are all the time puking—'

'Not *im*patient, Malinka. *In*patient. You have to check yourself in, live there. And that's not an option, since we haven't told Mrs. Taylor anything.'

'Wynn, I'm sorry, I tried . . . but that woman!' Peony's eyes bulge. 'I have successfully communicated with autistic children and outback aborigines, even crossed-over souls, but she . . . One minute she's chastising me over Kendahl's eating habits, and the next she's praising the Lord for her weight loss. Now our research has shown how poor parenting can contribute to an eating disorder, but shall we say it'll be a cold day in *heck* before JoBeth Taylor takes responsibility for warping that child's psyche.'

'OK, P – I didn't mean to imply . . .' Wynn says. 'Just maybe we should do another search for outpatient programmes only.'

Good idea. In fact, once we narrow the field to the New York tristate area, we hit the jackpot. Peony's all over the Osa Echo Centre since it takes 'a holistic approach to restoring equilibrium to our clients' relationship with food.' In other words, it purports to cure eating disorders through chanting, hypnosis, and other 'alternative therapeutic passageways.' Look, as long as 'clients' don't mistake healing crystals for rock candy, I'm down. Osa Echo's located in SoHo and runs morning and afternoon sessions, so Mrs Whackjob, aka Kendall's mom, doesn't need to know. (Brian, of course, has been filled in through the Peony-Gaylord network – he pulls the 6X purse strings, so the financing for Kendall's treatment will be vetted through him.) Plus, Osa Echo avows that with 'dedication and desire,' clients can achieve results in a month, which could feasibly put us back on the road with a non-chunk-spewing frontwoman by the end of July.

Fortunately Osa Echo is so revolutionary, they still have openings. Now we just have to get Kendall through the front door. The first step is our little soiree on Friday. Basically we're gonna strong-arm her with our female phalanx of love and compassion and understanding and solidarity. Yet when Kendall trots in toting the Vuitton overnight bag she scored in Paris and babbling blithely, there's a vice on my heart.

'Oh my gosh, Wynn, your home is just the most perfectly elegant place I have ever seen. This is a bona fide mansion, isn't it?'

I gotta tell you, I get choked up. We're a pack of wolves in sheep's clothing! Kendall has no clue. She doesn't even question Peony's presence. I bet she's got PJs in that LV; she thinks we're going to give each other facials and shit. We just kind of gape at her. Yeah, we've read up on what's supposed to go down, and it doesn't seem like vascular surgery – still, this is heavy, and we have zero experience.

So we make like it's a regular slumber party. Except, believe it, Wynn's mom really does spring for catering. A last hurrah, one final pig-out for our girl. Or maybe we hope she'll incriminate herself – we'll catch her in the act. First course is pan-Asian hors d'oeuvres – satay, dumplings, high-end egg rolls. Kendall digs right in, dipping a skewer in peanut sauce, and we follow like robots. Then Malinka – that savant – gets the party started brilliantly.

'You know what I want to do? I want to play the Truth or Dare! I have never played before this game. But that is what you do at slumber party, yes?'

Wynn leaps on it. 'Yes! Truth or Dare – that'll be great!' She gives me her imploring face.

'Yeah, oh boy – I love Truth or Dare,' I say.

Kendall's excited. 'You know what, Malinka? I don't think I've ever played it either. Can I go first?'

Damn, this is cruel! We play a round for real so we won't look too evil, but our hearts aren't in it. The worst dare they can think of for me is to flash my top on the terrace. When it's time for round two we all exchange the look: This is it.

'Dare!' cries Kendall.

Peony fields this one. 'Actually, Kendahl, you have to take truth.'

'Oh, is that the rule? If you pick dare the first time?'

We've all adopted the same posture, sitting on the floor in a semicircle around Kendall, leaning over expectantly.

'Not exactly, no,' says Wynn. 'See, Kendall, from here on out, there is no game. No pretence, no hiding. Just truth.'

'Huh? How come everyone's so serious all of a sudden?'

Peony knee-walks to where our victim sits; she takes

Kendall's hands in hers. 'Kendahl, this is a very important gathering. It has a purpose. It is an intervention.' She speaks slowly, pedantically. 'An intervention is when people who love you, and are concerned about you, confront you about what you're doing to yourself.'

Kendall's like: 'What I'm . . . ? I'm not doing anything.' She believes it too.

Now Wynn crawls closer to Kendall, peers into her face. 'Kendall, we know. We don't blame you, we're not judging you – we just want to help you.'

'But I—'

'Kendahl!' Peony moves out of coddling mode. 'You have an eating disorder. You binge and purge. You know you do. And it has to stop. That's what this is about.'

Kendall's like a feral animal – darting bright eyes, and she's quivering, scoping escape. She tries to stand, but Wynn gets on her knees and presses her hands on Kendall's lap to keep her seated and still.

'Ohhhh, Kendall, I know this is hard for you,' Wynn says. 'But this is us. Us . . .'

Then something happens that smacks me . . . shocks me . . . scares me. Lemme see if I can break if down. It's like drugs – you're not an instant junkie the first time you experiment. You're just curious, you dabble, and maybe it works for you. But if it doesn't, oops, one day you wake up and *you* work for *it*: addiction. Literally. Full-time. Your job is to protect and defend and nurture this insatiable parasite that's taken up residence in your brain and body and kicked the shit out of your soul. My brother had a junkie friend; he stole from our family and everything – JJ caught him with his paw in our mom's jewellery box, all right. The dude had no choice. He was just doing his job.

Eating disorder? Same thing. Soon as Kendall figures out what we're getting at, *it* puts her on lock. *Deny* . . . *deny* . . . *deny*. I can almost hear it seethe, smooth as steel, as this fake smile slides onto her face and this phoney tone usurps her voice. 'You guys!' she says. 'You are just plain silly!' All sweet and sincere – and about as real as a three-dollar Rolex. 'I don't know what—'

'Yeah. You do.' This is me talking. Standing on my knees, right in Kendall's face. Time for the tough love, straight outta Brooklyn. 'You know. You know damn well. You wanna know how *we* know? Exhibit A: Seattle, the tour bus – remember your little bagel-and-ice-cream binge? Exhibit B: London, the day we did *The New Ones*. And do not – do *not* – tell us some bullshit about an upset stomach or whatever, because, look, Kendall, game over for real. You lost twenty pounds since the Midwest tour, so forget about it. We know! All right? We know!'

I am not doing battle with Kendall, I am doing battle with *it*, and guess what? I don't know who's gonna win. So far she's being a pretty tough customer – she hasn't budged, just flat-out fronting, trying to make us think *we're* crazy. Then it hits me: I know how to make her march straight to the Osa Echo Centre. It's cold. It's cutthroat. But it'll work. Desperate times call for desperate measures. The way to this woman's stomach is through her man, so I'm gonna put her love on the line. Then another bolt from the blue. Chicks, we're all alike. Whatever the problem, love is the answer, always. Threaten our love, we'll do anything to protect it. Put our love on lock, we feel secure. *Flash! Bang! Boom!* Of course! I know what to do about Didion.

The Voice

I am . . . well, gosh, I am so many, many, many things. Flabbergasted, mostly. Angry too. How dare they?! Such an affront! Have they been spying on me? Listening at the bathroom door? Keeping tabs on my cookie consumption? The nerve!

Here's how I feel: superior. Yes, we are all God's children and all equal in His eyes, but I do feel cut from a finer cloth, because here they are flailing magazine articles about foolish girls who messed up their lives, and I think: *Now, now, now — that's not me. I'm Kendall Taylor. I know what I'm doing. It's just a little trick I use. And I like the results.*

Clever. All kinds of explanations occur to me, tales I can tell to get out of this. I've got it! I'll play dumb. How's that for smart? I'll tell them it's Britt's fault: She taught me the trick and I had no idea it was bad, but now that I know I'll just quit it. And they'll believe me.

Relieved. A smidge. See, there is this part of me that never quite felt right about the trick, always thought it was . . . against nature somehow. So that part believes it has a chance now that the cat's out of the bag. A piece of that part must peek out, too, since that's when Wynn and Peony start going on about how if we can nip this in the bud, treatment's a piece of . . . treatment's a snap! They're pulling out brochures for this facility, very spiritual and unique. All I have to do is pop in for counselling sessions. Only the second I start considering if maybe it's not such a terrible idea, the thing in my head clamps down with conviction: *No! Stupid cow! Do you want to get fat again?*

Scared. Because now they tell me how throwing up can ruin your teeth and your skin and even your voice . . .

Threatened. And that's what tears it.

'All right, Kendall, you wanna say nothing's wrong with you, that's cool.' Stella stalks away, then paces back. 'Because who are we to come to you with this? I feel you. So we'll just take it to someone whose place it is. Someone who has a right.'

I sigh. 'Stella, you think you're so smart. You're going to tell my mom on me? First, there's nothing to tell, and second, she wouldn't believe you anyway.'

'Your mom?' Stella says. 'Actually, Kendall, I have no intention of speaking to your mom.'

What *is* she thinking? I bet Wynn and Peony and Malinka don't know either – they turn to stare at Stella too.

'No, uh-uh, I was thinking about your *man*.'

My . . . ? Oh no! Oh, of course Stella knows my heart's secret – I told her so myself when we first went out on tour. But as far as recent events, she couldn't possibly—

'Yeah, mm-hmm, you heard me correctly,' Stella says. 'I know all about it. Your back against the tree trunk and the storm of purple flowers and him seeing you, finally seeing you . . .'

I go feverish. Yet somehow hearing this from a third party

confirms what I've only dared believe. It's true! A/B loves me! I don't know whether to hit her or hug her.

'Mm–hmm, that is right,' she goes on. 'He told me. In fact, you know that "family thing" he has tonight? Well, he lied. He's gonna break it off with E/D. Except, trouble is, he's pretty conflicted – that's why he came to me for advice.'

Stella gives me the staredown of all staredowns – it's like she's looking *into* me.

'So I steered him right. But what if I hit his cell right now, tell him he's nuts to throw away something good and sane and solid to take a chance on a fruitcake who not only hurls after every meal but is too far gone to admit there's something a little *strange* about that. I wonder what he'd say, what he'd do. Don't you, Kendall? Don't you wonder?'

Slap her, I think. Slap her mean, stupid, ugly face as hard as you possibly can before she ruins everything. But I don't. I can't. It wouldn't do any good. I look at Wynn instead. 'You know what? I think this is a bunch of crazy talk, but if it will get you people off my neck I'll be glad to take a gander at that brochure.'

The Body

Express checkout, register one . . .

Kendall: 'Now if you don't mind, I'd like to be alone!' Uh-huh, with her phone, so she can wait for A/B's call.

Peony: 'I'm just going to make sure she gets home all right.' And while she's downtown, hook up with Gaylord, I imagine.

Stella: 'Well, my work here is done . . .' So it's time for fun with Didion, no doubt.

Now it's just me and the Brutal Butterfly. Which is fine. True, Malinka may not be one to pore over and pick apart every aspect of the intervention with me – she's not the most analytical person on earth – but I don't feel compelled to do that anyway. The whole thing had me tense as a tightrope, and I don't need to relive it right now, or worry what will transpire next in the Kendall Taylor soap opera. I mean, I swear, I just want to blot it all out. By getting blotto perhaps? I give Malinka a look. 'Liquor cabinet?'

'I will race you!'

We peruse my stepdad's booze. 'Everything's so . . . *brown*,' I say. 'I don't know about scotch-y stuff – and we still have tons of food. Does – what's this? Glenfiddich? Does that go with blue stone crab?'

Malinka pokes her nose in a bottle. '*Blech-blech-pooey!*' She hands it to me. 'I am only making prayers your parents have vodka in the freezer.'

'You are a genius.' We run to the kitchen. 'Ta-da! Vodka, the wonder drink – goes with everything.' I gather ice, glasses. 'Cranberry juice OK?'

'Yes, OK.' She displays freshly filched Kahlúa. 'And for dessert I will make White Russians!'

We wander out to the living room. 'You want to hear the next big thing?'

Malinka shrugs. I pop in the Boy King demo – they really do do party music – and we bop around, sipping cocktails and sampling from the spread.

'This is great, Ween!' Malinka tells me.

'Boy King? You think?'

'Yes, they are OK – but everything is what I mean. Me and you in your living room, it is like our own club.'

'Mmmm . . .' I have to agree. 'Verrrry exclusive.'

She honks and squawks her car wreck of merriment, then strikes a pose holding an imaginary clipboard. 'Oh, I am very sorry, Lindsay Lohan, but you are not on the list. And who are you? Crimson Snow? No, I don't think so.'

She's too funny! 'No, we like her, Crimson Snow – come on, let her in.'

'Oh, but she has boyfriend Franklin K. with her . . .'

'And he used to put it in Britt Gustafson. Ick.'

'Back to the limo, Franklin K., you dirty man!'

We howl and keep it up, bashing celebs that sicken us, banishing them from our enclave of iniquity while inviting those we deem worthy to the VIP area to snort pretend cocaine off the coffee table. This is either very hilarious or we're very drunk, but eventually our pickled brains run out of gas. We each flop on a sofa.

'Do you want to go out?' Malinka asks.

'See people? Real people?' I reach for some snack mix the caterer called woodland mélange, eat a few cashews, and fling a loganberry at Malinka. 'Uch, no.'

'Not me either.' She rolls onto her stomach and into cobra pose. 'Here, throw it more – see if you can get it in my mouth . . .'

I roll over too. 'Goodbye tennis, hello circus.' I toss nuts and berries at her spazzily, but she actually manages to catch most of them. 'Linka, you are multi-talented. Verrry good eye-mouth coordination.'

She makes performing seal noises.

'Hey,' I say. 'Do you think it was uncool the way everyone beat a hasty retreat?'

'What is this hasty retreat?'

'You know, Kendall leaves, Peony leaves, Stella leaves.' I don't know why I'm going there – just griping, I guess. 'They all had to dash off to commune with their *boyfriends*.'

'Ah,' says Malinka. 'You are fortunate then, Ween, that I do not have boyfriend to beat hasty.'

I throw more dried snack product at her. 'Don't do that any more to me!' she moans. 'It is getting all in my hair, come on.'

'OK,' I say. 'Sorry.'

'When do your parents return to the house?'

I look at the clock; squint through slurpy vision. 'I don't know. Late, I guess. When my mother drags out the good diamonds it's probably some wee-hours wingding.'

Malinka rolls over again . . . and splat off the couch.

'Owww!' she yelps.

'Oh, come on.' I don't buy it. 'This is a verrrry plush rug.' Yet she's wonked, flatlining. 'Malinka?!' I sit up. 'Hey!' I get onto the floor with her. 'You OK?' I shake her shoulder. 'Malinka?!'

'Ha!' She opens her eyes and sticks out her tongue. 'I have idea – we should play more of the Truth or Dare.'

At this point I don't care what we do. 'Sure, OK.' We don't even bother getting off the floor, just lean our backs against one of the couches.

'You go first,' she says.

'Why? You're the one who wants to play.'

'Just go!' She's swilling straight from the Stoli bottle now. 'I want to play because I want to think up wicked truth or dare for you.'

'Oh God . . . OK: truth! No, dare! No, truth. Yes, truth.'

Malinka looks at me funny for what feels like for ever.

'OK,' she says. 'OK, Ween Morgan, tell me the truth: What would you do if I kissed you right now?'

'*What?!*' Ummm, I sober up in a hurry. 'Malinka . . . what . . . what did you say?!'

'Nothing . . .' she studies the intricate pattern in the Persian. Then she looks up. She says: 'This . . .' And she does it. Leans over. Puts her arm across my chest, bracing her hand on the sofa. Inhales once. And lays her mouth on top of mine. Her

341

mouth, not puckered or open or anything, just this pressure of her very specifically thin and sensitive lip skin on top of my very specifically thin and sensitive lip skin. For a few seconds that last an eon during which I am thinking: *Oh. My. God.*

Malinka pulls away just slightly, and I see this expanse of jaw. Smooth, fine, flawless, like porcelain or tightly woven fabric, only human and . . . and girl. And I don't move a muscle. I don't breathe a breath and I don't blink a blink.

'This . . .' Malinka whispers, and I can't believe it's her, whispering; I didn't know she was capable of whisper; I didn't know she was capable of kiss, but she is, she does.

'And this . . .' And she puts her mouth a fraction of an inch above mine, so the kiss lands astonishingly, remarkably off-centre. 'And this . . .' Now a trifle below, and when she draws back, tugs this tiny, tiny bit on my lower lip and I can't even begin to describe it except that I feel it everyplace, not just the concentrated ground zero of mouth but arch of foot and curve of hairline and base of spine and crinkle of belly button and lower and deeper and inside and out and on the floor and in the air and everywhere, everywhere, everywhere my senses sing in unison 'Ohhhhhhhhhhhhhh . . . !!!'

The Butterfly

Hello! It is me, Malinka Kolakova, coming at you live on camera from the bedroom of rock star Ween Morgan! I am talking to you because Ween says is OK. Right now she doesn't feel like talking. Right now she is in bathtub, turning into large white raisin. But I am going to slice her off some slack, and maybe you will, too, because oh boy Ween is having a crazy day let me tell you!

Today is Tuesday, and it is first time Ween and I have had chance for real hang out since the stop-puking party with Kendall – all weekend I've had big stupid tennis promotional conference in Madison Squared Garden. So I am glad Ween bangs my cell and asks: 'Do you want to come to practice?'

I am quick to reply yes!

'It's kind of boring, I don't know,' she warns. 'Brian wants us to change up the way we do certain songs, make the set more interesting, but you'll see, it's repetitive, we'll do the same number over and over and if we screw up it's my fault because the changes are a tempo thing and that's my job. When you're used to playing something fast it can be hard to slow it down.'

'Ween,' I say to her. 'It would be honour to be in the place where you practise.'

A/B is there already, and so is Kendall – who has already been twice to the centre for orderly eating, and I hope she is feeling better. I also wonder if A/B and Kendall are having hookup. 'So,' I say. 'Kendall and A/B – you are having hookup now or what?'

Kendall and A/B both blush very much, but they look happy to me for a quick second before Ween pinches my arm. 'Ma-LEEENK-a!' she says with hissy voice. 'Shut up, you silly! You can't ask . . .' Then she trails off, giggling, and when we look at each other we get just as blushy as A/B and Kendall.

'Oh, um, you guys don't mind if Malinka watches rehearsal, do you?' Ween asks, in covering our asses. 'I'm sorry, I guess I should have called.'

There is some silence and then A/B says, 'Hey, it's cool with me!' A/B makes big show of finding chair for me to sit on. 'Ween, did you bring extra earplugs?' he asks. 'Because, Malinka, it gets pretty loud in here. You're our biggest fan, we don't want you going deaf.'

Ween fishes into purse for a fresh pair. 'Here,' she says. 'They don't have any of my goo on them.' We both giggle at that. Then Ween realises something is not right. 'So where's Stella?'

'Weird, huh?' says A/B. 'The boss is never late.'

'She didn't even call? That *is* weird,' Ween says, then adds, a little bit with guilty: 'Either of you guys talk to her this weekend?'

'Hmm.' Kendall murmurs. I am burning up from curiosity – I want to know what occurred between her and A/B; I want

344

them to be in love and happy as I am wanting the whole world to be in love and happy. 'She certainly hasn't called me.'

'Me either,' A/B says, his eyes on Kendall.

Ween observes the clock on the wall. 'Wow, she's fifteen minutes late.' She rummages for her phone. 'I'll give her a call.'

This is not necessary at all since at that second Stella storms through the studio door. She is not alone. Didion is beside her, and they bring so much light and heat into the room it is like nuclear reactor accident except not terrifying. Big grins and big glows on them. Didion is wearing nice suit with white rose pinned to lapel. Stella is dressed up also in white minidress with small lacey cutouts, and stuck into her fuzzy short hair are those tiny flowers called breathing babies. This is so not Stella's usual style, and if it were not for the Doctor Martens boots I would not even be sure it's her. Well, everybody not just me is staring at them, and Stella wants to know why because she asks: 'What's wrong with you people? What are you staring at?' She has hands on hips like she is very exasperated with us, but she is faking, you can tell.

Nobody knows what to say in answer, unless A/B's cough counts.

'What?' Stella nudges Didion. 'We got parsley in our teeth?' To Didion: 'Baby, we eat anything with parsley up there in Rhode Island?'

Didion says happily: 'No, cherie, I don't think so. No parsley.'

Stella shakes her head like she is teacher and we are class of kindergartners. 'Whatsamatta . . . you never saw two newlyweds before?'

It is now screaming quiet in that room, until Didion and Stella start cracking up.

Kendall flies towards the couple: 'Good heavens! Oh my! Is it . . . ? Are you . . . ?'

'*Married?!*' A/B finishes. 'No! Really? Married?!'

'Read my lips.' Stella makes the word 'married' with her mouth very exaggerated.

'Holy crap! No shit? You are saying that you two actually went and got . . .' A/B has big trouble with the word.

Stella remarks: 'Maybe the champagne will convince them,' and Didion pulls a bottle from the paper sack he's carrying. At some point during this announcement I must have grabbed Ween's hand, because I am holding it and it is limp and clammy. I realise she still hasn't said a thing, and when I look at her she seems like wooden girl in shop window. I drag her towards Stella and Didion, shouting, '*Gor'ko! Gor'ko!*'

Now it is my turn to be stared at.

'*Gor'ko!*' I make explanation. 'Is Russian wedding toast! Does no one in this country say congratulations?' I let go Ween's lettuce-leaf hand and put big hug on Stella, then Didion also. Fortunately this is good ice cracker. A/B and Kendall start saying things like 'How wonderful!' and 'You crazy kids!' and 'When did this happen?' and there are squeezes and kisses. Stuttery sounds emerge from Ween, then she shakes herself intensely like wet dog.

'This is soooo amazing!' she finally says. 'I'm in shock still, but oh my God! Stella! Didion! You're married!' Her arms and legs come back to life, and she puts hug on bride and then groom and then bride again. Didion opens the champagne with a loud pop and mentions that he and Stella forgot glasses.

'*Pffff!* Glasses?' she cries. 'We don't need no stinking glasses! This is my *band*, baby!' She grabs the bottle and pours champagne on Ween's face and some goes into her mouth, and we cluster around to get doused until the bottle is empty and we are all very much completely wet.

Well, let me tell you, no kind of music rehearsal happens at all. We troop downstairs where two limousines are cramming with Stella's relatives (and one of Didion's – a doctor who is also an uncle). Off we go to very festive and noisy Italian restaurant in Brooklyn, and now and then little snickets of information stick to my ears about nobody being pregnant and that if you want to be married and are underage there is less tape that is red in the state of Rhode Island. There is much ravioli and wine and a garter is thrown and a broomstick is brought out over which Stella and Didion jump, and somebody tells me this is custom from when black people were slaves in America. What is coolest about party is even though it is a very rock-star thing to have secret wedding, it is also down-to-the-earth, regular family people having wonderful time. There is pop music on a jukebox in the bar of the restaurant, and we all make bad dance moves, even Ween who has been acting shy, I drag her out to finally shake some booty. Kendall and A/B also sort of move around each other, not too wiggly but with fingers touching, over by themselves in a corner. Towards the end I have arm wrestle with brother of Stella named JJ, and after I make two smackdowns I let him win.

Now we are back in Ween's house. Ween's mother is mad that Ween neglected to call and say she was at impromptu wedding celebration. Ween does not stop to make argument or explanation (I do – explanation, not argument); she just waves off her mother and goes upstairs. It is late and we are mostly exhausted but also hyped and Ween tells me she wants to take bath. I ask if I can play with camera and she tells me yes.

So Ween has been in bathtub a long time. Every few minutes she makes the water run loud. Maybe you think she just wants more hot. That's what I thought first. Only no! She wants sound to cover up her tears. Ween is crying in bathtub. Shiny salty bombs falling from her eyes onto her bubbles. The sobbing starts, she turns on water; it subsides, she turns off water. And on and on.

I start to pace back and forth in Ween's very beautiful bedroom, wondering what to do, which is very not like my normal personality to be with worry. I try to understand reason for Ween's tears, since this should be very happy day when your best friend gets married. Then it hits me like tons of sticks! Ween has had crush on Stella for long time. Even though she *knows* Stella is liking boys only. Even though Ween probably did not know she herself was not liking boys until a few days ago. Even though Ween likes *me* – I know she does and she knows she does. It doesn't matter what you know. What you know and what you feel can be so far away from each other they don't even live in the same country. But now that Stella has made big drastic move to be married, Ween must get in the face of the facts. She has to get over Stella. But can she? I wish that very much – only if she no longer has those feelings for Stella, can she really have them for me . . .

Wait, I must not be a person who is selfish! Because Ween is not being selfish. Yes, she has to deal with Stella and Didion, wife and husband, but not just in how it hurts on her heart. She is upset also because of what this marriage will mean to Seeks-X. With band, it is delicate balance – this thing Stella has done, what if it is bad for Seeks-X? So Ween cries also for her band – she cries because she is afraid.

Oh, no! This I cannot stand for Ween to be with fear. I pace back to bathroom. Should I burst in? Make knock? Say some words? I put ear against door of bathroom. I hear something – not tears, water swishing sound. And then *glug!* And then shower. This is good! Ween is taking shower now, bad feelings down the drain, good feelings from the spout. She is standing up, not lying down. Ween is strong person, she is good person, she wants happiness for everyone. She will not be afraid no matter what happens next – for Kendall and A/B, for Stella and Didion, for her and me . . . and for Seeks-X.